Praise for The Passionate Sister

"A marvel of imagination and creativity, not only in its premise but also in the author's writing, which is at times enchanting." — *US Review of Books*

"*The Passionate Sister* is a powerful and evocative tale of a woman's struggle to rebuild her life and mend the bonds of family" —*Readers' Favorite*

"An alcoholic fights to reclaim her life while tending to a dying friend and young children in Thorndike's luminous novel of recovery....A captivating story of midlife renewal." —*Kirkus Reviews*

"John Thorndike's finely wrought prose gleams in this boldly intimate fictional account of his mother's later years" —R.A. Moss, author of *Tobacco Republic*

"John Thorndike is an insanely good novelist. He writes gorgeously, and his characters take on lives of their own under his deft hand." —Henry Shukman, author of *Original Love: The Four Inns on the Path of Awakening*

"In *The Passionate Sister*, John Thorndike illuminates the ordinary with astonishing force. The lucky reader gets to experience loss, loneliness, joy, and redemption through one of the most fully realized characters in recent memory. Whether it's fiction, nonfiction, or a hybrid of the two, Thorndike writes beautifully about love and what it means to be human. --Rob Wilder, author of *Nickel* and *Tales from the Teachers' Lounge*

The Passionate Sister is a powerful, emotionally charged story of a mother's love for her grown sons; one, a gay man living in the shadow of AIDS, and the other, a member of a commune and husband to an erratic schizophrenic. The novel is a testament to the healing powers of love in a family fraught with conflict. —John Kachuba, author of *The Bottle Conjuror*

"Every word feels true in this extraordinary, wonderful, perceptive novel playing off the author's own family history. —Ray Ring, author of *Montana Blues*

"John Thorndike confronts grief by reimagining his mother's life beyond her premature death from addiction at 57. His compassionate narrative explores realms between memory and imagination, crafting an emotional testimony to maternal love and passion that transcends tragedy. He celebrates the resilience of the human spirit and the transformative power of second chances. —Mark D. Walker, author of *The Guatemala Reader*

"*The Passionate Sister* is a powerful novel of recovery. Thorndike has written a character based on his own mother in order to create a road to redemption for her long after her death. To be human is to err and Ginny Thorndike has erred mightily as a wife, mother, and lover. In Thorndike's brilliant book we become her character and her struggle is our own, balancing between a life of immorality and a passion akin to that of spiritual goodness and sacrifice for others. It is not an exaggeration to say that there are only a handful of writers, male or female, who inhabit women characters as deeply and insightfully as does Thorndike as he transcends the usual for the unexpected. He is in a league with DH Lawrence and Gustave Flaubert. —Marnie Mueller, author of *The Showgirl and the Writer*

"In this unflinching novel taking on some of the hardest of life issues, Thorndike draws from a deep well of personal experience to show us through his characters how we might navigate such issues ourselves. The result is a poignant and engaging work that leaves one more inspired than defeated." —Granville Greene, author of *The Mezcal Rush*

The Passionate Sister

John Thorndike

Beck & Branch Publishers, New York, NY

ISBN 979-8-9926682-1-6

Library of Congress Control Number: 2025915099

During the days, though, she was utterly at peace. Her life was like a single, well-spent hour. Its secret was her lack of remorse, of self-pity. She felt herself purified. The days were cut from a quarry that would never be emptied.

—James Salter

1

Virginia sits on a straight-backed chair, waiting for her son outside the main doors at Silver Hill. Her mug of coffee, that safe addiction, has grown tepid in her hands. The slate days of winter are coming, but today the meadows lie green and glazed in the pale sunlight. The sun warms her face and hands—but where the hell is Rob? *By midday* he said last night, and it must be well after noon. She stands and stretches, then walks around the circular drive. A pair of apples hang in the branches of a leafless tree and she snags one of them. It's too tart to eat.

She sits back down on her chair with nothing to read and only some birds to watch as they flit through the leafless lilacs. She should know these birds but doesn't. Wrens? Finches? Some day she's going to learn their calls.

She wonders if Rob will notice that she's lost some weight. Not much, and she's still too heavy. All right, she's fat. Not that it's her fault, it's the menopause. Well that's bullshit, of course it's her fault, because everything is. When *will* he show up? The birds keep hopping around in the bushes.

She's never been good at meditation, at just sitting. It's what she likes about her drugs, that they let her drift in slow motion. But she can't do that anymore. Now she can only use her mind to soothe her mind. Quietly she repeats, *Om mani padme hum* ten times, but it doesn't help. Of course not, because she's still in withdrawal.

She wants to be alone in her small, lovely, decrepit wooden house in Sag Harbor. But the house also scares her. It's filled with drugs and alcohol.

In the rooms behind her, patients are attending their meetings, doing yoga or beating little drums in a music session. How many of them, on a day like this when their stay is over, will be driven home by a friend or family member, only to relapse within weeks? From what she's heard, plenty. She's fallen off the wagon many times herself, but must not do it again. She smooths her trousers, woolen against the cold, and listens to the birds.

A green pickup rolls into the drive, and instantly all is well. She knows the truck from the week she spent at Rob's commune in Ohio. He parks, springs out and strides over to hug her.

"What a place, Mamá." He looks around, still holding her. "I'd imagined some big institution."

"It's more like a home. I think it *was* someone's home."

"Beautiful grounds. Are you going to give me a tour?"

"God no, my bag is packed and I'm ready." And only minutes later they're cruising down the Merritt Parkway, headed for the Throgs Neck Bridge.

"How come a truck?" Ginny asks.

"We only have one car and someone was using it."

She wants to stare at him, he's so handsome. His eyebrows and lashes are thick, and his long brown hair tied back with a bit of cloth. They talk about life on his farm and the commune's many projects.

"And the Six?" she asks.

"Always exciting. Always something to figure out."

She waits, but he says nothing more. The Six is his three-couple marriage, the commune's challenge to what they call the mononucleosis family. They've come through the sixties, and they're out to change the world.

The Merritt flows past, the leafless trees arching above them. When her boys were young she drove this road every morning, headed to the operating theater at Columbia Presbyterian. By 6:30 she'd be dressed and scrubbed, her masks and gauges laid out beside the cylinders of cyclopropane and nitrous oxide. When the surgeons were ready she administered the anesthesia, tracking the patient's every breath. Ten years have passed since she threw that life away.

"Have you talked to your brother?"

"We always talk when there's news."

"And I sure gave you some this time."

"You did. But you seem good now." With his eyes still on the road he lays a hand on the seat between them.

She rests her own on top of his. When he was younger they rarely touched, but these days everyone hugs everyone, and both her sons are quick to take her in their arms. *Thank you,* beatniks and hippies all.

Traffic slows to a crawl on the bridge. It's long before rush hour, but for twenty minutes they hardly move. Manhattan's towers loom to the west under a hazy sky. It's always been this way. If you don't take the ferry—and the ferry doesn't run this late in the year—there's no escaping the bottleneck.

"You know, I worry about your brother. Sometimes I think *he* drinks too much."

"Mom, forget it, it's not the same. He quits whenever he wants. He's done it plenty of times."

"*I* quit for Moon's birth."

"You did. You were great."

She hasn't had many triumphs in recent years, but that was one. Two weeks before Tasia, one of the Six, was due to give birth, Ginny gave up all alcohol and pills. Then she drove to the commune and guided Tasia through a difficult home birth with Moon, the child now loved by all.

They inch forward over the dark bay. The traffic eases, and by the time they reach the Expressway the lanes have started to open up. The truck rattles and its heater is weak, but now they're skimming over the earth past houses and lawns, on into the Long Island Pine Barrens. Ginny watches Rob relax, driving now with one hand draped over the wheel.

"How are we doing on gas?"

"We're good. I filled it this morning."

"What's in the box in back?"

"I brought some tools along."

She only asks questions so she can look at him. How long will he stay? What if he gets tired of her and wants to go home? What if he misses Moon? What if Natalia calls and insists he come back?

She goes quiet. She knows how it is with Rob, she has to wait until he's ready. And ten miles down the road he says, "Tell me what happened."

She thinks of what they told her at rehab, over and over: *Tell the truth. Don't keep secrets.*

"I got confused with my drugs, especially the Nembutals. I forgot I'd taken my nightly dose and swallowed some more. Same with the Seconals. And I was drinking. I finished off a bottle of gin. I thought if the bottle was empty it would help me stop. You know how addicts come up with these fantasies. I think what saved me was vomiting in my sleep and breathing in the smell. The stink woke me up."

"Why so many pills that night?"

"I wanted to go to sleep and forget about everything. But not for good. I don't think I wanted that."

"Don't ever do that Mom, please."

"I won't. I can promise you that today."

"But today you're sober."

"Today and tomorrow and the next day."

He watches her. He's seen her drink and medicate herself, and stop and start again many times.

"How did you wind up at Silver Hill?"

"I could have gone to McLean in Boston. They're good, I hear. But they couldn't take me for a week and I had to get out of that Southampton hospital. It was embarrassing there, because all the doctors knew me. It was bad enough when I lost my license, but waking up in one of the ERs was worse, attended by doctors and nurses I used to work with. And I had the worst headache of my life. It felt like the talons of some huge bird were ripping into my scalp. I think about that still. From now on I'll always be sober."

Rob watches her and nods.

The four-lane ends before Riverhead. They pass the store that looks like a duck, with a door in its white breast. They cross the Shinnecock Canal and drive on through the harvested potato fields, the ground ridged and lumpy. They can't see the ocean but it's never far off, and Ginny can feel it. From Water Mill they take the Scuttle Hole shortcut. When she and Joe first drove this road there were hardly any houses here. Now they dot the edge of the fields, and the old barns are falling apart. Every day at Silver Hill she wanted to go home, but as they get close to Sag Harbor her chest grows tight. They pass Otter Pond and turn at the Whaling Museum, and when Rob parks beside her house and gets out of the truck, she doesn't move.

He walks around to her door and opens it. "Come on, Mom. We're here, let's go in."

"I can't."

"What are you talking about? What are you going to do, just sit here?"

"I'm worried about what's lying around inside. The alcohol and pills."

"We'll throw it all out. I told you I won't drink while I'm here."

She pulls her coat close. "Could you do it for me? At least the bottles? The wine and gin."

He stands without moving, upright and stiff. The house waits beside them like an animal gone still, its dark shingles soaking up the sun, its windowsills low and peeling.

"Please," she says. "You know where the key is."

"I think you should do it."

"I'm afraid."

"You better get over it. You know I'm not going to stay forever."

Maybe he's afraid himself, of going into this house where she almost died. The truck's engine pings as it cools. The village is silent and the street empty. Rob slides his hands into his pockets, but his shoulders stay hunched.

"All right," she says. She'll go in.

It's as cold inside as out, and the kitchen floor creaks with every step. In the living room the ancient window glass bends the light as it spills over the wooden floor. Her downstairs bedroom stinks. It's the vomit on her quilt, lying in a corner on the floor. She asks Rob to ball it up and put it in the garbage can outside, then turns on her two small electric heaters.

There are bottles of wine in her bedroom, also in the living room and kitchen. She hands them to Rob, who opens them with a corkscrew and empties them under the smoke bush outside. Then the gin, the clear liquid gushing to the lawn. She watches through a window. When he comes back inside she says, "Now the pills."

This will be harder, because she's not sure where all of them are. Some small bottles sit in plain view. Others are hidden, wrapped up in a drawer or tucked behind books on the shelves.

"They have to go straight down the toilet. All except some Valium and Seconal. I want to taper off with those two. You could lock some up in the truck and give me what I need each day."

"Screw that." Rob turns half away and flicks a hand. "You've been in rehab, you've been clean, and now you want to take some pills? How stupid is that?"

"I'd be careful. I'd take three-quarters and then a half. People do this all the time, it's standard practice."

"You just want to get stoned again. So *no*, not while I'm here. If you planned to keep using, why'd you ask me to come help?"

Rob understands drinking. He drinks himself. But he has always hated her pills, the benzos and barbiturates. He hates to hear them in her voice, and he can always tell, even over the phone. They've just started and already he's had enough of her.

"The last day I was here," she says, "they took me away in a hearse."

"A *hearse*?"

Good, she has scared him.

"It was one of those combination cars with a red dome light. A hearse one day and an ambulance the next. It's what the hospital uses."

They stand for a while in silence, and the hearse story fades.

"Either we get rid of every pill," he says, "or I get in my truck and go home. You've been doing this too long. You're clean now, so stay that way."

She knows he's right. It was a desperate and hopeless plan. Still, she wants to swallow a Seconal now. She imagines the lovely ease of it as it spreads through her.

"I'm here, Mom, and Jamie is coming. But the only one who can stop this disaster is you."

"I just wanted some help."

"I'll help. I'll throw away every damn pill in the house. But what's to stop you from buying more?"

"Without my license I can't write prescriptions."

"Which is good."

"Except I can't practice, either."

He nods, and she watches him soften. He gives her the same appraising look as when he was five years old.

"You're right," she says. "About everything."

The sun pours in through the windows, but the house hasn't warmed at all. She loves Rob, and she needs him. If she were here alone she'd be shaving off part of a pill and swallowing the rest. It's a fantasy she better get over.

"All right," she says, "they all go into the toilet."

She pulls some Tuinals off her closet shelf, some Nembutals from among her sweaters, and a small brown bottle from amidst her collection of herbs in a kitchen cabinet: basil, oregano, cumin, diazepam. Altogether she finds over a dozen bottles. Rob goes through her car in the drive and comes up with three more, and she watches as he tips every pill into the toilet. Some bottles have only a dozen pills, some have a hundred or more. He pauses over a couple of them and inspects the labels, but doesn't pocket anything.

Still exploring, they climb the stairs and stand under the sloped ceiling of Rob's, then his brother Jamie's room, with their dormer windows, pipe-frame beds and a pair of upright dressers.

"It all looks the same," Rob says.

"But it's not. You know what they say, that you can never step into the same river."

"Ah hah, *philosophy*." He smiles. The sight of the pills swirling down into the toilet has relaxed him.

Downstairs again, it's clear that the heaters are too small to warm the house. Rob offers to buy a larger one in the village. "I'll go with you," she says. Even with her meds cleared out she isn't ready to stay here alone. They buy a heater at the hardware store and some food at Schiavoni's, then come back to cook dinner.

2

As Rob works the stove, Ginny cleans the kitchen. She sets two plates and glasses on the table, the same ones she bought at the Salvation Army in Riverhead years ago, only four of each. She has stuck to her plan ever since: no more than four people for dinner, and if you need another plate, wash it. She drops her four wine glasses into the trash can, finds a hammer and taps them until they break.

Her meals in this house haven't always been well balanced, but Rob prepares two healthy plates of sea bass, broccoli and baked potatoes. The new heater glows by the door, and they eat with their coats on.

"You never did go fancy out here," Rob says.

"Somehow I didn't care, especially after my two years in the Peace Corps. I liked that simple life."

"Mamá, you'd fit right in at the commune."

After Moon's birth they all invited her to stay, and they seemed to mean it. She never said how crazy that would make her, living with a dozen people and more.

"How's Natalia doing?"

"She's well. She has a part-time job with the Sprout Lady."

"And the Six?" Ginny asks again.

"One thing for sure, the guys are happy that the sex hiatus is over."

"The what?"

"It started because Tasia was no longer interested. She was breastfeeding Moon around the clock and sleeping with her every night, and she didn't care about sex any more. Natalia and Cynthia decided to pitch in, and we all agreed to put sex on hold. Five months it took, until Tasia was ready. And even then...."

"What?"

"I don't know where we're headed. We haven't been switching around the way we used to. The women don't want it. Even Natalia, who used to love it. And the real trouble is that we don't talk about it any more, which goes against everything we agreed on at the start. That's what the marriage was all about."

"It often happens," Ginny says.

Night hovers at the windows as they eat. Their times together in this house have all been in summer or early fall, with birds singing and insects whirring. Now, deep into November, they barely hear a car as it rolls down Garden Street.

"Have you talked to your father lately?"

"Sure, before I picked you up I spent the night with him and Melanie over in Westport."

This is a blow. Not that Rob saw his dad, but that he hasn't mentioned it all day. And worse, that she never raised the topic herself, never stopped to think that on a trip east of course he would visit his father. This happens too often. She doesn't ask enough questions, doesn't stop to think about others.

"How's he doing these days?"

"He's good. Of course we don't talk the way you and I do. But you know how supportive he is. I told him about some books I wanted, and he's going to get them for me."

"What books?"

Rob laughs. "One on plumbing and one on companion planting. I'll get my novels from you."

She loves it when he laughs.

She should have filched a few Nembutals before Rob flushed them all down the toilet. Then she wouldn't have to lie here awake at midnight listening to the hollies rub against her bedroom window, pushed by a night breeze off the bay. She lies under a blanket and another of her quilts, the room smelling faintly of vomit and Glade. At Silver Hill people often talked about these first nights back, and the inevitable craving. She hates that word, *craving*. She doesn't crave a drink, she just wants one.

Okay, what's the difference? Of course she wants a drink now, because when was the last night in this house she didn't have a cocktail, a nightcap, a double shot of gin before going to sleep? Over a year ago, she thinks, before Moon's birth. For months afterward she clung to the story of how she'd quit both alcohol and drugs, a tale they jumped all over at Silver Hill, given how she relapsed the very day she returned from Ohio. She stretches out in her bed, looking for solace from her skin. She palms her breasts, then her thighs, but her body feels inert. She could be caressing bolts of cloth.

How natural drinking is, she thinks. It's almost inevitable. Her parents drank, her first husband drank, she and Joe drank all through their marriage. At every dinner party they ever went to, everyone drank. Was there a single adult on Cantipauk Road who didn't? Joe was always a model of control, never stumbling or slurring his speech. On their trip to France when the boys were young they had wine with lunch, wine with dinner and there was never a problem. The French even gave watered-down wine to their kids.

She should go into the kitchen and heat up a glass of milk, which has sometimes helped her nod off. But in this uninsulated house, where anyone can hear everything, Rob might wake and worry. Too many times she has made things hard on both him and Jamie. Once in the middle of the night when they were teenagers, she opened her bedroom door to find them sleeping on pads on the living room floor, bedded down there to stop her from going into the kitchen and pouring another drink.

In a week Jamie will come from Key West. There, with his lover Miles, he paints, drinks, goes to art openings and lively gay parties. Both her sons are wrapped up with their partners, and maybe it was a mistake to ask them to come. Her counselors at Silver Hill all thought it was a bad idea. Don't ask them to help you stay sober, they said, that's your job. AA will help, NA will help, but don't ask your sons to protect you.

The hollies keep scratching. Except for Jamie and Rob, her life is empty. She doesn't have a job, she can no longer practice medicine, she won't have a man and sex would be a mistake, because there's none left in her. What a waste she has made of her life.

She wanted both her sons to come, but now she'd rather be alone. She will be, soon enough, and that scares her too. She used to love Sag Harbor in the off season, but somehow it all feels foreign now: Schiavoni's and the Paradise Grill and the movie theater and Long Wharf, all of it. She'll explore the streets tomorrow and see if she can recover her old affection. She and Rob will walk the beach at Sagaponack, and tonight, sleep will come. It always has. There's never been a night when she stayed awake until dawn. If she were alone in the house she'd get up and do something, step outside and stand in the moonlight for a while, listen to Chopin or Schubert, eat some grapes or boil an egg. Though she hasn't cooked in months, she'll start. She's supposed to make a new life for herself. She presses her pillow to her ears to block the scratching, and waits.

In his sleeping bag upstairs, Rob also lies awake. He has watched his mother come out of rehab programs before, then crash a month or three months later. But never before has she agreed to ferret out all the alcohol and drugs from her house. He turns on his bed and the mattress creaks. He has never slept here in cold weather. This has long been a summer house, with its ancient mullioned windows and the living room's bricked-up fireplace. Jamie will be flying up soon. They've talked it over and agreed that at least for now, one of them must stay with her. They've also promised not to get high in her house. No drugs, no weed, no alcohol.

One day he'll urge her to come visit the commune again. But not now, with the Six adrift and the couples keeping to themselves. Last night when he called, Natalia told him that Cynthia was sobbing in one of the back rooms. What about, he asked? Natalia shrugged it off and steered the talk to Moon.

He still loves the Six's friendly scheme. Why not spread sex around openly, instead of in secret? Why live the way his parents did? He still doesn't know how many affairs his mother had, he only knows that in the end she hooked up with Rich Villamano and tore everything apart.

She did have one more romance, in Chile after she joined the Peace Corps. On his visit there Rob was impressed by Alberto's farm. He was a friendly and devoted guy. He fenced his fields, seeded them to wheat and potatoes, harvested honey, milked his cows, made cheese and cider and grew most of what he ate. Still, Rob didn't want his mother to settle down at the bottom of the continent.

In recent years she has needed more care, and he hasn't given her much. Jamie even less. But it's not as if she's an old crone in a home, living out her life as their grandmother did. Ginny loves her house, and for much of the last ten years she has kept her job as a physician, and pretty much taken care of herself. Her friends the Brennans come out from Bronxville every summer weekend and stay in their house only a block away. It was the Brennans who discovered Sag Harbor, when Rob was only five. He remembers those early years, their walks to the wharf and drives to Montauk, their cheese and prosciutto picnics at the beach. Two families, five kids and everyone at ease, and no one splitting up. Every Labor Day weekend they sat before the tumult of the waves at Sagaponack, built sand castles meant to be smashed, watched the seagulls sweep over sea and sand. Some day he's going to write this all down. He should start now. There must be a notebook somewhere in this house. He'll look tomorrow, because now he's falling asleep.

Rob asks her over breakfast why she has chosen to come to Sag Harbor, instead of her apartment in Manhattan.

"I gave it up. I didn't sign the new lease. I can't bear the city any more."

He understands. He once lived there for a year himself, a good year, often thrilling, but he wouldn't want to go back to that packed and jumbled life with no woods, no creeks, no open land save for Central Park. Still, this house isn't ready. "If you want to spend the winter here," he says, "you need a furnace. These heaters aren't going to cut it."

"I meant to do that last summer. I even talked to a guy."

Before noon they drive to SwansonAir and meet with the owner. It's a quiet time of year on the South Fork, and he can start in two days.

That afternoon, at the local AA meeting, Ginny introduces herself. Hello, her name is Virginia, she's an alcoholic and her sobriety is almost five weeks. The group is small, ten local men and women and they only meet twice a week, if she needs more she can drive to Southampton. But this meeting, in the basement of St. Andrews Church, is only a five-minute walk from her house. She jumps right in, tells them that her son is staying with her, explains how he emptied out her bottles of wine and gin. After the meeting no one tells her she has laid too much of a burden on her son. They meet on Tuesday afternoons and Friday nights, and she'll be coming both times.

Even with three heaters running nonstop, her house is chilly. It's a small antique of a house, almost two hundred years old. These days in East Hampton, in Amagansett and on Shelter Island, people are building massive homes. Offensive homes, Ginny thinks. Whatever they're after, she doesn't need. She only needs to stay sober. She's leaning on Rob and that can't go on forever, but she's glad to have him now.

"The real danger for me is drinking," she tells him after dinner. "Alcohol is everywhere, no prescription needed, and for now I shouldn't get near it. Forget about persuading me of anything. Forget about will power. I just spent a month with everyone trying to convince me not to want what I want. And of course I stayed clean, because I wasn't going to find any booze at Silver Hill. But here I'm going to want it. I want it now. So please, make it hard for me to get near it. Except for meetings, I don't want to go out alone. I shouldn't drive my car."

She steps into her room and comes back with two keys. "Here's the original and my only spare. Keep them hidden. Treat me like a kid around cookies."

She can see this makes Rob uncomfortable. "You could always sneak out," he says. "How could I stop you?"

"Just make it difficult. Don't give in to me. When I'm lying in my room at night I'm going to want a drink. So if you hear me wandering around, come down and join me. We could take a walk."

"If I hear you."

"You'll hear me. You can't hide anything in this house."

"What happens after I go home?"

"Jamie will be here, I hope."

"And then?"

"We'll see about then. It's today I have to think about. That's what they say, over and over."

Rob rises from the table. He stands without a slouch in his sock feet. His hair has come loose. She watches him, trying not to look too hard. She could watch him all day.

"Okay," he says, "I'll keep you penned in."

In two quick days the furnace is installed in a back corner of the kitchen. Because there's no basement and only an eight-inch space below the floor joists, the ductwork is all exposed inside the house. Rob offers to close the ducts in, and at the lumberyard in East Hampton they pick up some two-by-fours and poplar one-by. No matter the mess they'll make, it's too cold to work outside, and Ginny watches as Rob lays out the tools from the box in his truck, then makes a pair of sawhorses in the kitchen, the sawdust flying. The noise and dust annoy her, but she keeps quiet about it. She resents the chaos, even as he devotes his days to her. He's come all the way from Ohio to help her out, and half the time she'd rather be alone. It shames her.

Perhaps Rob sees her disquiet, because after he frames the chases he gives her a job, helping him with the paneling. She's not very good with a hammer, so he shows her how to drill a small hole, then gently bang in the finish nail and embed it with a nail set. Over the next couple of days they enclose the ducts to her bedroom, the living room and the second floor. She winds up glad to have a project, to drill and nail and think less about a drink. The poplar is handsome, even more so after they brush on a light stain. But she can see that Rob's not much at ease himself. After their walk, after dinner, he hunches in his chair.

"You need to keep busy, don't you?" she says.

"Some days."

"Every day so far." She watches him. "Are you tired of being here?"

"There's a lot going on at home, and I worry about it."

"I shouldn't have asked you to come."

"No, you had to. And Jamie will be here, he'll take over."

"What a trouble I am."

"Not right now." Rob stands, looks over their paneling work, runs a hand over it. "You did well today."

"One day at a time. It's such a damn cliché."

"You'll keep going to meetings, right?"

"I will. But what helps me now is how close I came to dying. When I want a drink, I think about that."

"Too close," Rob says. "You scared the hell out of us."

3

Her sons flank her as they head into the wind, walking beside the Atlantic. Gusts stream sand against their ankles and tear the crests off breaking waves.

"*Damn*," Jamie says, pulling down on a woolen hat and clutching Ginny's old ski parka. "I can't believe you do this every day."

"We like it," Rob says.

"I need it," Ginny says.

A gull glides past, steering with the barest flick of its wingtips. The dunes haven't changed from midsummer, nor the strandlines dotted with driftwood and wrack, but ahead and behind there's no one on the beach.

"You *need* this?" Jamie says.

"I like watching something that hasn't changed in a billion years."

"And I'm stocking up," Rob says. "In Key West you've got all the ocean you want, but when I go back to Ohio I'll only have a creek and the woods."

"Maybe if it wasn't so cold."

"We'll get you some boots," Rob says. He steps behind their mother, claps him around the shoulders and gently roughs him up. "What kind of crazy gay brother wears a pair of Keds to an ice-cold beach in December?"

"I had boots but I left them somewhere. That's what happens in Key West. You forget about winter. You forget about most of the world."

On their way home they buy a Christmas tree from a roadside display and wedge it into the trunk of Ginny's car. They have no stand for it, but Rob makes a quick one out of two-by-fours. Then he's ready to take Jamie to the shoe store in Southampton.

"Are you coming?" he asks his mother.

"I have my meeting."

"Right. And then you'll walk home?"

"It's only five blocks. I'll be all right, I've done it before."

Rob studies her. "Okay," he says. "Straight back from the church."

"What was all that?"Jamie asks as they pull out of the driveway in Rob's truck.

"I haven't been leaving her alone at home. It was her idea."

"There's no booze in the house, is there?"

"She could go to a bar in the village, easy enough."

"What about her meds?"

"All down the drain. And she's been good about her AA meetings. I went to one with her

and they gave her a six-week chip. From how they talk, those people have been through some shit."

The roads are quiet and the potato fields empty. Jamie hunches up in front of the heater. "How's Natalia doing?" he asks. "And Moon."

"They're good. But I have to tell you, the Six feels wobbly. Natalia won't talk to me about it. She keeps telling me I have to get back for Christmas."

"Which is almost here."

"Right, and I want to spend it with you and Mom. But Natalia can be insistent. I do miss Moon, and it's her first Christmas."

"She's barely a year old. What's she going to know about Christmas?"

"It's Natalia who knows."

They pass the windmill in Water Mill. They talk about their father and his wife Melanie, and Rob's recent visit with them.

"She kept picking up a fly swatter as she walked around the house. There aren't any flies in December, but she kept swatting the windowsills and the backs of chairs. I couldn't help feeling she wanted to swat me."

"Same kind of thing the last time I went," Jamie says. "I've always made her nervous. I thought it was because of Miles."

"You never took him there, did you?"

"Hell no. But if I mentioned him I could see her pull back. Of course most of the world is like that. It's why we've never lived anywhere except Provincetown and Key West."

"The two of you should come up to Ohio some time."

Jamie shifts in his seat. "Would everyone feel okay about that?"

"Hell yes. Look at me, I'm married to five other people."

Jamie reaches across and knocks him on the shoulder. "But you're not sucking any dick, are you?"

"Okay, we might be a little uptight about that. But we do have a couple of women who I think are going lesbian, and that'll be okay. Everyone likes them."

"That sounds enlightened—especially coming from out there in the Ohio boondocks."

"You're a dog, Jamison. You're as prejudiced as some redneck from Georgia."

"So are you, Robbo. *Redneck. Georgia.*"

"Okay, you got me there."

A day later, after two more calls from Natalia, Rob explains his plan. He's going to spend Christmas Eve in Sag Harbor, and at five the next morning he'll take off for Ohio, arriving in time for the last of Christmas Day. Ginny nods, but it saddens her. Miles will be driving up between Christmas and New Year's. She's glad he's coming, she only wishes all three of them could be here at the same time. Rob has been a salvation. He came when she needed him, but his real life now calls him home.

In the afternoon they drive to the beach. Jamie wears his new boots, along with a sweater and Ginny's parka. There's no wind and the sea is almost flat, but it's colder than it was at noon. The year's shortest day has passed.

"Your father always loved the solstice," Ginny says. "For him that was the day the tide turned, and from then on everything was on the rise."

"Even if it was just the start of winter," Jamie says.

"It wasn't the cold that bothered him. He liked the cold. He thought it was curative."

Rob and Jamie glance at each other. This isn't like her, to speak so freely of their father.

"Do you know what he did at the end of every shower?"

They don't.

"He turned off the hot water and stood in the cold for thirty seconds."

"Bloody hell," Jamie says, and Rob nods in agreement.

"What softies you two are." She laughs. "Though it's true, I only tried it a couple of times myself."

Rob watches her.

"What?" she says. "*What*?"

"You were laughing."

"I can laugh."

"We should tell some jokes. Jamie, tell her the one about the javelin team."

"No, that one's as bad as *rednecks* and *Georgia*."

"Just tell it."

"All right, okay. Mom, did you hear about the Polish javelin team?"

"No, what?"

"They elected to receive."

"You guys are bad." But she's laughing again.

On Christmas Eve she reads them Dylan Thomas's *A Child's Christmas in Wales*. It was never Ginny who read at Christmas, it was always Joe, but she pulls out the 1950 *Harper's Bazaar* she has saved from Cantipauk Road, and her boys settle in. When they were young they heard this story many times, of Christmas and the close and holy darkness.

The three of them sit before their barely-decorated tree. Once they were a family of four. Once there was no divorce, no heartache, no Silver Hill, no early departure on Christmas morning. On Cantipauk Road their tree was laden with tinsel and surrounded by presents. Logs burned in the fireplace and the dog wore a new collar. Here in Ginny's house the ceilings are low, the floors are scarred and the furnace strains to keep them warm. There's no Irish setter, no old tuxedo cat, no gingerbread cookies, no eggnog laced with rum.

"Do you remember how my sister Carol and her husband would come over on Christmas Eve? How they'd both have four or five glasses of eggnog, then get in their car and drive home? We never should have let them. Joe and I didn't drink like that, but plenty of people did. There wasn't much talk about drinking and driving back then. Damn, I sound like I'm at an AA meeting."

"It's easier in Key West," Jamie says. "You get lit up and don't have to drive anywhere. We walk or ride our bikes."

"Out at the commune," Rob says, "I'm sure they've got a big bowl of eggnog set out right now, and they'll drink until it's gone. But then they'll sleep it off, no problem."

"People drink," Ginny says. "I understand. But thank you both for not drinking anything here. I needed this. Maybe later I'll be more relaxed. I can't ask everyone around me to stop forever."

"We could stop forever around you," Rob says, and glances at his brother.

Jamie hesitates. "Maybe I could do that."

"Miles knows the rules, right?"

"Sure," Jamie says. "We talked it over and it won't be a problem. Even in Key West he's been backing away from some of our parties. I think these days he could take it or leave it."

"Unlike you?" Ginny asks.

"I do love to drink. At least I don't smoke cigarettes any more."

"A miserable, dangerous, lowly habit."

"Mamá," Rob says, "now you're making *me* laugh."

"Tease away Mamá. I don't know how I ever started, after you showed us all those grisly photos of smokers' lungs."

"I did despair for a while, watching you light up."

"And then Miles got on my case. He quoted you on cancer stats, and if I smoked there was no kissing."

The three of them sit in a flickering light from the mantelpiece candles. How lucky she is to get along well with Miles. To like him. To love him, as she has told him several times. When she was growing up people vowed their love in movies, but not so much among friends and family. But she does love Miles. He kept Jamie alive through a painful time, and they've been a couple now for over a decade. In truth, she's far more at ease with Miles than she is with Natalia. Sometimes she imagines Natalia with a rope around Rob's neck. No, she shouldn't think that way. She just doesn't want him to leave tomorrow.

What she really wants is to hold onto both her sons. If only she had a huge bed, or a big soft pad on the floor where they could lie down in each other's arms. She's glad for the hugs they've shared, but hesitates to reach out and touch them whenever she wants. This whole time she's been holding back, because she doesn't want to scare them. Also, because she doesn't deserve it. She was the one, when they turned six or seven, who pulled away from them physically. How she regrets this now. She loved them but she was busy. She was good with their birthday parties, with Halloween and Christmas and the Fourth of July, but day to day she didn't hold them enough.

Now Rob must go to bed. He stands and tucks his hair behind his ears. He gives her a hug, then Jamie a hug, and goes upstairs.

Ginny sets Dylan Thomas on a shelf behind her. The candles flicker, and a faucet drips in the bathroom. The creaks from Rob's bedroom floor have stopped. She still hasn't talked to Jamie about how long he's going to stay. He might not know, but with Miles coming he's apt to stay longer.

"You and Miles," she says. "That was quite daring of him, to start something with you at Darwin Academy."

"We were careful. Neither of us wanted anyone to know."

"Still, he could have gotten himself fired. And you'd think anyone could have figured it out, from those paintings he did of you."

"He painted all the time. He painted lots of boys."

"Hey, I'm not complaining, you know how much I like him. I worried at first about the age difference, but maybe now who cares."

"I never think about it," Jamie says. "Okay, sometimes when his legs give him trouble. He's been trying to stay in shape, but he gets stiff."

"Don't we all?"

"Not me! I get cold but I don't get stiff."

Sometime she'll go back to Key West for another visit. Sometime she'll go back to the commune in Ohio, but for now she doesn't want to go anywhere. For years she traveled and loved it. She lived in France with Joe, she spent two years in Chile, she visited Rob in Guatemala after he too joined the Peace Corps. She can't imagine doing any of that now. She wants to stay sober, and stay here.

"...and he'll want to be painting." Jamie has been telling her something and she hasn't listened. "It's the same for me," he says. "In Key West we paint almost every day."

Ah, he's talking about painting *here*. "Take over the living room if you want, the house is yours. Is it too cold to paint outdoors?"

"The oils would be stiff, and I'd freeze out there. We'll see what Miles brings in the way of palettes and easels."

When one of the candles gutters out Jamie stretches, then covers a yawn with his hand. She doesn't want him to go upstairs. She wants a drink. At this hour she always had a drink close by. How comforting it would be if she could hold a drink, just hold it in her hand. Oh *sure*.

"What do you think about Rob and his six-marriage?"

Jamie wakes up to this. "I like it. But of course I'm prejudiced, I like every change to the old order. When the world doesn't work we should tear it apart."

"Do you think monogamy is on its way out?"

"Did we ever really have it? People take vows, then ignore them."

"You mean me."

Jamie watches her, then nods. "You did wander off."

"Did you hate me for leaving your father?"

"I'll never hate you, Mamá. I was pretty unhappy myself in those days. But even then I could see that you and I were alike. You wanted something forbidden and went after it."

"And three weeks after I left your father, Rich dumped me."

"He *was* a shitheel, wasn't he."

"And I couldn't go back after that. So maybe Rob and Natalia have come up with a better way. I just wonder if the world's ready for group marriage."

"The Mormons used to do it—though just with one guy, I guess. Rob tells me there are tribes around the world that do it."

A piece of Christmas music drifts in through the windows.

"How about your tribe in Key West?"

Jamie sits up, his legs folded under his chair. He's slender, like Rob. "What do you mean?"

"Miles told me about your hot tub parties. He talked about how intimate they are, and what happens with other men. He said it's common among gays."

"Miles sure likes to talk. He likes to talk to you."

"It's one reason I'm so fond of him. Really, I can't imagine a better person for you to have wound up with."

"Well, it could have been some girl, if I had a normal life."

"Fuck normal life."

"*Mom!*"

"Hey, I hear people say that word all the time."

"Not when I was growing up. Not from you or Dad."

"We were quite proper, weren't we? On the surface, at least."

"And you raised two proper boys. Who are now sticking it to the squares."

"How I love you, Jamie. Thank you for coming and keeping an eye on me. And I'm so glad Miles is coming too, and we'll get to talk about everything."

"He'll do that, whether you want to or not."

They watch each other face to face, smiling away like a pair of three-year-olds. Then Jamie stands and says, "Time to turn down the furnace, and say some words to the close and holy darkness."

As the moonlight filters in through the bushes outside, Ginny settles onto her mattress. In all these years she has never lain in this bed with anyone.

It's not drinking that's strange, it's sex, because no one can talk about it. Unlike when she was growing up, people now discuss menopause and cancer and death—but sex is still taboo, for her and everyone else. When has she ever talked about her sex with Joe, her sex with Isamu or Rich or Alberto? She steers herself away from even thinking about sex between Jamie and Miles, or sex among the Six. It's true these days that people are more at ease with their bodies. They talk easily about their heart rate and digestion and the state of their evacuations. But about sex they're never graphic, and she will be no different. She doesn't want to spook her sons.

The last man she lay down with was Alberto, three years ago in her house in Vilcún, Chile, on a bed too small for the two of them. The bed was too small because he was so large. Not that tall but round of belly, with big shoulders and arms. He was a gentle and attentive man. He loved to listen to her speak in what he claimed was flawless Spanish. It wasn't, because she too often stumbled with the subjunctive. Alberto loved to bring her food from his farm: a big round cheese, unshelled hazelnuts or *digueñes* from the forest. After setting his gifts on her table he relaxed, asking nothing in return.

It surprises her now to think that he and Joe were somewhat alike. Neither of them had to shore himself up with either knowledge or accomplishments. They simply went to work, Joe at his magazine and Alberto in his fields. When Alberto decided to plant more wheat, he chopped down the trees of another few hectares, then pulled out the trunks with a *tecle*, a giant come-along.

"This is how you make bread," he told her, extending his arm toward his latest project. "First you must clear the ground. Then you plow, and the oxen must be strong or the roots will defeat you. You plow again the next year, then seed the wheat. And all this comes before the first harvest, before the grinding and baking. Can you see the bread in this field?"

It wasn't just a list of what he'd achieved. His voice was full of wonder. And what a smile he had. When she spoke, he was always quick to listen. He paid attention to her moods, and sometimes asked her what was wrong.

¿Que te pasa, mi amor? He offered his life and assured her she could keep her own. She hasn't found anyone like him since. She hasn't looked.

She left Alberto, she left Chile and now misses them both: Alberto's comforting belly, and his broad fields lined with trees, and rivers so clean you could drink out of them. For the Peace Corps she ran a clinic, bringing medicine to a small town that knew no other doctor. She woke in the morning, thinking about her patients. She listened to Violeta Parra's heartrending songs. She drank only an occasional glass of wine. She sat on Alberto's lap. An overnight stay at his farm was like a trip to an earlier century. It was lovely, but too far from her sons.

Those days are done and her nostalgia for them useless. Instead, she needs a future. She needs something new, or at least to *want* something new. The trouble is, she can't figure out what. She has a goal, which is not to drink. But hoping not to do something is hardly a desire. When she drank she didn't care about the future. Alcohol and pills did away with all that. They softened her, they lowered her onto a deep cushion. No, what she needs now, what she wants to feel, are the drives and desires she felt as a girl, as a young wife, as the mother of two boys, as a woman in her thirties who went back to college and med school. How absorbed she was, how alive with hope. Now that has left her and she can't call it back.

Through most of those years she had a mate, but the idea of a steady intimacy now frightens her. She may well find peace, but that won't be enough. She wants to be close to her sons, but they have their own lives. Rob will leave tomorrow, and how long will Jamie stay? Right now she wants to sleep, but her worries keep her awake. She worries all the time. She worries about worrying. She palpates herself again, pressing palms against flesh. No, nothing. The furnace hums. Her clothes hang in the closet. Sleep will come when she doesn't know it.

4

A white mist blows offshore and the sound of the waves is comforting. Apparently immune to the cold, the gulls lift and pulse away, singly or in pairs. Jamie wears his Christmas gift, a new down jacket. They reach the harder sand close to the waves and head east past the dunes and a few visible houses. They all look empty. No sign of Christmas, no people, no lights.

"They're all in Manhattan," Ginny says, "opening presents. Which is fine with me. Don't you love an empty beach? Nobody to say hello to, no need for any comments. Life can't get much simpler than this. Either you stand still or you walk. Either you head left or right, and after that there's nothing to decide."

"At some point," Jamie says, "you have to decide when to turn around and go home."

"That's fine, I like going home. But all day there I have to choose to be sober, and here it just happens."

"Maybe we should keep going, all the way to Montauk."

"We could. Or we could come back here every day."

Miles shows up in his old Desoto, looking as relaxed after his drive as if returning from an errand. Hugs all around, and an hour later he and Jamie have taken over the kitchen to roast clams and sweet potatoes for dinner. Back in the days when she cooked, Ginny was rarely inventive. She boiled things or fried them. Miles now works the oven, the broiler, and a jerry-rigged double boiler for a garlic sauce. He's the same size as Jamie, spare and somewhat disheveled, his hair growing longer. The two of them talk about friends in Key West, about parties and painting and gallery shows. Broader topics—the Apollo 17 landing, Richard Nixon's second term, and an earthquake in Nicaragua—are touched on and dropped. Ginny sets the table. She folds cloth napkins under the forks. She moves the chairs and sweeps up with a broom. She takes her long-handled cobweb duster and cleans the room's overhead corners.

Over dinner they talk about clams and seafood and Miles's father, who is slowly failing in Delaware. After dinner they clean up together, then move into the living room and go on talking. There's little else to do in this house with no radio, no TV, no deck of cards. They sit on three chairs like mariners in a cockpit. Ginny rests a hand on the table beside her, thumbing a closed book.

"Do I make you nervous?" Miles asks.

"What do you mean?"

"Please don't think I've come to take Jamie away."

"Like the first time? When the two of you went off to Provincetown?"

"You weren't too happy about that."

"He was nineteen. And I hardly knew you then, but now you're family. If anything, the two of you relax me."

"You do seem a bit on edge," Jamie says.

"It's the hour. I don't do so well in the evening."

"Because that's when you drank," Miles says.

"Yes. But as I'm sure you've heard, there's not a bottle of anything in this house. And don't worry, I'm not going to start. I won't be slipping out to a bar behind your back. I'm just fighting a long habit."

"At least you never drank in the morning," Jamie says.

"I never needed to. I don't know why that was. Some people wake up with miserable hangovers and drink to get over them. But I rarely got them. Maybe they'd have taught me a lesson."

"How do you feel right now?" Miles asks.

"I've been sober for fifty-one days. I'm doing okay."

"But you still think about it."

"There are people in my AA group who've been sober for twenty years and think about it every day."

"So what do we *do* about it?"

"I don't know. You two cook. I get nervous and clean the house."

"Let's not forget the beach," Jamie says. He turns to Miles. "Every afternoon we go to the beach and freeze our asses off. Then we come back to our little house and have dinner, and talk."

Miles, warned in advance, has brought along his warmest clothes, and the next day wears gloves and a cap pulled down over his ears. On the beach, after only a few steps, he stumbles in the loose sand. He goes down to his knees, then struggles to his feet.

"The sand's not so mushy in Key West," he says. "It has more coral."

They walk half way to East Hampton, sometimes abreast, sometimes in file as they pass close to the waves. There's not a boat in sight, nor any ship on the horizon. A recent high tide has washed up tangled streaks of seaweed, fish ribs, broken balsa floats and an occasional bottle, its glass ground smooth. On their way back the wind is behind them.

"Again we took to the beach," Ginny says, "for another day walking along the shore of the resounding sea, determined to get it into us."

"What's that?"

"Thoreau, from *Cape Cod*."

Beside them, the slow heartbeat of the waves. To the west, the mist has lifted under a streak of blue sky. When they get back to Ginny's car, Miles can't open his door, and Jamie goes around to open it for him.

"It's the cold," Miles explains. "These gloves are too thin."

"Maybe, but I've seen the same thing happen at home when it's eighty degrees."

"Not very often," Miles says.

They drive home through the potato fields, side by side on the front seat of Ginny's Chevrolet, which soon warms up and blows a stream of hot air across their legs. The road is empty. All the way to Sag they don't pass another car.

Jamie is annoyed, she can tell. She watches him slice some beets from the market, thwacking through them to the cutting board below. All through their dinner prep, he and Miles say almost nothing. As Jamie serves the curried chicken, Ginny asks him, "Are you angry about something?"

Maybe she should have waited. They could have eaten first. Now they sit down and no one picks up a fork.

Jamie doesn't answer, and thirty seconds pass before Miles says, "It's me."

"What did you do?"

"He left all our paints and brushes at home," Jamie says. "He didn't bring anything. He knew I was going to want to paint. We talked about it before I flew up here."

"Jamie, I'm sorry. There's something I should have told you. I should have told you a month ago."

"What the shit, you're supposed to tell me everything."

"I know, and I didn't. I was trying to figure out what was happening." He holds up his right hand. "My fingers are messed up. They look all right, but they don't work."

He closes and opens his fist. It all looks okay to Ginny.

"I pick up a brush and start to paint, and I can't. Or I can, but not the way I want to. If you were watching me you might not even notice. I could paint a seascape or something, and you'd just think I was going impressionist. But it's been driving me crazy. I know the brushstrokes I want to make and I can't do them. My left hand's okay, but I can't paint with my left hand. I feel like a two-year-old."

"You haven't shown me any canvases lately," Jamie says. "Is this why?"

"I was trying to do one of you as a kid, working off some old photos. I kept at it but it was all screwed up."

"And this has been going on for a month?"

"Maybe two."

"Let me see," Ginny says. She stretches and folds his fingers, then rubs his palm with her thumb. She looks at his other hand. "I'm no expert, but I don't see anything wrong. Does it hurt?"

"No pain at all."

"How about your wrists, and your elbows?"

"They're fine."

"Have you seen a doctor about it?"

"No offense, Ginny, but I try to stay away from doctors."

"I know a couple of orthopedic surgeons in Southampton. I could get you an appointment."

"Surgery on my hand? Forget it." He holds it up. "I started painting with this when I was six, and painting is my life. That and you, Jamie. I'm sorry, I should have gone to your studio before I drove up. I got lost in my own troubles."

Jamie slides his chair closer to Miles and puts an arm around his shoulder. The two of them sit side by side, their eyes down and their heads touching. Ginny watches them, looks away, tries not to stare. She thinks about Joe. Did the two of them ever, at a table or in bed or watching a sunset, sit or stand beside each other with their heads lightly touching? For ten seconds? For two? That wasn't Joe's way. She wonders how her children ever learned to do this. From the bohemians and hippies, she thinks again. And from the gays, coming out of the closet.

On the afternoon of New Year's Eve they head down the beach under clouds so low and thick there's no sign of the setting sun. When they get back to their car at five o'clock, night has fallen.

Dinner, their one busy activity at home, is again a lively affair. Ginny prepares a butter sauce for the scallops, Jamie a ginger sauce and Miles a remoulade. Though it's nothing she'd do on her own, she's getting used to all this work in the kitchen. If she were here alone she'd just drop the scallops into a frying pan with some olive oil. Or more likely she wouldn't have any scallops, she'd just heat up some soup from a can.

They eat in the kitchen at her round oak table. They talk about Rob and his commune, about the many painters in Key West, about Jackson Pollock just down the road here in Springs. As they move into the living room with their mint teas, Ginny checks the time on the clock in her bedroom. Eight thirty. She should buy a clock for the kitchen, or fix the grandfather clock beside the fireplace. Left by the previous owner, its hands have been stuck for years at ten after ten.

She sits down facing Jamie and Miles. "I don't think I'm going to make it to midnight."

"No reason we have to," Jamie says.

Miles ignores their disavowals. "Ginny, tell me about the AA meetings you go to. Are they helpful?"

"I like going, usually. It's a little community and we all share some history. Though last night I had my doubts about some of it."

Miles watches her and waits.

"There were too many drunken stories. I think they're worried about tonight—you know, this night when the champagne corks fly and everyone's toasting at midnight. As we went around the circle, half the people wanted to tell some old New Year's Eve story. The preface was always the same, how you had to get sober and stay sober, and nothing was more important than that. But what they really wanted to do was talk about how crazy they got one year, and how much trouble they got into. The usual recovery stories get pretty dull, and it's more exciting to tell how drunk you got and how you screwed up. But it started to feel like a competition. Who had messed up the worst? *Enough*, I wanted to say. I almost got up and left."

"Did you say anything when it was your turn?"

"No, I passed. I didn't want to hear all those stories, but I didn't want to rain on them."

"Other times you talk?"

"Sure. You don't have to, but I usually have something to say."

"Like what?"

"Miles! If you want to know something, you can ask me."

"I want to know what drinking was like when you were married, and how it changed. You know Jamie and I drink at home, and sometimes I worry about it."

"You're not drinking now."

"No, and I don't miss it. Jamie?"

"I think I'll miss it at midnight. In Key West we'd be sloshed at some club. But I'm okay."

"Joe and I did not get sloshed. We drank but not too much. Maybe sometimes I got a little tipsy, but it wasn't like the stories I heard last night. It was never like that. But then, after Rich...."

She stops and looks at Jamie. "I don't know if you want me to talk about this."

"It's all right, Mom. Do you think Rob and I haven't talked about every inch of it? Miles, too. He always wants to know everything."

"But there's plenty I haven't talked about," she says. "Alcoholics lie and cover things up."

"Homosexuals lie and cover things up," Miles says. "What happened after Rich?"

"I totally went off the rails."

She tells him about her drive from Miami to Savannah after Rich left her, and about the lost weeks that followed. "After a while I settled down. I kept a lid on it, but I also had pills. I mixed them up. Benzos and rum, barbs and gin. After I went back to work it got to be a routine. I'd usually wait until I came home. Then I'd have my first drink and take a Tuinal and lie down in bed. There's not much to describe. I don't have any of those raging stories, I just lay there not wanting to feel anything, not wanting to think. It's about as interesting as that movie Warhol made of a guy sleeping."

"I think that was his lover," Miles says.

"But a five-hour movie of someone lying in bed asleep?"

"You never know, Mamá. If someone filmed *you* sleeping for five hours, I'm sure I'd watch it."

"Jamie, you're a charmer. Though would you make it through an hour?" She closes her eyes, opens her mouth and bends her neck to one side in mock stupor.

Jamie laughs. "Miles would watch it with me. Ask him how much we talk about you."

"All the time," Miles says.

"Sure, because I've made so much trouble for everyone."

"Not any more," Jamie says.

"Well, I'm about to set a record. I think this will be my first completely sober New Year's Eve since I was a girl. Since I was fourteen and my father started giving me a taste of his brandy. How about you, Miles?"

"I guess I drank most years. But then one time when I was first teaching at Darwin I went up to northern Maine and spent Christmas and New Year's in someone's cabin. I thought the isolation might cleanse me of all naughty thoughts. It was just me and the woods and no alcohol."

"What kind of naughty thoughts?"

"I think you can guess."

"Did it work?"

"For about ten minutes the first day."

Jamie reaches over and punches his arm. "Incorrigible," he says with a grin.

They sit for a time in silence. Then, like a student in class, Miles lifts his hand. "Can I ask another question about Rich?"

"Sure."

"You can always tell me to shut up."

"Except you've probably figured out that I like to talk about him."

"Why did he leave you?"

"That's what I wanted to know. He never said it, but let's start with the obvious. He was thirty-four and I was forty-seven, so maybe he woke up to where that was headed."

"Did he have to wait until you left your husband?"

"Maybe he did. Maybe for him it was some kind of competition. And having won, by separating me from Joe, he was done with me. As long as he was chasing me he couldn't get enough. Once he had me, it was over."

"Do you ever hear from him?"

"I don't even know if he's alive. He must be, but I don't know where he lives or works. Miami, probably. I wish I could wash him out of my mind forever."

"But you can't," Miles says. "So instead, what if you don't hold back? What if you talk about him any time you want? To us."

"I'd embarrass myself."

"Maybe embarrassment is better than obsession."

Jamie lifts his palm. "You see what I live with? He's like a resident shrink."

"And how is that for you?"

"I love it. Most of the time."

Ginny stands up, steps into the kitchen, turns off the overhead light and comes back. She stands beside the Christmas tree with its five small ornaments and a paper angel on top.

"Okay, I'll tell you a story. Not exactly about Rich, but something I never talk about."

She feels safer standing up. If she gets half way through and doesn't want to go on, she can leave for a glass of water.

"I had a psychiatrist once. I saw him every week."

Jamie leans forward. "When was this?"

"In that first bad year, when you two were up in Provincetown. He was a help, once I got used to it, because he got me to talk about everything. About Rich and Joe and how I'd torn our family apart. Then one day I got a call, canceling my appointment. They said the doctor was sick. Later they called again and told me that he'd died, of a heart attack. I was miserable. I'd put my life in his hands, and now he was gone. Later his office set me up with another psychiatrist, and I tried to ease into that. But this second guy knew something he wanted me to figure out. He kept giving me hints, and finally I had to face it. My first psychiatrist didn't die of a heart attack, he killed himself. He walked into the woods behind his house and shot himself in the head."

A long silence in the small house.

"Afterward I thought I should have guessed what happened, because he'd asked me so often whether *I* thought about suicide. Of course I had, but then *he* did it. I wanted to talk to his other patients, but no one would give me their names. I lived with it. I drank and took more pills."

Ginny sits down. In the quiet room they hear a few small explosions in the village, the distant sound of New Year's Eve. Maybe they'll make it to midnight after all. They sit and watch each other. This too seems new. People don't just say more these days, Ginny thinks, they look right at you.

"How about you, Miles? How's your father? You said things didn't go well with him on this trip."

"I already told Jamie what happened."

"So now tell me."

He's slow to start. He glances out the windows into the dark, running his palms up and down his thighs. Then he stands, as Ginny did, with his back to the fireplace.

"Delaware was on the way and he wanted to see me, so I told him I'd stop by for a few days. You have to understand, he hates me. Or he hates that I'm a faggot. That's his word. He can't stand what I've done with my life. He thought I should be a lawyer, because when I was ten or eleven I started arguing with him, and I was good at it. I knew he was running around on my mother. She never told me, but I figured it out. Then she got sick. Her heart, her physical heart went to pieces. And I have to say, he looked after her. He was good about that. But after she died he fell apart. I don't think he knew how much he depended on her. My sister went to live in Alaska, about as far away as she could get, and I was always the black sheep. He's a bitter guy. He never wants to hear about my painting, and not a word about Jamie. I don't slap him in the face with it, but occasionally I mention Jamie's name, and whenever I do, that's the end of the conversation."

"But you still go to see him."

"I have so far."

"What happened this time?"

"My dad was a builder for forty years. He knows everything about construction, and though his knees are giving out he doesn't really need my help. But when I got to his house he told me he'd started a project in the garage. He's converting the whole thing into some kind of studio or den, but he doesn't want the town to know about it, because he doesn't want his taxes to go up. He already had the two-by-six joists and now he needed some ply for the subfloor. He was paranoid about it and only wanted to bring in three or four sheets at a time, and he wanted me to go out with his pickup to three different lumber yards. Okay, I went along with that. But really, he wanted me to finish the whole job. And when I told him I couldn't, that I was driving up here to see you—I didn't even mention Jamie—he wouldn't listen. He ignored me when I told him that I was leaving in three days. We went to work on the floor, and as long as we didn't talk about anything other than the layout and what to cut, everything rolled along. But the morning I was leaving, I packed my suitcases and put them in my car. I didn't even know where he was until the garage door opened and he came out with a piece of two-by-four, holding it like a bat. I don't know if he wanted to hit me or my car or what, but he scared me and I grabbed him. I pulled him to the ground and he started blabbering about how I had to help him, he was too old to do this work by himself. So I got him up and took him back inside and made him a cup of coffee, and we sat there and I told him the truth, that I was coming up here to see the two of you, and I'm gay, and I'm an artist and I'm never going to be a lawyer, and I'll try to look after him if he needs help but I can't come and move in with him. He calmed down a little and listened to what I said. But the only word he spoke the whole time was *Okay*. After a long silence I said goodbye and went outside and got in my car. He didn't come out, and I drove away."

Miles stands in front of the fireplace, swaying from foot to foot.

"Do you think he learned anything? Will he ever be agreeable?"

"If he reaches out again I'll probably go see him. But I can't imagine stopping by with Jamie on our way back to Key West. What do you think, Jamie? Want to meet my dad after all these years?"

"Doesn't sound like a good idea."

In the quiet that follows, Ginny watches herself. She's seen before how she responds to stories about parents ill at ease with their son's or daughter's homosexuality. Compared to the rest of them, she's the enlightened parent. But now it feels pitiful, how she pumps herself up this way. She's been doing it for years. *Let it go*, she thinks. Why can't she listen to stories—both this one from Miles, and those she hears every week at her AA meetings—and not compare herself to everyone else? Why have to prove that she hasn't been as bad as some others? She's been bad. Work on that, she thinks.

"Look," Jamie says, "it's snowing."

They go outside and stand coatless in the yard, the soft flakes swarming down onto their hands and faces. They don't stay long, and as they come back inside the phone rings. It's Rob in Ohio, calling from the commune in the midst of a noisy party.

"Natalia sends her best," he says, but she's off talking to someone else.

After a few bland comments, Ginny passes the handset around, sharing Rob though she doesn't want to. When she gets the phone back the noise behind him is even louder. She can practically feel the alcohol. Rob describes the game they're playing with Moon as the football, passing her from one to another as she screams with delight.

"Moon is the *football*?"

"It's safe," Rob says. "We just pretend to throw her. Listen to her, she loves it. And tomorrow morning she'll have us up at six wanting to play some more. You've done all this, Mom, you know how it is. But someone else wants the phone and I better join in. I just called to say happy New Year to everyone." And with that he's gone.

Has she done all this? No, from everything she hears, Rob and Natalia and the four other parents are more fun-loving and more devoted to Moon than Ginny ever was as a parent. Now she lies in bed wearing a pair of flannel pajamas, listening to the grumble of the furnace. She sips from a glass of water, then sets it down on the bedside table beside her latest book, Mary Renault's *The Persian Boy*. Though it will lead him to naughty thoughts, she'll pass it on to Miles after she finishes it. He and Jamie have gone out for a walk, perhaps hoping to catch some piece of New Year's in the village. Maybe they'll have a drink and keep it to themselves.

In a way, she owes Miles everything. Ten years ago he saved Jamie's life. That's how Jamie puts it, and Ginny has always believed he would have died without Miles. It was Jamie's second year at Dartmouth, and he was desperate. Chad, the classmate he loved, after months of friendship, had realized that Jamie wanted to hold and kiss him, wanted more than that.

He turned on Jamie and screamed at him. He told him if he ever *looked* at him again he was going to kick the shit out of him. "*I don't have fucking fags for friends.*"

Others heard them, and Jamie wanted to die. He figured out how. He'd walk up into the mountains before a big storm, taking no blanket or tent. Somewhere up on Mt. Adams he'd sit down on the snow and let himself go numb, and soon it would all be painless. He'd read that the Eskimos sometimes did this, when age overtook them and food was scarce. The storm would cover him up and no one would find him until spring. What saved him was Miles, his old teacher at Darwin, who persuaded him to fake his death instead, to leave his car on a mountain road and let everyone think the snowstorm had engulfed him. After Ginny figured that out and tracked them down, she let Jamie go off to live with Miles in Provincetown. Well, he didn't need her consent, he was nineteen. But he was always clear about it. He'd have died without Miles.

In this house where there's almost no privacy, she better give them some time alone. It's a selfish plan of course, because she wants them to stay longer. She's confident enough now to go out by herself. She could take a solo walk at the beach, that's safe enough.

Her feet are cold. She gets up and puts on a pair of alpaca socks, then nestles again under her quilt. Her boys are a comfort, but eventually she will live here on her own. She'll have to do something more than walk beside the ocean and cook dinner and clean her house, but she hasn't figured out what.

She's thought about re-enlisting with the Peace Corps. Not in Chile, where Alberto is now married to someone else. Maybe in Peru or Ecuador, but that feels too far away. This is her home—this country, this town, this house. This house where she has never spent a winter. People did, decades ago. They kept fires going in the fireplace and in the kitchen's old cookstove. They were stronger than she is. They must have piled on the blankets at night and gone off to work in the morning, fishing or harvesting oysters in the bay.

After Rich she could no longer practice anesthesia. In her broken state it would have been far too delicate to hold a patient's life in her hands all through an operation. She worked as a general practitioner in Chile, and later at Shinnecock Urgent Care. But all that is finished. No clinic in the U.S. is going to hire her now, not even for nursing duties. No one is going to let her get anywhere near their drugs.

She's been frugal all these years and has money saved up. But what is she going to do next? Take a job at an old age home for two dollars an hour? Work for a medical journal, writing that turgid prose?

She better stop worrying about it. Even thinking about it, because it never helps. She should go outside with a sleeping bag and lie under the sky, staring up at Cassiopeia, at Cygnus and the Pleiades, at a world that neither needs nor rejects her. Even as she imagines this, she hears some fireworks from the village, then car horns joining in. She has made it to midnight.

5

It's Miles who guides their after-dinner talks. One night he steers them to
Jamie's years at Dartmouth, another to Ginny's mother and her dementia.
He looks good as he sits on his chair, but during the day Ginny watches
him move. She watches his right foot after it bangs against a table leg. She
sees how hard it is for him to open jars, how slowly he eats dinner, how he
slurs occasional words.

"Miles, I think you should see a neurologist I know."

"Why?"

"Because of the troubles you're having."

"What troubles?"

"You told us you can't paint, and sometimes you knock into things."

"I'm a little clumsy. It's no big deal."

"And you have trouble swallowing."

"I can swallow."

"But it's getting harder, isn't it?"

"So what? What are you worried about?"

He stares at her hard but she doesn't tell him. "It would be good to see
an expert. It's why we have neurologists."

"What do *you* think is wrong?"

She looks away. She wants the diagnosis to come from someone else.

"*What*? What *is* it? Tell me the truth, why don't you?" He gets to his feet
and half lurches into the Christmas tree. Jamie jumps up and grabs him.
He stares down at Ginny. "Just *tell* me."

She stands up to face him. She wants to reach out to him, to touch him, but Jamie still has him wrapped up.

"I think you might have Lou Gehrig's Disease."

At eight in the morning she drives him to the neurologist's office in Southampton, where the doctor asks a hundred questions. He asks if his sense of smell has changed. Has he lost weight? Does he sometimes drool? The doctor inspects his mouth and tongue, has him drink and swallow, then chew and swallow. He taps him, presses him and takes him out of the building into the parking lot to watch him walk. A few snowflakes are in the air. One seagull, then another swoops over the lot, flares and lands. Miles looks tired. He looks defeated. The doctor leads them back inside, sits Miles down and says, "I can't say for sure, but I believe it's most likely Lou Gehrig's Disease." He nods toward Ginny. "ALS, as we know it. Amyotrophic lateral sclerosis."

Miles tucks his long legs beneath him. "Are there any tests? So we could know?"

"They have an EMG machine at the Mayo Clinic in Minnesota. That's where Lou Gehrig went. But until the symptoms are more pronounced, it's hard to be sure. There's a chance it could be Parkinson's, but I don't think so."

"How bad is it?"

"So far it's mild. From the way you describe things, I'd guess you've had it for six months or so."

"It doesn't hurt."

"No, it's a painless disease. It's not contagious, either."

"Does anyone survive it?"

"Not in the end."

"When *is* the end?"

"It's hard to say. For Lou Gehrig it was only two years, but people do live longer."

"Are there drugs for it?"

"I'm afraid there's nothing yet."

The doctor looks down. He writes something on his clipboard. Snow is coming down in the parking lot and the empty fields beyond. Miles slumps in his chair. He stares across the room at a poster of a brain. Minute by minute, he seems to be shrinking. He says in a whisper, "Jamie isn't going to like this."

Ginny explains to the two of them the unsure timeline of paralysis. She says that both speech and the ability to swallow will end. Miles sits backward on his chair, his hands gripping the spindles. Their house in Key West is going to be a problem, Ginny says, with its stairs to the second floor.

"I could move to my studio."

"No kitchen," Jamie says. He paces around the room, the most distraught of the three.

Miles unfolds himself from his chair. "Look, for now I'm okay. I can still do everything." He stands up and gives them a small pair of jumping jacks, his hands almost touching the ceiling. "We need a project. Okay, *I* need one, and it's right in front of us. Even with your new furnace, it's freezing in this house."

"Probably because it's ten degrees outside."

"I bet there's no insulation in these old walls, and none in the ceiling upstairs."

Before an hour is up they have chewed into a wall in the pantry to take a look. Behind the lath and plaster, the only insulation is some balled-up newspapers from the 1920's, faded and brittle. "Useless," Miles says. "We need some batts of R-13. I can't paint, but I can build."

In the days that follow he turns away from all questions about his health or how he feels. After his steady interest in delicate topics, this seems strange to Ginny. In the evenings the three of them sit with their tea and speak of anything other than Lou Gehrig's Disease. During the day they tear the house apart. The plaster knocks down without a fight, but they have to pry the lath from the framing studs, stick by stick. Miles and Jamie make a run to the hardware store in Southampton and return with hammers, pry bars, a tape measure, a circular saw and a stapler.

To Ginny, Miles seems a different person. Of course, because he's been told he's going to die. He's been told he'll never paint the way he used to. He and Jamie work all day, and Ginny can't keep up. On the second afternoon she drives to the beach and takes a walk. Perhaps they take a break when she's gone to make love in one of their beds upstairs. Ginny doubts it, because when she gets home they're still hard at it.

Miles has installed insulation before, working with his father years ago. But this house is unique. The studs are rough-cut oak, randomly spaced. Along with the pink batts of insulation, Miles has some 2X4s delivered for horizontal blocking. Instead of drywall, they're going to panel the rooms with poplar tongue and groove to match the chases.

Amidst the activity, Ginny finds an unexpected peace. For years the misery in this house has been all hers, but Miles's troubles now dwarf her own. That he and Jamie have come to Sag Harbor to take care of her is all but forgotten. Miles and his future is now their focus, even if they rarely speak of it.

Ginny tries a few times. One night she suggests that a visit to the Mayo Clinic might be worthwhile.

"I can't see why."

"So you'd have a better idea of what's coming."

"They can't be sure, that's what the doctor said. Can they tell me how long I'll live? Are they going to pin that down?"

"No, I don't think they can."

Miles sits backward on his chair again, as if fending off the world. "Why even talk about it?" he says. "We all know what's happening to me."

They settle into a gentler routine. They work until one or two, eat lunch, then head out for a walk at the beach. Miles is game, but his foot keeps catching in the sand. If it were summer they could walk close to the firmer sand by the water, but now they can't let the streaking waves touch them. Still, Miles's draw to a daily walk is now as strong as Ginny's.

In two weeks they finish the wall paneling, then start on the sloping ceilings upstairs. Under the splintery painted boards they find no insulation at all, only the ancient purlins that support the shingles above. Everything slows down as they work off a pair of ladders. Ginny has chosen a darker cherry for the new ceiling, which they drill and nail into the two-by-six rafters, over thicker batts of insulation. As the end of the job nears, Ginny worries about what will come next. This work has become the backbone of their lives. It's too bad, she thinks, that they can't start in the late afternoon and work into the evening. That's when she needs a distraction from the drink she always wants. Of course she's not going to drink, but what a battle it is.

She has her guests, two people she loves, but sometime soon they'll be leaving. At the end of the day their thoughts are elsewhere, with their own troubles. After dinner one night Miles starts in with some questions. He wants to know about swimming, about walking, about pissing and taking a crap. He's especially worried about eating.

"It can get bad," Ginny tells him. "Many patients wind up with a feeding tube."

"Down my throat?"

"Through the nose, usually. Or there's a fairly simple surgery, a gastrostomy, that inserts a catheter directly into your stomach."

"Don't do that to me."

"You should write out your wishes, Miles. Make them clear and have them witnessed. And even so, you might change your mind. I've seen it happen plenty of times. Someone decides against a level of care, they forbid it absolutely, and later they want it. It's why you need to be able to tell us what you want, which can be a problem when you lose your speech. If you can still write, fine. If not, we could use an alphabet board and you can point to the letters. Or if you can't point, Jamie can do it, and you can nod or blink your eyes when he lands on the right letter."

"Shit on this disease."

She has said too much. *Just answer his questions*, she tells herself. Why did she have to skip to the end like that, to the worst of it? Why does she have to prove she knows all about it? Which she doesn't. She's never seen one of those alphabet boards, just read about them. Unless Miles asks, she doesn't have to lay out all the bitter details.

"And Jamie," he says, "I'm not going to put you through all this."

"Don't worry about me. We've gone over this already."

"I *am* going to worry about you. That'll be the last thing that goes. But I don't want to drag you down into it. You're young. You have to paint and live."

"I will. I'm going to paint and live and take care of you. And for once, you old bugger, you won't be able to stop me."

Miles laughs at this, and the two of them watch each other. Of course he's going to drag Jamie into it, Ginny thinks, and her, too. That's what happens.

After all the ceiling boards are up and lightly oiled, they vacuum and dust every surface in the house. And then, as Ginny has feared, they don't know what to do. The furnace has an easier time of it and the house warms up, but the relentless gray days wear on both Miles and Jamie. At night they reminisce about Key West and its sunsets. Miles pulls back from their beach walks over the cold and difficult sand. He's ready to go home, and so is Jamie. They hadn't planned on staying this long.

The time has come, Ginny agrees, and she assures them she'll do fine on her own. She won't drink, and she'll still have people to talk to. She'll go to both weekly AA meetings, and drive to East Hampton on Sundays for a Narcotics Anonymous meeting she's heard about. But it's all a false front. She's afraid of how she'll feel when she's alone, at dusk, at seven at night, at eight and nine and ten. She wants to say, *Don't leave me.* But the troubles they face are so much greater than her own, she's ashamed of her desperation.

The three of them sit in the quiet living room, surrounded by the comforting new walls. It's the end of a campaign. Jamie and Miles will leave, they decide, in a couple of days. Their relief at the plan is clear, though they try not to show it. They want to be back in Key West in their own small wooden house, with time to themselves.

On the night before they leave, Rob calls from the commune. He talks first with Jamie, and he's clearly worried about Ginny staying alone in her house. When she takes the phone she lies to him. She's doing fine, she says, thanks to all three of them. She doesn't mention Miles's disease, because he's asked her not to. Rob wishes he could come back and spend some more time with her, but there's trouble on the farm.

"The Six has fallen apart. We're done. Tasia and Barry aren't even here, they took Moon with them and left. They're the birth parents, not one of the original couples. The rest of us are in mourning, and Natalia is furious. But you could still come out for a visit, Mom. You know everyone loves you here."

"When would be a good time?"

"Well, maybe not right now. These are hard times for us. In the spring might be better."

"In the spring? It's still the middle of winter."

"Mom, I'm sorry. We're pretty confused just now."

"Yes," she says. "Me too."

6

Her house is clean but empty, and Ginny restless. She calls her sister in Connecticut and suggests a visit. "I'd just come for the day," she says. "We could go out for lunch."

"You're welcome to stay over, I'd be happy with that."

She wants to see Carol but she's not going to stay overnight in her house, because Carol drinks. Most nights, Ginny knows, she goes to bed half soused. "How about lunch at the Red Barn?"

"I like the Red Barn," Carol says. "They always have fresh lobster."

"But can I ask a favor? You know I've been sober for two months now. Could you not have a drink while we eat?"

"Their Manhattans are so good. But of course, Ginny. We'll have a completely sober meal."

The traffic is oddly thin as she skirts the city and heads out to Connecticut on the Merritt. Still, she doesn't drive as fast as she used to, and it's a three-hour trip. When they both lived in Westport they got together often, but now it's been almost a year. A lonely year for Carol, after her husband Milton died of a heart attack.

Carol is also a smoker, and lights up on their way to the restaurant. Her car, her house, her clothes all smell of cigarettes. She has confessed to smoking in bed at night, and Ginny fears that sometime she'll fall asleep and set her bed on fire. But they've talked about this before, several times, and for now Ginny lets it go.

She's happy to walk into the Red Barn, where she used to come with Joe for a rare night out. Swayed by Carol's enthusiasm, she joins her in an order of lobster tails. But as the waiter walks off, Carol calls him back and makes what seems a coy, even flirtatious request. "Could you make me a Shirley Temple please?"

In two minutes it's on the table. "You see," Carol says. "No alcohol for me!"

Ginny wants to slap her. The bright red drink looks like a strawberry daiquiri, and Carol hovers over it, sipping it with pleasure, giving it all the attention she would an actual cocktail. Her voice even sounds a bit tipsy as she calls up the many Thanksgivings their families shared, meals always prefaced with gin and vermouth.

Even as her sister annoys her, Ginny is aware that she's a helpful distraction. There are dangers in a restaurant, where drinks can be had so easily. As Carol talks, Ginny stays safe by feeding her grudge.

Carol chats on about a shopping trip she made to the city, about a walk she took in Riverside Park in front of their mother's old apartment, about the bulbs she planted around her house last fall. She barely pauses between one story and the next. *She's afraid,* Ginny thinks. Maybe afraid that Ginny will start reciting the Twelve Steps, then launch into some evangelical plea for sobriety. And in fact, Ginny would like to talk about drinking and how she's leaving it behind. But the topic is already a barrier between them, and she doesn't want to make it worse. At a pause in the stories she says, "You look good, Carol."

"I don't know about that."

"No, you do."

She's a good deal thinner than Ginny, and her hair has been styled. They have the same chestnut hair they had as young girls, but Ginny, unwilling to bother with hers, wears a shorter cut. And while Ginny has come in a sweater and an old pair of slacks, Carol wears a handsome dress. Ginny asks about their younger sister, Lauren, who lives in New Brunswick and whom they rarely see. They talk about the dances and plays the three of them put on in Ohio when Ginny was a young teenager, Carol two years younger and Lauren only seven or eight. Lauren has always been the guileless and unaffected sister. Ginny has never seen her drunk, nor the least intoxicated.

This is clearly the lens through which she'll now see everything. The world is made up of drinkers and abstainers.

After the meal they drive to Sherwood Island, walk out onto the sandy sweep of the beach and stand close beside each other, looking out over the rustling water. It's cold, but Ginny is glad to be outdoors, where Carol's cigarettes stay in her purse and no one is sipping cocktails. The seagulls have vanished, and the waves are so small they barely slurp in.

"Are you going to keep this up?" Carol asks. "No liquor, ever?"

"No liquor and no meds."

"I couldn't do that, it's a sleeping pill for me every night. And I do love a drink. Though look how good I've been today!"

"You have, and I thank you."

"What about Joe? Do you ever see him?"

"We write sometimes."

"What about other men?"

"In the last couple of months I've been focused on staying sober. And I have to figure out what I'm going to do next. I'd like to go back to work, but you know I lost my license. How about you? Have you been lonely without Milton?"

"I've been quite the proper widow. But I doubt that I'm finished with men. Don't you look around?"

"I guess I don't."

"And you were always the passionate sister."

"I remember that."

Some gulls appear in their colony, a dozen of them pouring down onto the sand to alight not thirty feet away.

"Don't you need to be held sometimes?"

This is so surprising from Carol, so direct, that Ginny steps in front of her and says, "I'll hold you."

For a full minute they embrace in silence. But Carol isn't done. "I want to have a man," she says. "In my bed, and sometime I'm going to. I haven't given up."

"I guess I have."

"Ginny, don't. You're only fifty-seven. That isn't old."

"Old enough. I think about other things. About Jamie and Rob and their troubles."

This is delicate, because when she speaks of her sons it raises the specter of Janna, Carol's daughter, an only child who killed herself five years ago, leaving a husband and two young sons. Carol almost never talks about her. Ginny wants to ask now how she kept on living after Janna's death. She drank, of course. Now, though Janna is gone and Milton is gone, Carol seems the more eager sister, the one hungry for more life. How does she do this? She's a better drinker than Ginny ever was.

This line of thought dismays her. She wants to believe that she and Carol can help each other, but maybe not, because everyone who drinks now scares her. The two of them share a quiet few minutes, their shoulders touching as they watch the gulls and the gray waters of the Sound, and say nothing more about their children.

At home the next day she regrets that she didn't stay in Connecticut for a night. She could have taken a motel room and had breakfast with Carol in the morning. Now she sits in her living room's single armchair. Jamie and Miles are gone, the house is quiet, she has no job, the beach is cold, she doesn't want to cook, she must not drink.

Why didn't she and Carol talk more about their mother? It was their natural topic and somehow they said almost nothing about her. Gran is fading from the world. When does anyone recall her love of elaborate tea services, velvet dresses and all things English? Do either of Ginny's sisters remember the curtain she drew over the bathroom mirror whenever she undressed to take a bath? What do they think of Pop, who let Gran do all the work of raising them? And did they sense Gran's relief when he died? Of course she mourned, but Ginny also saw the release from a marriage that had gone on too long. Someday she'll ask her sisters about it. But it bothers her that she let Carol ramble on, and rambled herself, and they said almost nothing about Gran's marriage, her dementia, her death.

Ginny goes into her room and lies down. She has avoided doing this in the middle of the day, but now she needs it. She wants to drift back to her childhood in Columbus, to their backyard with its peach and pawpaw trees where they put on Ginny's plays. Plays about princesses, toads and gazelles. For their dances, Gran sewed them long white dresses with many buttons and sashes, worn over ballet shoes. They pranced and flung themselves about the yard, sometimes getting their feet wrapped up in their skirts and tumbling onto the grass. They wanted to wear tights and tutus, but Pop would not allow it.

Do they remember the time their uncle came for a visit, a bachelor with no kids of his own, but who loved to play with the three of them? He got down on the floor with them and had them teach him jacks. He played for an hour, as enthusiastic as a kid himself, then drove downtown to buy a Parcheesi board. They played that for an hour, then he sat back down on the floor and said, "Who's ready for more jacks?"

Do they remember the Sunday trips in Pop's old Ford, or the Circle Line Cruise they took around Manhattan, or the time they were driving back from New Brunswick and got a flat in Vermont, late in the afternoon and far from any gas station or motel. Pop couldn't get the lug nuts off, and no one stopped to help. Finally Gran changed out of her heels into a pair of walking shoes, set the tire wrench, held one side and stepped on the other, bouncing on it until the nut let go. She brushed Pop back and wrenched all the nuts off herself.

Ginny stretches out on her bed, feeling not like an outcast, but a loner. Most of the people she's been close to are paired. Jamie is, Rob is, Joe is, and Rich Villamano must be. The Brennans are. Not everyone at the commune is, but they have their close-knit group. Down in Chile, Don Alberto is married. Her sister Carol hasn't found anyone, but she's looking.

Floating along on her nostalgia is now her only intoxicant. Again she strokes her breasts and the inside of her thighs, and feels not the least quiver. Carol was right, she was always the passionate sister—but not anymore. Can she really be done with men? Sexually they could be blocks of wood. What if she found a woman she liked? Women do that. She's read Gertrude Stein and Alice B. Toklas and Djuna Barnes, and none of them shocked her. But women have never aroused her. It feels like nothing will again.

No wonder she loved her meds. With them none of this mattered. She didn't care about sex and didn't miss it. And why care now, she thinks, when the feeling has left her? Still, it's troubling to lie here so inert. She runs over her list of men, the ones she slept with. Not Mike Blake, her diving coach. Justin Tidwell was the first, before they married. Then Osamu Noguchi and Robert Capa, Joe Thorndike, Henry Bergheim, Ricardo Villamano and Alberto Fernandez. Not that many, really. But sex to her was always vital. It lit up her life, then destroyed it.

7

After a windy walk at Sagaponack, Ginny heads home via East Hampton, where she stops at the drugstore to pick up a notebook of lined, empty pages. Late in the afternoon she sits down in her armchair with the notebook and a fountain pen.

97 days

The beach always calms me, but not today. The wind was in my face the whole way to Georgica Pond, and two minutes after I turned around it started blowing in the opposite direction. How does that happen? It's freezing out there, but that won't stop me from going back tomorrow.

I haven't kept a diary since I was thirteen. I stopped then because no matter where I hid the book, my sisters were going to find it, and it was full of the feelings I wasn't supposed to have. We all knew what we weren't supposed to feel. Even my sisters were starting to know. But today I'm not so sure. Are any feelings wrong? Was it wrong to feel what I did for Rich Villamano, or just wrong to act on it?

I assume no one will ever read this. And if they do, too bad. Like a surgeon with his scalpel, I like the feel of this pen and notebook. I'm going to do this every day.

101 days

After yesterday's dead calm the waves today were so big the foam blew in and flecked me as I walked. As I waddled, I should say. That's how it feels every time I set out across the sand. Sometimes it doesn't bother me, sometimes I can think of nothing else.

Rob, Jamie, Miles—they were all polite about my weight, and kept telling me I looked fine. Yeah, sure. Soy vieja, pero no soy estupida. Well, sometimes I am. I was stupid yesterday when Patty Brennan called. She wanted to come see me, or for me to drive in to Bronxville and stay with her and Bill. I was stupid and cowardly. I didn't dare tell her how afraid of her I was, how after all this time I'm still leery about being around people who drink. And Bill will always drink. He is one smooth functioning alcoholic. Like me, for years.

After waiting until the end of April, she takes off for the commune. There's bound to be room at the farmhouse now that Moon's parents have gone, and she'll show up unannounced. She hasn't gone anywhere in months, but this is her new freedom. She has no dog or cat or anyone to take care of. She has no job or prospect of one, but she has money in the bank. She turns off her furnace, locks the door behind her and heads out in her Chevrolet. Now that she's calm and sober, she can drive as fast as everyone else. Of course they all wind up crawling as they approach the city, and it's almost as slow going out the other side. She thought she could make the trip in a day, but doesn't come close. She takes a motel room in Pennsylvania and reaches the commune the following afternoon.

Outside the farmhouse there's only one car in sight. Ginny's tired, and suddenly afraid. Rob's world is crowded, and the thought of facing everyone exhausts her. She steps out of her car and quietly closes the door. She wants to take a walk, a slow walk by the ocean with only gulls and terns for company. She knows how hectic the commune can be, and now feels it's a mistake to have come. But she's here. She steps up onto the porch and looks inside. As if waiting for her, Natalia stands in the living room with a white cloth bag in her hands, and waves her in with a swing of her head. Ginny opens the door and goes in.

"Hello, Natalia."

"Hello."

"I came for a visit."

"Yes."

It's always been hard to get much out of her. She's as beautiful as ever, with her thick hair and smooth dark skin. She's short and trim and not one to smile quickly. She doesn't now, and says nothing more until Ginny asks if Rob is around.

"He's building. Everyone's off in town, because we all have jobs now. We had to make some money."

"You're growing sprouts, I hear."

Natalia holds out the wet cloth bag. "I brought some back for dinner."

"I don't think I've ever eaten sprouts."

"I pretty much run the business now. They're good for you. Better than meat, that's for sure."

As she steps into the kitchen and sets the bag on the counter, Ginny notices her belly's small bulge. She's barely showing, but she must be pregnant. Her stance makes it clear, Ginny thinks, how she offers her profile. Or maybe it's how calm she is, how assured. But then, she was always like that. It seems she has nothing more to say.

Ginny asks, "Is there a room I could sleep in?"

"Sure, Tasia's room. No one has stayed there since she left."

After Ginny brings in her suitcase, Natalia leads her down the hall. It's the room Moon was born in. Ginny sits down on the bed and lays her palms on the cover. The house is old and musty. There are cobwebs in the corners of the ceiling. The afternoon sun pours in through the window. "Would it be all right if I took a nap?"

She wakes to find Rob standing in the doorway. "What the hell?"

"Spring is here, so I came."

"Usually we agree about visits."

"So agree and get over it."

She tosses off the bedspread and rises. Rob comes over and hugs her, as he's supposed to, but she feels his resistance. "I'm going to be busy," he says. "We're framing another house."

"That's all right. I'll find things to do."

"You didn't start drinking, did you?"

"I told you, I'm done with that."

"How long are you going to stay?"

She glances around the room. "How about as long as I want?"

"No, you're not the one in charge here."

"Why don't you put it to a vote. See what everyone thinks."

Natalia might resist her, but no one else, she's pretty sure. Her last time here Ginny was the savior, the one, after the birth, who coaxed out Tasia's resistant placenta.

"It's the hippie way," Ginny says. "You don't announce your plans, you just show up at someone's door."

"Face it, you're no hippie."

"Face it, I'm your mother and you invited me months ago."

He looks stiff and unfamiliar. Can he be this afraid of her? It's true that she's made trouble for years, but surely five sober months must be good for something.

At the big table she says hello to everyone already seated: the third couple, Cynthia and Mike, and Jerry who plays the piano, and big Lisa, and Flora who helped at the birth. She can't remember the names of the others, but nods at them. She sits down, and is immediately aware of the glasses on the table.

"Beer," she says.

"So? Now everyone has to stop drinking?"

Having suggested a vote on her tenure, she better not say yes. "Don't worry about it," she tells Rob. In fact, she wishes they would.

Dinner is an arugula and spinach salad, a soup of last year's potatoes and onions, and deep-fried tofu blanketed with the pale sprouts. Rob sits across from her at the round table, and for a time only talks to others. Then, during a rare silent pause, he catches her eye and says, "Have you noticed about Natalia?"

"No," she lies. "What?"

"We're going to have a baby."

"How about that."

The announcement stimulates everyone else. They already know, but they like hearing it again. Big quiet Lisa smiles like a volcano in eruption. Jerry slides over to the piano and taps a few notes, a song he seems to be inventing. Flora, in her robe, holds an imaginary child in her arms and rocks it. "It won't be Moon," she says, "but we'll be happy to have another baby girl here."

"A girl?" Ginny asks. "You already know?"

"I can feel it," Natalia says.

It's almost ten o'clock by the time Ginny gets to her room. She unpacks her bag, puts everything into a dresser, and lies down on the bed. There's still some talk from the living room. Perhaps they're drinking—then she catches a whiff of dope. They drink and they smoke, of course. Marijuana doesn't worry her because she was never a smoker of anything. And then the miracle. The realization that all evening she hasn't once ached for a drink. There was so much else going on that she didn't even think about it. She takes out her journal and pen.

May 2

Enough keeping track of my sober days, I have almost six months.

I made it through the evening. I talked with almost everyone, because they all wanted to talk to me. Natalia not so much. She's polite enough but doesn't reach out. Maybe it's because she's pregnant. I remember feeling something like that with both my boys—that I was on a mission and didn't have to take any shit from anyone. I was bringing a child into the world, and no job was more crucial.

Rob is unhappy with me. I hope he gets over it soon, but

if he doesn't I'll just talk to everyone else. Hah, the benefits
of a commune. I'll keep being cheerful, or as much as I can
manage, and wear him down.

May 3.
Just like that, I have a job. I'm head of the garden. Not really,
but everyone else is busy during the day, and I said I'd take
over. There are whole beds of lettuce, arugula, spinach and
kale, the broccoli and cauliflower plants are taking off and
the greenhouse is full of starts. Tomatoes, peppers, melons
and eggplants. Vegetables are much easier than people.

May 5
Natalia can be prickly. I asked her this afternoon if she was
planning on seeing an obstetrician and she said, "Don't talk
to me about that." She doesn't care if I weed the garden
and manage the greenhouse, but god forbid I should talk
about anything medical. I don't think she's going to want
me anywhere near the birth of her child, which is fine with
me. I won't get involved this time, the way I did with Moon.

Rob has softened, and one night after dinner, in the long May evening,
they go out for a walk. At first they're silent as they follow the gurgling
creek, then head up a path through the trees, threading their way past
maples, oaks and hickories, up into the last of the sunlight. The path is
steep near the top and Ginny breathes hard. On Long Island the most she
ever climbs is a forty-foot dune. At the top they emerge into a meadow of
new grass, green as felt and already knee-high. Rob takes off his baseball
hat and his dark hair spreads out. He says, "Mamá, I apologize. I shouldn't
have been so upset when you came. There's just so much going on, and
I felt guilty about not inviting you sooner. And I knew that Natalia was
bound to make some trouble."

"Maybe she's afraid of me and my addictions."

"But you aren't an addict anymore."

"Of course I am. I'll always be one, I just won't be using."

Far above them a pair of turkey vultures circle, lifted on a breeze Ginny can't see or feel. At home she has seagulls, but nothing flies like a vulture. She tells Rob that she talked to Natalia about seeing an obstetrician. "She didn't want to hear about it."

"She can be stubborn, I know, and she steers clear of doctors. It's not you, Mamá, it's every doctor and all medicine. After that labor we went through with Tasia, it worries me. But when it comes to childbirth my opinion doesn't count for much."

"Did you plan this, or did it just happen?"

"It was pure Natalia. Only a couple of days after Tasia and Barry left, she took me into one of the bedrooms and said, 'We're going to make a baby.' It was pretty much a decree."

"And you were ready?"

"I guess I was. We went right to work, morning and night for two weeks. We could have been a pair of rabbits. And that did it, she never got her next period. She'd always talked about having a child some day, and you know how she is when she decides something."

"So now it's just the two of you in the marriage?"

"She didn't want to keep it going with Cynthia and Mike. And those two were crushed. They both lost their original partners. Natalia and I, we had an adventure and now we're back together."

"But without Moon."

"That's been hard on everyone. We've had some after dinner where we all huddle up and cry. It's good, and last night after you went to bed we had a different ritual. Natalia lay out on the table, and everyone put their hands on her belly and said little prayers or sang something. We were really getting into it until she sat up and said, 'Thanks, that's enough.' She knows what she likes and makes it clear. It can be awkward sometimes, but I've always loved how blunt she is. It's a kind of courage."

"Will she be a good mother?"

"I'm sure she will. She's already made her plan. She'll quit her job at eight months and won't go back to work until Sophie is two or three."

"Sophie? You've already named her?"

"We tried out a few names, and this one seems to have stuck."

"What if it's a boy?"

"Mom, don't mention it. She's convinced."

They head home in the fading light. This was the right place to come, far from everyone. The tension between them has vanished. From some perch in the woods a whippoorwill calls out across the meadow. Calls again and again and again. What dedication, Ginny thinks.

She has adjusted. She's been here two weeks, almost three. She talks to people morning and night and it hasn't killed her. She retires to her room and no one comes knocking. But she can't go on like this forever, sharing her life with a house full of people. If she's going to stay in Ohio much longer, she'll need a place of her own.

After a drive to the McArthur supermarket to pick up some cooking oil and rice, she stops by the hotel in town and asks to see one of their rooms. The old bearded man at the desk takes her upstairs and shows her what he must think is a good one. A single minute inside and she's had enough. The windows look out on the town's main street, and the sound of tires and engines is unrelenting. She'll need a more secluded place than this.

> May 21
>
> Just when I was thinking I needed a break, Jamie called from Key West. Miles isn't doing well. He gets around with his walker but sometimes falls. He eats slowly and his speech has started to slur. Jamie didn't come out and ask me, but it's clear he needs help. He was effusive when I said I'd come.
>
> I've already told Rob that I'll be leaving. He sees how stiff things are between me and Natalia, but he has come around. "Come back any time," he said, "no invitation needed."
>
> It's what everyone said, except Natalia.

8

A hundred years ago she and her sons would probably have lived in the same town and she could have talked to them every day. Now she drives six hundred miles to see Rob and twice that to see Jamie. Sag Harbor, Vinton County and Key West, her expanded triangle.

Semis dot the road, but otherwise the traffic is light. Fields of winter wheat and newly-sprouted corn border the highway. No coffee this morning, she's saving that for later. A car trip shares something with a walk on the beach. There, her only decision is where to put her feet, and here, what lane to drive in. Beyond that her thoughts are free to wander, and it isn't long before they land on Rich Villamano. Their four years together, and the ten in which she tried to drink him out of her system. How could she have been so blind as to think he was going to marry her and stay with her forever? He was thirteen years her junior. He had told her often—was it always a lie?—how in love with her he was. Then, only days after she left Joe and her Westport home, *I've decided I don't want to marry you after all*.

She can wander through her old life, but can't get far with the future. It would be good to practice medicine again, but she'll need years of sobriety to get her license back. For that exam she'll have to memorize again the many thousand names of bones, tissues, diseases and drugs, most of them from Latin or Greek. And with a license will come a job, a schedule, an endless busy flow. It's what most people do, and how she lived herself most of her adult life. Just imagining it now makes her shaky.

She listens to the radio with its news at noon, then music of the Car-
olinas. She naps at a rest stop, fills up with gas and coffee and pushes on.
After twelve hours, just north of Jacksonville, she pulls into a Motel 6.
Six bucks for a room, pretty good. After dinner she slides into bed, but
sleep doesn't come. Her success these days is sobriety, but there must be
something more.

South of Miami the road narrows and runs beside the water, then over
the long bridges from key to key, spilling finally onto Key West. Ginny
tracks down the pale wooden house she knows from earlier visits, with its
green shutters and spreading palms. She climbs the three steps onto the
porch and peers in through the screen door. Miles sits in a living room
chair, staring at the floor.

"Miles," she says, and opens the door.

He looks up. "Ah, Ginny. So glad."

His speech sounds okay, but he doesn't move from his chair. She bends
to take him in her arms. "You look good," she lies. He looks subdued and
cautious, which was never his way.

"Jamie stepped out for some bread. We have a friend who bakes."

She pulls up a chair so they can speak at the same level. "That's good,"
she says, "that you can still eat bread." Immediately she regrets the *still*.

"I have to munch it like a cow. Meals take forever, but that's my life. How
was your trip?"

"You get to Miami and you think you're close, but no."

"Welcome to Mile Zero."

He speaks slower than before, and *zero* sounds like *cero*. She looks around
the room. "I've always loved this house. Wood everything and these tall
windows."

"I don't help much with it now. I can't stand up as easily as I used to."

"Sit, stand, do whatever you like Miles, it's fine with me."

"Really? Whatever I like?" He clears his throat and watches her. "No, it
just makes for trouble."

"What?"

"Telling the truth. Saying what I want to. I try not to make it hard on Jamie."

"Jamie isn't here, just me. So tell your friend."

Miles pushes up from his elbows, then settles back in his chair. One of his legs starts twitching and he smooths it with his palm. "What I really want to do is complain. Sometimes I want to yell. I don't want to be cheerful when people come around. I hate this damn disease."

"It's bad, isn't it."

"Just this once, I'm going to tell you how bad it is."

"Okay."

"It sucks. It sucks donkey dick."

She can't hold back a laugh, which starts Miles laughing. She takes his hands and holds them in her own. She moves closer and slides an arm behind his neck. The day will come when he can no longer speak, when he'll barely be able to move. But always, inside his decaying frame, will be this same lovely guy, her son's lover of a decade and more.

She goes out to her car and brings in her suitcase. "You get my old room upstairs," he says. "I sleep down here now." He gestures to a cot and mattress beside the door to the kitchen. "We even have a new crapper, just inside the back porch."

"Why was I worried about you two? You've got it all worked out."

"Not really. Take me for a walk on the sand and you'll see. I keep falling. Okay, that's it. No more complaints today."

He's definitely talking slower, and *complaints* sounds like *complens*.

The walls in the living room are hung with paintings. Unlike in her own house there's no paneling, only the exposed studs and the unpainted back side of the clapboards. In this benevolent climate there's no need for insulation. Though the windows and doors are new, the house was built in the 1890s. Someone once told them that Winslow Homer lived here one winter. They don't know if it's true, but at the foot of the stairs they've hung a copy of his "Undertow" with its gleaming lifeguard bodies.

Jamie walks in with two loaves of bread wrapped in cloth. "*Mamá,*" he says, "look at you, you're almost skinny!"

She's not, of course, he's just trying to make her feel good. But she soaks up the comment as they hug, the warm bread pressed against her back. In his T-shirt and shorts, Jamie is the skinny one. He puts down the bread and hovers over Miles.

"You hungry? You need anything? Do you want a glass—no, never mind."

She didn't talk to them this time about alcohol in the house, she just assumed they wouldn't drink around her. Miles shouldn't be drinking anyway, it will slow his speech even more. If Jamie wants a drink, she can surely handle that, but did he have to bring it up in front of her? Two minutes in and she's annoyed with him. She better watch herself.

He cooks pink shrimp for dinner, with rice and a salad. Later, as she washes the dishes, she glances at the two of them in the living room, Jamie's chair drawn up beside Miles and their heads once again touching.

When she joins them Miles says, "You see how good Jamie is? All he needs is four or five hours a day in his studio, so he can paint."

"Even three or four is good."

"Also, a few nights off to party and see his friends."

"I don't need to party. I don't want to without you."

"Tell the truth."

Jamie straightens up. "Okay, I do miss it sometimes."

What a job he has taken on, Ginny thinks.

"I tell him to go out and carouse a little," Miles says. "I'm only being selfish. I depend on him and I want him happy."

Ginny's having more difficulty with Miles's speech. She barely catches *carouz* and *selfsh*.

Bicycle bells sound from the street, and an occasional song from a passing car. It's Miles who leads them into the back yard for a look at the moon and stars. No palms back there, for just that reason, to see the sky at night. The waning moon has risen, dimming the Milky Way, and for ten minutes the three of them stand and say nothing. Even with Lou Gehrig's disease, it's going to be more peaceful here than at the commune.

As soon as he finishes breakfast, Jamie goes off to his studio. He's light on his feet, he smiles, he turns at the door and says "Thank you, Mamá." She's glad to spend time with Miles, which is also a gift to Jamie. She has felt at ease from the moment she arrived, perhaps because of how much Miles and Jamie love this town, where they can be gay with hardly a thought. As Jamie ambles off, Ginny stands on the front steps soaking up the sun. The next-door neighbor waves, no need for any words as he mounts his bike. Night and day, the temperature is always mild. In the air, a hint of salt.

Miles wants to walk the beach. "I still fall," he says, "but on the sand it doesn't matter, and I can still get up on my own. Usually I can."

The ocean is wide and blue, the waves mild and the sand, it seems to Ginny, as soft as Long Island's. They plod side by side along an almost-empty Smathers Beach. Miles stumbles and falls once, then again, and won't take her hand as he gets to his feet. "Let me do it," he says, "while I can." But he's also ready to complain some more. "A little groaning each day," he says, "but only with you. To the rest of the world I pretend I'm coping and all is well. That's my frontal, what I'm supposed to feel, how people like me to feel. Of course it's horseshit." *Horsit* he says.

"Groan away, Miles. I would."

"No one wants to hear it. They want me to keep up my spirits. No one wants the truth. With all the gay rugs it's the same."

"The gay rugs?"

He stops hobbling. He purses his lips and pushes out the word. "Row-gs."

Ah, *rogues.*

She remembers what he once suggested to her about Rich: *What if you talk about him any time you want?* All right. "What if you complain as much as you want," she says, "but only to me? You can moan, you can curse, you can scream if you want, and I'll listen."

Miles steps toward her and wraps his arms around her shoulders. "Ginny, you're perfect."

"You can start now if you want."

"No, I feel good now. I'll wait until it builds."

A couple of days later it has. They walk the same beach and he tells her how unhappy he is that he can't paint. He'd damn well give up on his legs and feet if only his right hand worked the way it used to. And why was that the first thing to go? And why *him*? Why not that asshole Richar Nisson? And why is there no medicine, no treatment, no hope? He knows what's coming. He'll get worse and worse, and then he'll die.

After his tirade he does seem more at ease. She wonders if screaming might be even better for him—though where are they going to do that? In the car, perhaps, with his face in a towel.

They walk every day, early, before families and tourists show up on the beach. They walk and he falls. He's always slow to get up, sometimes he sprawls on the sand and turns his head to stare at the lapping water. After all, it's what people do on a beach. They stretch out on the sand and watch the gulls and pelicans stream past. Sometimes she thinks he stumbles half on purpose—and one day he turns it fully to a game. "I love the beach with its sand," he says. "This is the only place I don't have to be careful when I walk." He drops to his knees, keels over, then rises with a smile.

"Miles, you're a treasure."

"You could knock me over yourself."

"What are you talking about?"

"Push me."

"I'm not going to push you."

"Go ahead. It's safe here." He takes her hand and puts it on his chest. "Push."

All right, she pushes lightly and down he goes. Then he lies there with his arms and legs spread, making angel wings in the sand. No help is his rule. He gets up slowly, then tells her to do it again. She does, but this time a woman in a halter and shorts runs up to them and stops in front of Ginny. "Is he bothering you?"

"No, no, it's a game."

"It's all right, you can tell me."

"He's my son-in-law. We're fine."

The woman is middle-aged but strong. A runner, maybe a body-builder, and she clearly doesn't believe what Ginny says. Miles has risen to his feet, but his grin only sets her off. She tells him not to get close to her.

"It's okay. I'm just dying."

"Oh sure."

"He is," Ginny says. "We were playing a game. He has Lou Gehrig's disease. I was life, pushing him around."

Miles holds up both hands as if in surrender, and the woman takes a step back.

"I can call the police if you want."

"Please don't do that. You don't understand."

"I saw him come at you. He grabbed you."

"He wanted me to push him."

"You better be careful."

Miles has had enough. "Screw this," he says. "It's more goddamn donkey dick."

"*What?*"

"Please let us walk," Ginny says. "We've got troubles, but not what you think. It's Lou Gehrig's disease."

"What are you talking about?"

"It kills you," Miles says.

This seems to get through to her. Slowly, she turns away and heads for the street, looking back over her shoulder as she goes.

"Such a helper," Miles says.

"For a minute there I thought I was going to have to explain about donkey dick."

He's smiling again. "I'm sure she'd have loved to hear that."

Ginny offers her arm and slowly they walk toward the harder sand beside the water.

July 12

How is it going to be for Jamie, after I leave? I'm here now, I pitch right in, but I'm not going to stay forever. At some point I'll go home and it will all fall on him. He pretends that nothing else in his life matters—but Miles can see the truth and so can I. He misses his friends and their lively times. He'll do the right thing, but he's torn. And it's going to get worse, it's going to be brutal. How much easier this all is for me, because I'm not giving up anything to take care of Miles. I get up in the morning, I fix him something that can slide down his throat, I fit him into my car and take him to the beach. We come back and I read to him, just now from *Midnight Cowboy*. Jamie shows up in the early afternoon and I take a walk around town. I like to walk Duval from ocean to bay, then back again. Sometimes I stop and talk to people. I almost never did that in Sag Harbor, but people are friendlier here—except for that creature at Smathers, and I suppose even she meant well. It all works for me because it helps with my other job, the one I'll have forever, staying away from alcohol and pills.

Two jobs and they're not enough. I get along, day to day, but I can't figure out what I want. I used to want adventure and sex and success, and now I don't even miss them. This sounds like depression, but it's not. It's just—floating. I'm sober but half burned out.

What an insult it would be to complain about this to Miles. Because I'm going to live and he's not. I won't say this to Jamie, either. Last night he stood up after dinner and left the house without a word. He was tearing up and didn't want Miles to see. The three of us should get in a pile and weep, but when I suggest anything like that, Jamie steps back. I can't blame him, after what I put him through in my drunken years. But too often we hide from each other.

9

The three of them plan a party, a wake while he's still alive as Miles puts it. They invite fifty people, most of them gay, some lesbians, a few straights. At the gathering they'll announce what everyone already knows, that Miles has Lou Gehrig's disease, then talk about it.

Much has changed in the last few weeks. If steadied with a gait belt, he can still walk a few steps on solid ground, but not on the sand. They've installed a wheelchair ramp from door to sidewalk. Miles's speech comes slower and often garbled, and they've planned for that during the party. Jamie or Ginny will stay by his side to help with conversations, and sometimes he'll do the best he can on his own. He still likes to try.

It's one of September's perfect days, with no temperature at all. The whole town could go naked and no one would be too hot or cold. The first guests arrive just before sunset, some by bike, some on foot, and for thirty minutes it's just as Miles predicted, that people would be quiet and respectful, that it wouldn't feel like a party at all. Jamie puts on a Doors album, then John Lee Hooker. Ginny has been firm about allowing some alcohol, and on this one night there are bottles of beer on ice. Food as well: shrimp, conch fritters, miniature crab cakes and tiny squares of key lime pie. Mother and son spent half the day cooking.

Conversations sprout as the crowd grows. Ginny drifts from group to group, but it's been years since she felt at ease at a party. As she talks to two or three people, she overhears another conversation and wonders about that one. She's fully aware of the beer bottles tipping up and down, but watches them like an anthropologist. The mood lightens and the talk turns lively. They have planned for this too, and soon, instead of twenty conversations, there will be just one.

After Miles gives them the nod, they wheel him onto a tiny platform Jamie has built out of two-by-fours and plywood at the far end of the room. Everyone goes quiet fast, and Jamie announces, "Miles has some things to tell you, and my mother will help him." He hands a pair of typewritten sheets to Miles, and a carbon copy to Ginny.

Miles looks over the silent crowd. "You know I have Lou Garug...." he stops.

"Lou Gehrig's disease," Ginny says.

Miles's right arm is visibly twitching. Though sometimes a smiling presence, he looks hesitant now. What he wants to say is all written down, and he glances at his sheet. "You know me. You can relass. I hope you won be narvss."

"I hope you won't be nervous," Ginny repeats for him. She looks around at the crowd and goes on. "Inside, he's the same Miles you all know. He just wants to explain some things about this disease."

"I hope you have fun tona...."

He stops, glances at Ginny and nods to her. She reads what follows. "Please don't get somber around me and have less fun. The less fun you have, the less fun I'll have."

Miles looks out at the crowd. "When we talk, you don need to showt."

Ginny explains. "His hearing is fine, and you don't need to shout when you talk to him. Some people get loud, but it doesn't help."

"I can always...." The paper in his hand is half scrunched. He looks up at Ginny. "Better you."

"I can't always respond," Ginny reads. "Often I can't say what I want. But I can listen. And you might be able to figure out what I say. Work on it with me."

She goes down the list. "Please don't offer Jamie's mother a drink. She's stronger now and has nine months of sobriety, but please don't press her at this or any other party. Don't put a cocktail in her hand, or a glass of wine. If you're drunk, talk to someone else. Dope doesn't bother her, and here, tonight, she's going along with the beer. If that seems thin, liven it up with jokes and stories and hugs and kisses. By the way, I wrote everything else here, but she wrote all that.

"Don't shut me out. Invite me to your gatherings. I probably won't go to many, but now and again I might.

"Invite Jamie to everything. To walks, to dinners, to parties. He likes to get out of this house sometimes. Wouldn't you?

"Tell me your secrets, because that's what friends do. That's what I'm doing now. Of course you can see how I can hardly walk anymore, how I have trouble swallowing, how my tongue gets in the way when I try to talk. And now, here are some other things you might have wondered about.

"There is no cure for this disease, but it's not contagious. It stops the brain from telling my muscles what to do, but it doesn't affect my stomach, my bowels, my heart, my sight or hearing. Or my dick. Pardon me, but you're a loose crew and I bet you've wondered. Sex is still possible, and still lovely. It isn't always easy.

"My brain is pretty much the same. It isn't dementia when I talk, these are just bulbar symptoms, my tongue and mouth making me sound like an idiot. I'm not an idiot yet. It could happen, but not tonight."

Ginny turns to the second page.

"I'm going to die, but who knows when. Lou Gehrig lived for two years. The faster the onset, they say, the faster the progression. When the time comes, throw my body into the ocean. I know you're not supposed to do that, but maybe you could. Some of you have boats, and you could take me offshore some night and tie me to some concrete blocks and toss me over. Okay, I won't be there, I won't care, and Jamie will decide. Listen to what he says.

"I love Key West. I love our world here, there's nothing like it. Even Provincetown wasn't as free, so keep it going. Embrace our sisters, too. I hope you all live it up.

"And please, don't look at me and look away. If you want, come close and we can try to talk, and if that doesn't work we can just stare at each other for a while. You can see a lot in someone's face. If I don't look at you, it probably means I don't want to talk to you. When you don't look at me, I think you don't want to talk to me.

"Come back to our next party, whenever that is, and I'll pontificate all over again. Now there's a word I'll never again say out loud—but I can still put it down on paper.

"And that's it, except for the two people I want to thank. First Ginny, who understands my speech better than anyone. Who used to take me to the beach every day, and now wheels me around town. I don't know how long she's going to stay with us, but what a blessing she has been. And second, my lover Jamie, who's the hottest guy in town. Hotter than any one of you. No insult meant, just the truth. And who's a beautiful man, inside and out. Once, years ago, I saved his life when he was depressed, and since then he's saved me from despair and misery a thousand times. He does it every day, and I love him.

"Okay, one final word before I get too sentimental. Just in case you haven't been watching close enough, *this disease sucks donkey dick.*"

10

For a time Miles tried to paint with his left hand, but never finished a canvas. He even tried once with the brush held in his teeth, but after ten minutes he spat the brush on the floor and let out some rare curses. Soon after that he gave up his studio.

Most of his canvases are now in the house, a dozen of them leaning against the wall in the living room and many more upstairs. He doesn't talk about them, rarely asks to look at one, but doesn't want to sell them. Ginny remembers being unsure about his paintings of teenaged boys, back when Jamie was in school at Darwin. But starting in Provincetown, and continuing here in Key West, he began to paint what Ginny thinks of as house portraits. Simple houses, most of them, but each accompanied by something unexpected: a pair of long-necked egrets, a man passing by on crutches, a porpoise idling in unlikely shallow water just in front of the house.

For all these years, art has been vital to both Miles and Jamie. But now, far too often, Ginny feels numb around the art that surrounds her in this town. There are paintings and sculptures she enjoys, but they rarely touch her deeply. In all her life, has she ever bought a painting? She can't remember one. Well, a print of a Tahitian woman once, by Gauguin. In her Sag Harbor house there's not a single piece of art. At least she could have hung something by Jamie, but she never asked for one of his paintings. This shames her now. And these days, when she stops by his studio and looks over his latest work, she's curious but often puzzled. She shuffles through several canvases: some older seascapes, and more recent evocations of life inside some fruit. A formal dinner table inside a papaya, a small boy and his scooter inside a melon, a nude man playing golf inside an avocado.

"What's this?" she asks, looking at a bulging red-leather suitcase with tiny socks poking out of it, all lodged inside a peach.

"My favorite fruit," Jamie says. "At first it seems so feminine, but you bite into it and find the pit, hard and knobby with the flesh clinging to it, the pit of the world. Do you like that one?"

"I do."

It's not a lie. The painting is inventive and she does rather like it. But there's nothing about it she could put into words. She can't imagine how a painting like this could change her, or illuminate something about her life. As always with Jamie's paintings, she feels inadequate and disloyal.

On a Friday night they go to an opening at the Zur Gallery, pushing Miles down the street in his wheelchair. The gallery's two rooms are filled with people talking, but Ginny, because she thinks she ought to, starts a full round of the paintings. Two artists are displayed, apparently a couple, one who works in oil and the other in watercolor. They've painted Key West streets with chickens and crows, some crinkly figures with skinny legs and hair like fire, and a number of canvases that are pure abstractions. Beneath a painting of some severed trunks of palm trees, surrounded by a ring of mud turtles with their heads protruding, she reads the artist's statement.

My goal is to make the personal the universal. I choose my subjects by walking through our town, finding sights that inspire me. Palms should be eternal. Turtles should be eternal. My goal is to reach the deeper consciousness of the viewer, to lift him into a larger world, to show with my brushstrokes our connection to everything around us. We have much to learn, I believe, from palms and turtles.

It sounds sincere, but she doesn't really follow it. She moves on to the next painting by the same artist, a mash-up of deer antlers and high-heeled shoes. No, she's no good at this.

She does better with books. She's been reading her favorites again: *Anna Karenina*, Durrell's Alexandria Quartet, and *Madame Bovary*. They're all stories of marriage, infidelity and dissolution. The women have all transgressed, and all will suffer because of it.

A man approaches her, someone she doesn't know. He introduces himself and she promptly forgets his name. Frank something. He's polite, tanned and closely shaved, and wears a shirt that might be a blouse. Yes, looking at the buttons, it's a woman's shirt. A precise haircut, soft beige pants and white shoes. He was at the party for Miles, he tells her, but she doesn't remember him. He compliments her on how helpful she was when reading Miles's explanations, and he wants to tell her something about his father, who lives up in Pennsylvania.

"He has some kind of dementia. His speech isn't failing him like Miles, but he goes around in circles. He repeats himself. He can't remember where he put his socks. He keeps telling me that someone is sneaking into his house and stealing things."

"How often do you see him?"

"Only a couple of times a year. That's why I want to talk to you. How do you and Jamie do it? Don't you get exhausted?"

"Do you have any siblings?"

"A brother, but he's never going to help."

"There are homes, when the dementia gets too bad."

"I think it's too bad now. My father has sworn he's never going into one of those places, and I don't want anything to do with Altoona. I want to paint and give tango classes and live in Key West. It's why I'm so amazed by you and Jamie. That you're so generous."

People swarm around them, but no one steps in to interrupt what's clearly an intense conversation. What a turn her life has taken. Here's someone who thinks she's generous. She better straighten him out.

"I'm an alcoholic. I guess everyone knows that. I screwed up my life for ten years. I help out here because I love Miles, but also because I need something steady. This helps me. With your father—how much do you love him?"

"Not very much. But he is my father."

"Jamie and I just found ourselves in the middle of this disease. Maybe you could go stay with him for a while, see if the two of you can stand it. It would be easier if you didn't have any other life, like me. Or if you were signed on, like Jamie. But you could give it a try. You could do now what you can't do later. Let your father reject you if he has to, but don't make it the other way around."

The conversation goes still. She has offered no more than commonsense suggestions, but Frank watches her and puts his palms together. They stand facing each other, occasionally glancing at Jamie and Miles. All around her, so many hard stories. It makes her own life feel normal.

11

Almost always, Jamie gets up first in the morning. His steps wake Ginny as he passes down the hall or descends to the kitchen. There he has a bite to eat, a bagel or muffin. Sometimes, as she lies in bed, she hears some low talk. Eventually the front door opens, closes, and he's off to his studio.

For years she was an early riser, headed for work before seven at a hospital or clinic. After losing her license she lost the habit. She sipped her drinks late into the night and didn't wake until eight or nine. Now she lies in bed, listening to the occasional murmur of a dove. If Miles needs her she doesn't want him to wait, so she rises, slips into her blouse and shorts and goes downstairs.

He's lying half upright in his hospital bed. He sleeps that way, breathes better that way, and at first they don't bother with words. What's he going to say? That he needs to pee? She knows what comes next, she must help him to the toilet.

At this hour he's a frail walker. She helps slide his legs off the bed, then stands him up. He limps back to the toilet, then hangs on her as she pulls down his underpants and lowers him to the seat. They've done this many times. She hears him tinkle. Though he doesn't usually crap in the morning, if he does she'll have to wipe his ass. That's more likely to happen in the afternoon during Jamie's watch—and these days, with his growing constipation, he may not move his bowels for two or three days. When the cleaning falls to Ginny, either she has him stand and bend forward, which never feels safe, or she reaches down from in front, past his testicles. Only a couple of months ago he could do the job himself. Now, with such a tremble to his hand, he'd likely smear the shit all over.

He's had a sweaty night, but when she takes off his shirt and underwear and cleans his body with a warm wet cloth, he shows no embarrassment, so she hardly feels any herself. They need to install a shower downstairs, and Jamie has been talking to a plumber. Before dressing Miles, she gently rubs some Vaseline over a couple of inflamed bedsores.

Once in his wheelchair, they work on the mucus that has built up overnight. His cough has no power, so she slides a finger into his throat and his gag reflex brings up what he can't swallow. She cleans that up, then shaves him, then wheels him to the breakfast table. A soft-boiled egg, some yogurt and his three mashed pills, for pain, swelling and constipation. Grape juice as well, though thin liquids are now more difficult for him. It's almost an hour before he finishes. She brushes his teeth. She'll wash his sheets later in the old wringer washer out back, or else wait another day. And finally, a walk to the beach.

With hardly a car passing by, she rolls him down the street, glad again for this easy climate. No chill winds of autumn and rarely a cloudy day. At the beach the wheelchair can't go two feet onto the sand, can't reach the pier at Higgs or the palm trees at Smathers. She wheels him instead through half-empty parking lots, the ocean a radiant blue beyond the pale sand.

They stop and talk, or try to. Miles tells her something about his restless night. He tells her a story she can barely make out, about a visit he and Jamie once made to Nova Scotia and its beaches, and a hospital there. Was one of them sick? It takes her some minutes to figure out that the shoreline was inhospitable. Miles usually stays clear of such difficult words, but occasionally, as his speech disintegrates, he mounts a campaign.

In spite of the obstacles, Ginny loves these outings on which they have no chores or plans. A pelican glides past, its wings barely moving, an utter contrast to the disease Miles is fighting—until the bird lands and starts waddling about. Forty terns sweep in, land with a flair and strut. Ginny lies down on the sand beside the pavement and makes angel wings, as Miles used to do. She wonders if he'll be happy to see her do this, or will he only regret that he can no longer do it himself? Should she talk more to him about the disease and its progression, or just keep quiet about it? In the past he often spoke of delicate subjects, but these days he rarely mentions his symptoms. Then again, these days he talks less and less.

She's still stretched out on the sand when she hears him groan. She scrambles up and finds him twisted in his chair, grimacing. "*Crmp*," he says, with his hands on his left leg.

His cramps can be severe. She does her best with his thigh, massaging it, unsure of how much pressure to use. His pain eases, she thinks, then returns. It's hard to tell, because in these recent months his face has been showing less of what he feels. She rubs him slowly and gently. She should have brought along some of his pain medication, but doesn't like to walk around with it.

"I'm okay," he says, finally. "What a pissr."

Back in the sunny house they eat some cream of mushroom soup. Miles lowers his mouth to the bowl, then works his spoon. All eating is now a chore. Jamie comes home at one, and ten minutes later Ginny gives Miles a hug and heads back to the ocean, to sit on a bench and think through her everlasting worry, that she has no life of her own.

Every day, even on weekends, Jamie goes to his studio and paints. Ginny has no such focus. In the afternoon she reads at the library or wanders through the easy streets of town, past stores, past brightly painted houses and porches, the concrete sidewalks leaking bits of seashell. *I'm still recovering,* she thinks, and *I need this quiet time.* But after Miles, what is she going to do?

Through most of her drinking decade she was able to work as a doctor. Some day, some year, she might get her license back—but before that, what? She watches the waves break onto the sand. She watches the gulls pulse left and right.

All her life until the day Rich left her she was deeply involved in something. As a girl she loved to dance, then dive. As a young woman she worked at newspapers, then at *Stage* and *Vanity Fair.* She had her children, and in her thirties went back to college, then med school and an anesthesia residency. If she didn't have a job, she had a project. But she's not a young woman, and Miles is not a project. She wants something to absorb her, the way Jamie's art is a backbone to his day. Here she's a helper and still trying to get used to it.

For dinner she cooks a yellowtail snapper, keeping it simple, frying it with some mango sauce. Jamie coaxes some phlegm out of Miles's throat, then takes him back to the toilet. When Miles returns he's drooling, but not from hunger. He often drools or yawns, and now he starts laughing hard. It's not that anything is funny, it's a pseudobulbar affect. Sometimes he laughs compulsively for five minutes, unable to stop, and other times he cries. It's not connected, Miles has told them, to any real emotion. Soon he'll look calm again, though distressingly so, with his face stilled.

Ginny serves the fish with zucchini, and Jamie recites the toast they've adopted, made up months ago by Miles: *Let us now be grateful for something, even if we have no idea what.* Then Miles sets to, focusing like an inmate. He chews and chews, with small bites and long waits. Each bite can take a minute to get down.

Jamie raises an old topic. "It wouldn't be that hard to put in a surgical feeding tube."

"No, don wan."

They're not going to force him. He has also let them know that while he might accept a face mask and breathing machine to sleep at night, he wants no part of a tracheostomy. "No mo lie," he said, and eventually they figured it out: when he gets to that stage, no more life.

"Don wan," he says again now, and closes his eyes. Often that's his sign of rejection. When he wants to say *yes,* he opens his eyes and nods faintly, up and down, and when he closes his eyes he means *no.*

After going through a third of the food on his plate, he raises his head. He looks at Jamie, then at the door. "You go," he says.

What kind of command is that?

Jamie explains. "He's reminding me about the hot tub party tonight. No, Miles, I'm not going. I'm going to stay home with you."

Miles closes his eyes. "Go," he says, and opens them. "I wan you go."

"I don't think so."

"Go. Go. Go."

"He'd like to get rid of me," Jamie says.

Ginny knows this isn't true, but a tiny smile appears on Miles's face. He's always made it clear that Jamie should have a good time when he can.

"A hot tub party," Ginny says, after Jamie has left and Miles has taken his last bite. "You told me long ago what that means."

Miles nods. His face has gone back to its half-frozen look, but his eyes are wide open.

Yes and no questions are the easiest for Miles, and she tries to stick to them. "You send him off to a hot tub party where the guys will be fooling around. You know what will happen, right?"

He looks straight at her.

"How's it going with you and Jamie? Do you still—engage?"

He nods.

"What a disease this is. It takes so much from you but leaves most of your organs intact. Heart, stomach, and that one."

He looks toward the door that Jamie walked out of, nods his head and glances down at his lap.

"Miles, you've been a randy guy ever since I met you."

"An you? Wha...?"

"What do I do with men? Nothing, for years now. I don't know if it'll ever come back."

Miles wriggles in his chair, then sits up as straight as he can. "You luh guh."

Is he saying she looks good? She knows that isn't true. But better than before, when she was fat and drunk.

"Miles, how bad is this for you?"

His face goes still. Of course he can't answer this. She has to feed him questions he can answer with his eyes, with his head, with a *yes* or *no*.

"Do you worry about dying?"

He nods slowly.

"Are you still glad to be here?"

"Som...."

"Sometimes," she fills in for him, and he nods.

It's past time for an alphabet board. What she wants to know is how he feels, but the veil of his face, his bland half-frozen expression rarely gives her a clue.

"What can we do to help?"

Damn it, it's another question he can't answer.

"You tah..." he says. It takes her a moment to figure out he wants *her* to talk.

"If I were lying there with that disease, I think I'd be worried about the mistakes I made. Choices I regret. But maybe it's different for you. I wound up alone, and you wound up with Jamie and you've had a great time. That's true, isn't it?"

He nods.

"If only you could have more of that, on and on without end."

He nods.

"But everything ends. We'll go on loving you, but you won't be here. Is it all right to talk about this?"

He watches her, eyes open.

"I think about this a lot. About how much we never say. Of course that's how I grew up. And then I picked a guy, Joe, who didn't need to talk, who rarely wanted to. There's a little of that in Jamie, even. Hell, it's in all of us. But I think about it more, now that it's so hard for you to speak. You were always good at talking about things. You were the best. We need one of those alphabet boards. It takes time, but it lets you say everything."

"Gd."

"And Miles, there's something I need, too. I need to take a break and go back to my house in Sag Harbor. Just for a month or so, then I'll come back. Will that be all right?"

He watches her for twenty seconds, then nods.

"I'm trying to figure out what comes next for me, what I'm going to do. I have no idea, and it wears on me. I need to sit still in my house and think about it. And I want to see my sister in Connecticut. I want to talk to her about our mother, and how we didn't take care of her enough."

She can't read his expression, because he doesn't have one. This damn disease. Finally he responds. "Yss. Kay."

Later that night she reads to him from Mary Renault. Perhaps he could still hold a book and turn its pages, but he'd rather listen. Ginny has to pause, often enough, to help him cough, to wipe the drool from his chin, to move his feet and legs to a different position as she tries to limit his bedsores. Life is hope, she thinks. It hardly matters what trouble you're in as long as things are getting better, and this disease is the opposite of that.

12

Rob calls with another invite for her to visit the commune.

"Do you mean it this time? Are you going to go distant when I get there?"

"I won't. I want to see you."

He reports no emergency, but there's an edge to his voice. She can't be sure about it, what with the background noise, the chatter of other people at his end.

"I could come up on my way back to Sag Harbor. First we have to find someone to help look after Miles. This is a terrible disease. I'll fill you in when I come."

As quickly as that it's decided, and only three days later she and Jamie find a young woman from Honduras, straight off a migrant boat. She speaks some English, almost enough to follow their guidelines for Miles, and she's glad to move into one of the upstairs bedrooms. The morning Ginny leaves, Miles cries hard and loud. It could be a compulsive bulbar affect, but she knows he's torn to see her go. She slides into his chair with him and holds him close. She'll come back, she promises. She only needs to visit Rob and to have some time alone at home.

The commune has shrunk again. A young woman took off with a drummer traveling west in his van, and Jerry joined a rock and roll band in Pittsburgh. Of those left, Natalia is now clearly the commune's queen. She sits with her back to the kitchen, unconcerned with the cooking and serving of the meal. With her due date only a month off, she has a greater mission. She doesn't flaunt her belly or talk about it, but its swell seems the focus of all attention.

"Is the squash good?" someone asks her.

"Good enough."

Ginny forgets herself and asks, "How's your digestion? Any trouble with gas or constipation?"

It's a doctor's question and Natalia doesn't look up from her plate. "No troubles for me," she says.

They eat almost in silence, which is not how Ginny remembers the commune dinners. A pair of cats parade about the floor, their tails straight up. As short-spoken as Natalia is, she seems to hold everyone's attention. Maybe it's her composure and self-absorption. When dealing with her, Rob often seems the supplicant. He's been courting her, Ginny thinks, since the day they met.

Natalia eats half her dinner, pushes her plate away and stands up. "A nap," she says, and disappears down the hall.

Big Lisa says, "It must be tiring."

Flora says, "She's got to take care of herself."

It's a Sunday morning and no one goes off to work. Rob and Ginny walk up to their meadow, the path steep and dry, a red-tailed hawk crying out above the trees. As they walk, Rob tells the story of the group's last acid trip.

"It was in June, after you left. I told Natalia it didn't sound like a good idea, but someone had sent us a sheet of hits on blotter paper, and without a word she ripped off a tab and ate it. You know how she is. She decides something and it's done. We all joined her, but after it came on we drifted apart. Some people stayed in the house, I think some came up here. Natalia and I walked down past the garden to the creek. She took off her shirt and scooped up some dirt to rub over her belly. Then she made some mud and smeared it all over and let it dry."

"That doesn't sound so bad."

"No, I liked watching her. After a while I did the same and we lay beside the creek with our feet in the water. We held hands for a while and didn't talk. I was flying for hours, and it all felt pretty good. But the next morning something was different. Natalia looked at me like she hardly knew me, and she's been distant ever since. You saw her at dinner last night. In the past, acid trips joined us, but this one took her somewhere else. She doesn't want to connect."

"With you?"

"With anyone."

"There's no trouble with the baby?"

"I don't think so."

They reach the far edge of the meadow and sit down in the tall grass. How flexible Rob is, Ginny thinks. He drops to the earth like a two-year-old. Ginny puts a knee down, a hand down, stretches out one leg and then the other. "I don't know anything about acid," she says, "but I'm glad she didn't get drunk. There are dangers to that."

"She hasn't had a sip in months. No dope either. There's no more acid, and if there were I'd make sure she couldn't find it. But I worry about how abrupt she is, how isolated, even when we're all together. And the way she talks about Moon, it's as if we didn't take care of her well, and that's why Tasia stole her. That's how she puts it."

"Could you get her to talk to a counselor?"

"She won't."

"And clearly, she's not going to want me around for the birth."

"No."

Above them, clouds puff by over a big shagbark hickory, and birdsongs float in from both woods and meadow. Rob asks about Miles, and she describes how difficult his life has become. She's only taking a break, she says. After a stay in Sag she'll go back to help Jamie, perhaps into the final days. Impossible to say when that will be.

"And after that will you go home, back to Long Island?"

"Yes."

"You'll be okay there? Alone?"

"I'll welcome it. I think I will. And I'll have the ocean. In Sag and Key West there's always the ocean. I do know you miss that."

Rob lifts a palm into the air. "We have our ocean here. It's the trees."

Oct. 14

Things aren't as lively on the farm as they used to be. We gather each night, but after dinner people drift off. Some leave even before I do. That's fine with me, of course, and during the day I have work to do. I've been digging up sweet potatoes before the first frost.

I'm going to be a grandmother, and this time part of the bloodline. Not that I'm ever consulted about raising kids. And maybe I shouldn't be. I've never told Rob or Jamie this, and they've never asked, but I was derelict about feeding them when they were infants. I only breastfed them for six weeks, then put them on a strict schedule with bottle and formula. The hippies have trashed all that. Flora reports about a big commune down in Tennessee, about Ina May Gaskin and the midwives there. Formula for babies? It's practically child abuse.

Oct. 17

Rob and Natalia and I were sitting on the porch last night on a lovely cool evening. I've stopped saying anything to Natalia about the baby, but Rob had some suggestions. He thought they should get a carrier for her, and a stroller and a baby swing. Natalia swept it all away. "Forget it. We have the chest sling Tasia left, and we don't need the rest of that crap." After that, silence. It was a beautiful night with some doves cooing—but what's it going to be like after they have this baby? Is Rob going to have a say in anything? I won't be here, so for now I just shut up. I can talk to Natalia about beets and kale and the garden, but I better keep quiet about kids.

13

Ginny likes the autumn calm in Sag Harbor. Though she's hardly a Bonacker, she shares the locals' view of summer's tumult. The beaches, the roads and the village streets are all quiet now. In her first week back she creates some work for herself, repainting the kitchen and bedrooms. She returns to her AA meetings and finds many of the same people in attendance. She doesn't really need to attend, she thinks. In Key West she didn't go once. But she's back in the house where she almost died, so it's probably a good idea. Besides, it's an easy walk, and the meetings lend some structure to her week.

She buys a radio and listens to the news as she cooks dinner. Even living alone, she cooks, preparing whole meals with fish or chicken, potatoes or rice and a salad. It's a routine meant to convince her she's living a normal life.

She thinks about Frank, the guy from Altoona. She has heard from Jamie that he moved back to look after his father. Ginny had been full of advice for him, urging him to act so he wouldn't feel sorry later. In fact, she was thinking about herself, and since then has wondered many times if she or her sister, instead of consigning Gran to a nursing home, should have looked after her themselves. She makes another trip to Connecticut, and suggests this to Carol as they sit in the Red Barn waiting for lunch.

Carol shakes her head. "She didn't even know who we were."

Carol's Manhattan sits in front of her, ordered after Ginny assured her it would not be a problem. The restaurant is quiet and half the tables empty. As ever, Carol smells of cigarettes.

"Maybe not in those last couple of years," Ginny says. "But imagine how alone she was."

"She was never alone. She ate in the dining hall three times a day with all those attendants. She was surrounded by people."

"People who didn't know anything about her."

The waiter brings their plates and sets them on the silent tablecloth. Ginny ignores the lobster tails, the gleam of Brussels sprouts and mashed potatoes. Carol touches her fork but doesn't pick it up.

"Back then," Ginny says, "I didn't think about it. But now, as I watch Miles down in Key West, I see how hard it is on him. That disease takes away so much of what he loves. It isolates him, and that must have happened to Gran too. I know we can't do anything for her now, she's dead and gone. But how hard it must have been for her. I can't stop thinking about how rarely we went to see her. I want to go back to that nursing home. With you."

"Why?"

"Today. Let's go look at it."

"What could that do for anyone?"

"She was our mother."

Ginny waits. She has always been the guide, the older sister. "All right," Carol says, "we'll go after lunch."

No one at the reception desk has any memory of Anna Taylor Lemont. Not surprising, for the staff turnover must be high in these places. But after some explanations, Ginny and Carol are allowed to walk through the dining room, the meeting and exercise rooms. Then a young woman named Anabel escorts them to the second floor, though not into 216, the room Gran lived in for years. The door is closed and a resident, they are told, is sleeping inside. They walk up and down the corridor, then sit near the second-floor desk and talk about their mother, until Anabel leaves them and goes downstairs.

"What is it we're supposed to be learning here?" Carol asks.

"I don't know. I just want to soak up what it was like for her. I want to know how she felt."

"How can you ever know that?"

Silent nurses and attendants pass by on the polished stone floor. A few patients shuffle past as well. Some of them look more lost than Gran ever did.

"Would you want to live in a place like this?" Ginny says.

"God no. But you were the one who suggested it, when she was forgetting everything in her apartment."

"Which is why I feel so guilty. I didn't think she could take care of herself on her own."

"She probably couldn't. And we were both busy with our kids."

And Ginny in those years was having her affair with Rich Villamano. "I made a lot of mistakes," she says. "That's probably why I'm so obsessed about it now."

Though of course they can't, Ginny wants to spend a whole day here, a day and a night, feeling the enclosure, watching what Gran saw.

"Do you remember the old woman who used to park herself here in her wheelchair?" She gestures toward the elevator. "She said the same thing to everyone who passed. 'Can you help me? Please help me. Can someone help me? Please help me get out of here.'"

Carol nods. "I remember how unhappy she was."

"I keep thinking about Gran's dementia. I never learned anything about it in med school, I don't think I read a single paper on the subject. It was just something that happened to old people."

"Plenty of them do go senile."

"And what do we do about it? There's no cure and no medication. The only drugs they ever gave Gran were to help her sleep. And now they don't have anything to help Miles. It's a misery."

"Is that why we're here, because Gran is like Miles?"

"No, Miles has it worse. He needs a lot more care than Gran ever did."

"And you're giving it to him."

"Except when I leave. Jamie's the one who's locked down, who never gets a day off. Can you imagine one of us doing that for Gran? I can't get over how we abandoned her."

"I can. It's past, it's done. You know what they say these days, *Be here now.*"

Here is Gran's nursing home, the very thing in which Ginny wants to immerse them. But it's hopeless. Carol doesn't want to wallow in their family history.

Though invited to stay over, Ginny opts again to drive home. Better to go back to her solitary house and sink into her memories. As she drives, she wonders if she could go back to school and become a neurologist, the field that now intrigues her. A hopeless plan most likely, for it would take years, and soon she'll be turning sixty. Still, how many people are there, in thousands of nursing homes or living with their families, whose brains are disintegrating? It could happen to anyone. It could happen to her, or Carol.

Even before she gets out of Connecticut, the traffic builds on Route 95. The Throgs Neck Bridge will be jammed, so at the last minute she turns off the highway and heads for Bronxville. She'll just appear at the Brennans. She's been invited to do so often enough.

Bill answers her knock, and Patty jumps up behind him. With cries and hugs they urge her inside. They're dressed in their cool-weather standards, Bill in a jacket and tie, Patty in a polka-dot dress and white sneakers. Their cocktails sit on the coffee table, and Bill picks up the shaker. "A daiquiri?" he says, then immediately corrects himself. "Oh Ginny, I forgot."

Patty starts to carry off the two glasses, but Ginny stops her. "It's fine, don't worry. Go ahead and drink, it doesn't tempt me now."

Of course it does, but these days she almost welcomes such trials. She just passed one with her sister at the Red Barn, and every time they prove her sobriety. She accepts some grapefruit juice and they talk about their kids. Patty fills her in on the two oldest, both doing fine, and on Tommy, whose anxiety still pursues him from job to job and girlfriend to girlfriend.

Ginny tells them about Rob. They've heard about the Six, but not that the marriage has broken up.

"That's unfortunate," Bill says with a small laugh. "I'd come to think that might be a solution to the world's problems."

Patty gives him a stare, and the topic is closed. Ginny moves on to Natalia, soon to give birth, and to Jamie and Miles in Key West.

Patty sits erect, her dark hair falling on her shoulders. Bill is neatly shaven and hardly seems to have aged. They are the couple that stayed together, the other face of her and Joe. For decades the four of them lived in much the same world. Joe and Bill both worked at *Life*, and occasionally they all went out to dinner in the city or made it to a Broadway show. At Christmas the Brennans came to Westport to ice cookies. For twenty years and more they met up in Sag Harbor over Labor Day weekend. Their kids were all friends.

She and Joe were the problem. *She* was the problem, because she ran off with Rich. As they reminisce now about Sag Harbor and the beach, she wonders if Patty has ever had an affair. If so, Ginny would not have heard about it.

The Brennans look happy enough, sitting at either end of the couch. They drink their cocktails, and wine glasses await them on the dinner table. Ginny wonders if the two of them still curl up in bed at night, glad to be lying flesh to flesh. Does sex still matter to them? Does it matter equally? Can that happen?

After dinner Bill makes himself a cup of coffee, because he's about to start writing. These are his best hours, he explains, from Patty's bedtime until two or three in the morning. He's working on an article for *The Atlantic* about the Kennedys on Martha's Vineyard. He's had to branch out, now that *Life* is effectively finished.

"Do you remember," Patty asks, "how you once told me that Tommy should be careful of the benzodiazepines? Sometimes now I take a diazepam for sleep."

"Sometimes two," Bill says.

"If I don't, I worry about Tommy. I can lie there for an hour, for two or three. But with a pill I drift right off. Is this a bad idea?"

"I wouldn't make it a daily habit. They're addictive, and obviously I know about that. And they can wind up making your sleep worse. Try some teas instead. Chamomile and lemon balm. Ease your way over to those."

"Is that what you do?"

"I don't know why, but sleep is rarely a struggle for me. Most nights I drop off the way I did when I was ten. But I couldn't do *that*." She points at Bill's coffee cup. "No coffee after noon is my rule."

Bill laughs. "No coffee after two AM for me."

Here she is, handing out advice as if fully sober and dependable. Well, she is fully sober. She knows what to say about diazepam, but wishes she had some advice about Tommy's anxiety.

She asks for an alarm clock and says goodnight and goodbye to both Brennans. She won't see them in the morning, because she'll be crossing the Throgs Neck bridge before five.

14

The public library is only a two-minute walk from her house, and she drops in one morning to read about dementia. There are no copies of *The Lancet* or *The New England Journal of Medicine*, so she turns to the Encyclopedia Britannica. There she finds that her mother's trouble has a name. She's never read the word before, or heard it spoken: Alzheimer's Disease.

Alois Alzheimer, she reads, was a German neuropathologist who first discovered the brain's ravages from "presenile dementia." After one of his harrowed patients died he opened up her skull and found evidence of atrophy, of plaques and neurofibrillary tangles.

Ginny remembers nothing from med school about plaques and tangles. But clearly something went wrong with her mother's brain, something worse than mere old age. She reads about the invention of the electron microscope in the 1930s and how that helped scientists look at brain samples from patients who had died and whose skulls could be dissected. For walking patients, such as Anna Lemont, it was still pretty much guesswork. But Ginny is convinced. Her mother must have suffered from Alzheimer's.

Rob calls with the news. Natalia has given birth—to twins! A girl and a boy. Again it's a noisy call with lots of excited talk in the background. Natalia is busy nursing, and Rob elated. "They're like a couple of little walruses," he says. "No tusks, but slithery! *Ay Mamá*, this is where it all starts!"

He doesn't invite her out for a visit. It's clearly too soon for that, and probably just as well, for while babies are born in Ohio, Miles still suffers in Key West. "It's getting worse," Jamie tells her. He calls twice a week with the news. Miles can barely speak, his muscles have grown weaker and his face more immobile. It will end, but when? Jamie hopes that she'll come down before Christmas.

"Before New Year's," she says.

"You're going to spend Christmas there alone?"

"I want to."

"You're not drinking, are you?"

"You'd know it if I were."

It's true. On the phone, within a few seconds, both her boys could always tell. She was never able to hide it.

"Miles misses you. He told me that today with the alphabet board. It's good we have that."

She can't explain, even to herself, why she wants to spend the darkest days of the year, including Christmas, alone in her quiet house. To prove she can? To feel she has a home?

"I'll get there by New Year's at the latest."

"Okay, Mamá. We miss you."

On the afternoon of Christmas Eve, as on every day, she walks the beach. The gulls are fewer, the sandpipers gone, the last high tide is marked by a curving line of wrack. She's still no good at meditation, but as she walks beside the resounding sea, she's as determined as Thoreau to get it into her.

At home she has no Christmas tree, nor any gifts. In the late afternoon she bakes some gingerbread cookies, more than she'll ever eat. When her boys were young she baked them every year. Now she sits in her low-ceilinged kitchen and calls up the Christmas Eves of her past: the trees, the cards, the piles of presents and *A Child's Christmas in Wales*, year after year the same. All that flows back to her, unlike the years when she drank. Those memories are erratic, and what she cannot remember becomes a life she never lived.

She understands, finally, why she has devised this solitary Christmas Eve. Because whenever others are present, what she feels stays half buried. Even with Jamie or Miles or Rob, something is inhibited. She'd like to share with her sisters her grief about Gran's death, but when Carol or Lauren are with her she doesn't feel it. Not the same way. The piercing loss only comes when she's alone. It's the same with her misery and rage over Rich Villamano. Talking about him to the Brennans or Miles or her sons, she can only allude to how she feels.

She eats a small dinner, the windows dark beside her. It's cold but not snowing. She goes into her bedroom and lies down. There's life ahead of her, but she can't imagine it. A year ago today she was sober, with both her sons here in the house. None of them could have imagined that on this Christmas Rob would be holding a pair of newborn twins, or that Jamie would be looking after Miles, half-strangled by Lou Gehrig's Disease. She lets the future go, because what she imagines never comes to pass. Instead, she lies down with her past. She gives in to everything that has led her here: her marriage to Joe, her love affairs, her drinking and drugs. She rolls over, puts her face in her pillow and weeps. It's why she had to be alone on this night.

15

Miles has changed. His face is more masked than ever. He watches as she sets her suitcase down and crosses the floor to hug him. After a long embrace and a kiss on his forehead, Jamie says, "He's glad to see you."

"How do you know?"

"That steady look. He stares at things he likes, and looks away from the rest. Besides, he told me on the board last night that he wanted to see you soon."

Ginny feels awkward, talking about Miles as if he weren't here. "Let me settle in with him," she says.

"Good, I'll take a walk. We need some bananas and yogurt."

She sits down in a chair in front of Miles, and they stare at each other. This terrible disease offers something rare. It makes it easy to lock onto Miles's face, to watch him as he watches her. She holds his hands and says nothing, and in three or four minutes she's back inside his life.

It's amazing how long he can watch her without blinking. She's aware of her own blinks, and can't stop them. It's his hands that clench and relax, in small repeated spasms. Miles was always an active guy. He walked, he ran, he swam—and now this. How does he bear it? She tries to imagine how she'd feel herself, locked into a frozen body. She thinks it would drive her mad. She wants to ask him about it, but maybe shouldn't. Last fall she could ask him anything, but that might have changed. They go on staring.

When to stop? If he's had enough, will he look away or close his eyes? She's ashamed to have spent so much time away—though even now she finds herself waiting for Jamie to return and interrupt them. This is more than she can handle. She sits back, then rises, saying she must use the bathroom.

Jamie returns and they talk, staying close to Miles in his reclining chair. Jamie says, "What he likes most is to go outside, to be out in the open air. He'd sleep out there if he could. I take him for three walks a day."

It's quickly agreed, Ginny will take him now. They lift him into his wheelchair, Jamie doing most of the work, and she rolls him down the front ramp. "Where should we go?"

"Anywhere under the sky."

She heads for the sea, the clouds a pile of puffballs ahead, a breeze ruffling the palm trees. The street is so level and the wheelchair so smooth, pushing it is almost effortless. The only trouble is that she can't see Miles's face. When they get to the beach she bends around to look at him. He seems calmer—or does she only imagine that? The day is ending, the ruffled water growing dark. The wheelchair is an elegant contraption, a blessing and at the same time an affront. Everything they do he could once do on his own, in the days when he could walk and skip and jump. The memory of his former life must always be with him.

Parked on asphalt, she stands beside him for some minutes. Then she lowers herself to the nearby sand and stretches out her arms the way he liked to do. She wants to honor him, but how does he feel about it? Everything she does is something he no longer can. She wants to be given the news of his reactions. His face changes minutely, but it could be just the twitch of a muscle.

"Do you want to stay here, or keep moving?"

No, when is she going to learn? "Should we keep moving?"

His eyelids lift, and he stares at her.

She wheels him down to the Southernmost Point, then across town past Hemingway's house to Mallory Square, then back on Duval. By the time they get home Jamie has dinner prepared and he sets it on the table. He sits next to Miles and helps him with every spoonful. He grabs his own bites on the fly, the fish and sweet potatoes they have cooked so many times, the potatoes now mashed and pooled with butter.

The house is still and the talk at first desultory: the weather here, the weather in Sag, the basil and parsley Jamie has been planting, the leaking roof now replaced. Ginny asks about the woman they hired, from Honduras.

"She was great, I could never have had any time in my studio without her. But you were coming and she found a job cleaning someone's big house. She has a ten-year-old boy in Tegucigalpa and she wants to bring him here."

They talk about Jamie's father in Connecticut. They talk about Miles's father in Delaware, who hasn't come to visit. The town is quiet. They draw closer.

"*Alf,*" Miles says, in what sounds like a growl.

"He wants the alphabet board."

Jamie brings it and holds it up on the table. He moves a small wooden pointer over the letters, stopping when Miles grunts or blinks.

TLK, Miles says through the board. ABT EVTHNG. I CNT TLK SO YOU. He doesn't need every letter, and Jamie skips ahead when he can, saying the word as he figures it out.

All this time, of course, Miles has been thinking—but the words come as a shock to Ginny, they're such a contrast to his immobile face. She'll learn the board. She must become as quick as Jamie with it. She asks for the pointer and holds it ready.

I LOVE YOU Miles signs, with no abbreviations.

"And I love you, Miles. I'm going to talk to you and read to you and take you for walks. I love hearing you now, hearing what you're thinking."

He stares at her hand, and she lifts the pointer to the board and starts running through the letters.

I INTND TO LIV FREVR.

"Do you?"

SO FAR SO GOOD. NOW TLL ME THNGS.

She tells him about Rob and Natalia and the six-week-old twins, Sophie and Chilo. About her uneasiness with Natalia, her quiet days in Sag Harbor, her walks on the frozen beach and her solitary weeping Christmas Eve.

She and Jamie read aloud, taking turns, from Rechy's *City of Night*. Jamie comes to the end of a chapter and sets the book down. The three of them sit for a while in silence. Then another growl from Miles, *Ouk*.

What's that? she asks Jamie with a glance.

"Ouk—outside. He wants to go out."

"Again?" Ginny says.

"In the morning, in the afternoon, at night."

"I can do that."

Downstairs the next morning, she finds Jamie seated in front of Miles with a large sketch pad and a charcoal pencil. He shades in the brow of the portrait, then goes to work on the eyes. Ginny sits down to watch. How deft Jamie is, and quick. He was the only one in the family who could ever draw anything, the rest of them could make little more than cartoons. Now as Ginny watches, a recognizable portrait of Miles emerges on the pad. Except then, with a few quick strokes, Jamie adds a cigarette to his mouth.

"Jamie, you can't! Miles never smoked."

Miles grunts and Jamie, with a laugh, shows him the drawing. Then he puts it down, slides his arm around Miles and kisses him on the forehead, on his cheek, on his mouth. After he stops, Miles says *Alf*.

SO CRUEL he signs, but he's almost smiling.

"In the old days I couldn't always get him to sit for a portrait. Now I can do one every day." Jamie picks up the pad and shows Ginny a dozen other sketches, some in black and white, others in color. There's a Miles riding a bristly pig, a Miles with half-folded angel wings, Miles frowning and Miles smiling and Miles laughing hard, all things he can no longer do. "I told him if he dies on me I'm going to put these up in a show. How about it Miles, would that be all right?"

He utters no sound, but his eyes stay open.

They move him from day chair to wheelchair. He's thinner now, but even so the move isn't easy. Jamie enfolds his torso, lifts and pivots him to his feet. Ginny could never do this on her own, and Jamie is sweating by the time they get him settled. "We need that Hoyer lift," he says. "I'm going to order it today."

Five minutes later he's off to his studio, and Ginny hasn't asked enough questions. What about his diaper? What if he shits his pants? In the fall that rarely happened in the morning—but now? What a cleanup that would be.

Crustless bread, soft-boiled eggs and apple sauce for breakfast. Miles eats even slower now, and before he's half finished her patience grows thin. She tries not to let it show. Her first meal feeding him and she's impatient. It's pathetic.

A walk is easier. Out to the shore at the end of Duval, then east to Smathers Beach. They sit for twenty minutes there and watch the seagulls and the half-pint waves, with Ginny on the ground beside him. Talk isn't part of it.

Back in the house Miles signs, PLS READ.

She has brought some books from home, including favorites by Durrell and Cather. Also, James Agee's *A Death In The Family.* With some hesitation, she suggests this now to Miles. He stares at her, which means yes, that would be good. Sitting in front of him, she starts at the beginning, with Agee's evocation of summer nights in Knoxville, Tennessee, of people sitting on their porches, of a street car passing with its iron whine and the sound of its bell growing fainter, disappearing. "Now is the night one blue dew."

She loves this line and repeats it to Miles. Slowly, she's learning something about his face. The changes are subtle, but she can see him relax. His body stays rigid, but his expression softens. She thanks James Agee.

That night after dinner she and Jamie leave Miles on the porch and take a short walk. Jamie wants to explain something. "It's getting harder for Miles to piss."

She has watched him pull Miles's penis out of his pants and press his belly, to help him urinate into a jug. It's not something she wants to do.

"And most days he can't crap on his own. I don't think we even need the diaper anymore, because he's always constipated. I've tried prune juice and Dulcolax suppositories, and nothing works."

"So you wait?"

"If I wait too long it gets painful for him, so every two or three days I dig it out of him."

"*How?*"

"I go in with my fingers. Don't worry, I have rubber gloves and I'll take care of it. But I

thought you should know."

She does want to know. She wants to know everything. "I can't tell how he feels. I can't see it anymore."

"Me neither," Jamie says. "I can only guess. You know Miles, he was never a complainer, but I think this must be driving him crazy. With his face so quiet it's hard to say."

"The alphabet board is a help," she says.

"But it's slow."

It is. It's slow and clumsy. Lying alone in her room that night she thinks about it, and remembers her Christmas Eve at home, how she needed to weep, and did. So the next morning after breakfast she brings Miles a pillow and lays it on his lap in the wheelchair.

"I want to know how you feel," she says, "and I can't tell. I imagine sometimes it's not so good."

He stares at her without a blink. His nod has gotten fainter.

"If words are too hard you could still make some noise. The pillow's just for the neighbors, in case it gets loud."

His eyes turn left, right, then down at the pillow. He can't pick it up himself, so she does it for him, holding it over his face, and in ten seconds he goes from growling to screaming. The scream turns into a cough. He quiets down, then starts again, even louder. If anyone came to the door it would look like she's suffocating him. When he goes still, she pulls the pillow back so he can breathe, and when he screams she holds it over his face. His body is bent, tears run down his red and mottled face, he screams again and again, then sits still and slumped.

It's too much, she thinks. Could this kill him? But slowly his face smooths out and he opens his eyes. He looks at her, then tracks the room until he finds the alphabet board. She pulls it up and he signs, slower than usual, EVRY DAY.

On New Year's Eve they wheel him downtown. Throngs of people, distant fireworks, young and old men in drag, lots of alcohol in bottles and cans and paper cups. Ginny doesn't worry, it's a celebration from another planet. She wonders what Miles makes of all the faces that come at them as they roll down the street. There are people who know him, and know about his disease. Others probably not, and a few, after greeting him, are visibly puzzled by his lack of response. Jamie tries to explain Miles's condition to them, but the topic is too complex, too deadly, and soon he's had enough.

"Let's keep moving," he says. "Or is that what you want?" He kneels beside Miles. "Is this too much? Should we turn around and go home?"

Miles closes his eyes. No, they should not.

He's drooling, and Jamie cleans him up. His hands lie on his lap, the right one curled tight. His breathing seems good, so they move on through the crowd, his wheelchair the prow of their ship. Ginny watches from a step behind. Lively faces, people laughing and talking and singing, it's a communal New Year. But how communal can it feel for Miles?

She takes him out the next day for another long roll. When they come back they sit on the porch and watch the quiet street. Talking is work and they don't do it. But she wants to know, almost every minute, what Miles is thinking and how he feels. His face shows so little, and she steps inside to get the alphabet board in case he wants it. When she comes back to the screen door there's a dog standing close to the wheelchair, sniffing. A stray, surely, because it has no collar. It gives her a glance but goes on sniffing, closer now to Miles, it's nose to his thigh. She steps outside and the dog freezes. For thirty seconds they stare at each other. Then it turns slowly and walks down the ramp and off along the sidewalk.

She offers the board to Miles, but he closes his eyes.

They've written his father and tried to call him, but no response. They think he should know what's happening, but from how Miles has described him he probably wouldn't want anything to do with them. Nor would they be eager for a visit from him, the fag-hater. And though they work with the alphabet board every day, Miles has never used it to talk about his father. Much of their days is passed in silence, and occasionally there's a benefit. If they don't like a topic, they let it lie.

One late afternoon they get a visit from Frank, who's taking a week off from looking after his own father in Altoona. He puts his arm around Miles and seems relaxed with him. Miles signs with his board, HOWS ALTOO.

Frank tells them he hardly knows anyone there anymore. Like Frank himself, his childhood friends have all moved away and the town is slowly shrinking. His father has clung to their narrow three-story house and claims he's never met the neighbors, who have been there almost as long as he has.

"He's confused," Frank says, "and sometimes completely lost. But I'm glad you gave me that push, Ginny. I might not have gone without that talk we had, and I'd have missed out on some surprises."

He explains how his father, who sometimes speaks only a few dozen words in a day, can also come out with a longer story. His memory is better about the distant past. One snowy night after dinner he talked about someone named Carl, a guy he knew from the war. They were on Guam before the invasion of Iwo Jima, and one quiet night they lay down on the sand, side by side on their backs, talking and watching the moon through the palm fronds.

Frank listened to his father tell the story, with its uncommon details. The rising moon and the softness of the sand. It didn't sound like his father at all, and he had no idea where the story was headed until, without changing his tone, his father said, "And then we did a little cocksucking."

In all his life Frank had never heard such a word out of his father. "He sounded calm, like it was no big deal, but a few minutes later he came apart.

He started rambling and repeating himself. I had trouble following him, but the heart of it was that he'd done something terrible. And when he figured out I was gay, he was convinced it was because of him, because of what he'd done that night. It was a sin, he kept saying, a terrible sin. I tell you, taking care of him gets crazy. From one day to the next I never know how bad it's going to be. Sometimes he looks at me like he doesn't know who I am. I wonder all the time—how long can it go on?"

It's what they wonder in this house, Ginny thinks. In the silence that follows, Frank turns from Jamie to Miles to Ginny, with a hesitant look. "I'm sorry, sometimes I talk too much. I didn't even ask how you're doing here."

"We're getting along," Jamie says. "We like to hear stories from the rest of the world. We've about run through all our own. And let me say something about Miles. He looks kind of distant, but that's just the disease taking over his face. Underneath he's as alert as ever. He's here, and thinking away. He hears and understands everything."

As if to prove it, Miles gurgles again for the board. Jamie holds it and Miles signs, TANGO U TWO.

Miles has remembered that Frank is the town's tango dancer. Frank and Jamie both laugh, but neither stands up.

Miles stares at the board, then signs NOW.

"How are we going to do that?" Jamie asks.

TAPE.

"He must mean that Carlos Gardel tape I gave you," Frank says. "You remember it?"

"We played it for a month straight. But here? Now?"

Miles gurgles and nods, and after Jamie digs out the tape and they clear the floor, Frank guides him through some first steps. As the teacher he's completely at ease, leading Jamie left and right, forward and back, into spins and reverses and finally a slow dip.

It has always surprised Ginny how Miles keeps soaking up the world. He wants to watch what he can no longer do. It's the same with food. He wants to smell the bacon cooking, even though he can't eat it, or not until they run it through the blender. And speech. He can't speak but he'll listen for hours to a book read out loud, or just to people talking. He can't dance the tango or anything else, but watches every step as Frank and Jamie gambol about the living room, knocking hips and toes into table and chairs.

16

Jan 23

I was reading Lawrence Durrell to Miles last night, and he had me repeat one of the lines about marriage as "a magnificent two-headed animal." It made me think about me and Joe. We had something of that animal, though I don't know how magnificent it was. Then we lost it. Or my affairs destroyed it. I was delusional, thinking I could find the animal with Rich Villamano. Do we only have one chance at it, and everything that follows is doomed?

When Miles screams, which he does every day or two now after calling for his PILW, his face also loosens up. I wonder if I'm inventing this. It would make me feel good, that I've come up with some kind of therapy. But later, with his face as flat and static as before, I'm not sure if I've only seen what I wanted to.

Miles makes his decisions, and I see no doubt on his face. But then, I can't see anything on his face. Is it truly a given for him that he's never going to accept a feeding tube, or even worse a tracheostomy? The only thing he and Jamie have talked to their doctor about is some morphine, if the pain gets too bad at the end. And when will that be? In the meantime Miles is alive, and off we go to the ocean for another look.

Rob calls. He wants to come down from Ohio, but life with the twins is chaos and Natalia needs him. When he tells her he'd like to make a trip to Florida, she takes hold of his shirt and doesn't let go.

He has called this time because he wants to tell Miles a story. Jamie holds the phone in the air, and it's just loud enough for all to hear.

"One summer Jamie and I made a bet, I think he was eleven or twelve. To win it he had to walk the whole length of our road at night stark naked, then stand in front of Debbie's house for one minute. What I didn't know at the time was that he didn't care that much about Debbie. I should have made him stand in front of Nick's house. Well, he did it and won the ten dollars. Miles, I want to tell you, you stepped in at just the right time. You've been great for him, and Ginny and I both believe that you can never do wrong in life."

Miles has heard him, Ginny's sure, but his face remains a mask. Unless he starts to scream into a pillow, that's how it is now. She has spent her life, as everyone does, trying to decipher the expressions of those around her, the feelings that are often hidden. Now, with Miles, she can never do it.

Jamie and Ginny take turns sleeping on the cot in the living room. Miles sometimes needs attention at night, and they have a Hoyer lift now, indispensable when moving him anywhere. Ginny's asleep one night when Miles wakes her at 3 AM, saying *Ouk, Ouk*, the end of the word half strangled.

It's not the first time he's insisted on a nighttime walk. She gets up, puts on a pair of light cotton slacks, a blouse and a sweater she won't need, and engineers the move to his wheelchair, all without words. Out the door and down the ramp. She's already glad that he's torn her from sleep, because no one else is around to share in the silent beauty of the streets. The only sounds are the run of the chair's rubber wheels and a faint rustling of the palms and flame trees overhead. She avoids the bumpy sidewalks and cruises down the middle of the pavement toward the beach at Higgs. As far as she can tell, Miles seems content. She can only guess, until she stops and asks, "You doing okay?"

He stares at her. The ocean lies before them, it's waves stronger than usual. She parks him at the beach as she always does, on the lot closest to the water, and after a time sits down beside him. How long will he want to stay? Maybe she can nap on the warm sand. She stretches out on her back and watches the stars. She knows them no better than the birds and flowers and shells that surround her every day. Well, that's Orion above her, and those two might be Castor and Pollux. She'll wait Miles out. But first she needs to urinate. Simple, she walks off into the darkness, drops her slacks and squats on the sand. Life with Miles is a steady return to the elementals: eat, drink, piss, shit, read, walk, talk. All of which Miles needs help with. Standing beside him in the starlight, then in front of him, she tries to guess at his wishes. She doesn't want to ask him outright. All questions are coercive, she reminds herself, and she doesn't want to put any pressure on him. In the starlight she can barely make out his face, but as she watches he says *Ouk* and closes his eyes, which means he's had enough of being here.

She doesn't believe him. "Are you only saying that for me?"

He gives the faintest nod. Or she reads it as a nod.

"If you'd come alone, would you stay longer?"

Another nod and an eyes-wide stare. But again he says *Ouk*, and closes his eyes for ten seconds. He's ready to go back. She's taking care of him, and he's still taking care of her.

Visitors come by the house. The twins come. They aren't actually twins, or even brothers, which is a good thing because they're lovers. But they look remarkably alike and often play with it, dressing in the same linen shorts and half-unbuttoned Hawaiian shirts. They're still in their twenties, decades shy of all disease or impediment. They take Miles in stride, rest their hands affectionately on his shoulders, speak a little too loud and tell stories from some legendary parties they all attended. They promise to come again, but don't.

A group of six come by with a thermos full of margaritas. If they know about Ginny's history they've forgotten it, and offer her a plastic glass. She turns it down, and before long they're out the door with Miles, headed for the sunset pier. They're gone for a couple of hours, and while not quite somber when they return, they don't seem as festive. Ginny can't tell if it's just that the margaritas have worn off, or if the time spent with Miles has sobered them. She knows how it goes. It's hard to laugh it up with Miles.

After they leave he signs, LFE SUCH FUN FR SOME.

Old Barnaby comes to visit on a Tuesday morning, wearing a skirt. He seems relaxed with Miles, and with himself. He walks with a limp. His skirt is long and mildly flowered, nothing like the showy garb of the drag queens on weekend nights. When Ginny says the skirt looks good on him he says, "I doubt it. But I'm eighty-two years old, and from now on I wear what I like."

"I might start wearing more skirts myself," Ginny says. In recent years for her it's been mostly trousers and shorts.

"Do you know what Miles did for me one year?" Barnaby says, glancing back and forth between the two of them. "He worked a miracle with my daughter. He called her and persuaded her to come down to visit me, and after a few days she wound up relaxed about everything." He cups Miles's neck with his hand. "Thank you, Miles. You're a good one."

Miles watches him. They watch each other. Few visitors, Ginny thinks, are so relaxed with him. "Let's hear his response," she says, and holds up the alphabet board.

LOVE YOU. HOLD ME.

And Barnaby does, putting his chest as close as he can get to Miles and staying there for a long minute. After pulling back he says, "If you and I could trade the time we have left, I'd do it. You could have my stretch, and I'd live as long as whatever you have in store. Of course it wouldn't be much of an offer. My diabetes isn't getting any better."

Later that day, off on a walk to the Southernmost Point, Ginny thinks about Barnaby's offer. Would she do that herself? It would be the right thing, to trade Miles's death for hers and let him live on. Of course it would actually be for Jamie, so Miles would not be taken from him. Oh, it's ridiculous, it's all a fantasy. Yet she wonders about it. She'd never have thought about such a crazy bargain when she had young children, when she was married to Joe, when she was in love with Rich. Even when she was drinking and blitzed half her days, she wouldn't have given up her life for anyone else. Well yes, for one of her kids. But now, today, she's older and doesn't see that much ahead of her. What a gift it would be for Jamie. But then, what about Rob and his twins, who would miss out on a grandmother? No, there's no sense even thinking about it.

Miles sits in the back yard in his wheelchair, and if he wishes for anything more he doesn't show it. Geckos scurry up and over the fences, and a seagull passes overhead, staring down into the yard. Miles has grown even thinner. It's been days since he said a word she could understand, but she knows what he likes. He likes it when she reads to him, and telling a personal story is even better. So she tells him another. He likes stories about Jamie as a boy.

One summer, she says, when Jamie was four or five, her sister Lauren brought her kids down from Canada for a visit. Shelley, the daughter, was seven, and quite organized for a little girl. She wouldn't unpack her suitcase, because she liked everything kept as she'd placed it. One day Ginny walked into the guest room and found Jamie there with both hands down among her clothes.

"'Jamie, don't mess with your cousin's things.'"

"I didn't."

And it was true, he hadn't pulled anything out. He'd just slipped his hands in.

"Can I have a dress?" he said.

"What for?"

"To wear."

"I don't think so. You're a boy."

"So what?"

She never did let him wear a dress. "That was as far as it went," she tells Miles, "But I should have known right then. Maybe I did. Looking back it seems a small thing, but I was afraid of it."

She would like to hear, in return, about Miles's childhood, what he felt about girls and boys, what attracted him. But the alphabet board is too cumbersome. So she talks and he listens. They settled on this long ago. She tries to come up with stories he'd like, and sometimes he guides her. He signs, YOU WHEN BAD.

"Oh you *would* want to know that." She laughs and thinks it over. It's late in the afternoon. Birds wing past overhead and the eternal bicycle bells ring in the street. "Okay, here's one. You remember that photo of me and my dorky boyfriend? He's wearing a sweater and a tie, I'm as tall as he is and he's got his arm around me. I took him on one summer because I was having an affair with my diving coach. Or almost an affair. He wouldn't sleep with me, but everything else. I was mad for him and couldn't let my parents see it, so I pretended to be interested in poor Franklin. I let him kiss me but nothing else. I went around with him arm in arm sometimes, but it was only a screen. Later I ditched him and he was hurt. I've been ashamed of that for forty years."

MORE, Miles signs.

She thinks about it. More of when she was bad, he means, or that's her guess. She's been bad plenty, but it's some minutes before the next story comes to her.

"One time I stole someone's boyfriend. This was back in eighth grade, and what did it matter? But it did, to all of us. My friend Katie had latched onto this kid Bruce, who was also a little dorky. But not really, he just didn't like the usual sports and movies and cars the other boys liked. He was into woodcarving, which made him pretty odd at the time. He learned it from his father and he carved all kinds of things. Bowls and spoons and fish and birds. He was great with birds. He had a full-sized owl in his room, Katie said it was amazing. And sometimes he'd bring a smaller wooden bird to school, a little robin that fit in his jacket pocket. But what started everything was when Katie told me a secret. She just had to tell someone, and she chose me. I guess she knew I'd be interested, probably more than anyone else. People already guessed that about me."

Ginny pauses. She watches Miles, his unblinking stare, his body inert in the wheelchair.

"It's always sex that's bad, isn't it? I must have been bad about something else, but it was the body that gave me trouble. The secret was that Katie, who was a nymphet like me, had gotten Bruce to carve something for her, something none of us had ever seen. You can guess what it was. A penis. Bigger than I'd ever imagined, smooth and dark, carved out of cherry. To have something like that in your room was as bad as it got. She kept it hidden behind some insulation in a little dormer closet. She showed it to me and I just stared at it, until she put it in my hand. That was too much. It was just the way a penis is, an erect one—though it was a few years before I really knew that. Oh, Miles, I *was* bad. Once I'd seen that thing, and held it, whenever Bruce was around I couldn't keep my eyes off him. Katie told me she'd never touched *his* penis, but he obviously had one and I imagined it was like that carving."

She goes still. What a world that was, girls and boys of thirteen, desire rising like the tide, and all of it a secret from adults.

Miles grunts and signs, WHAT BAD.

"Miles, you're terrible! You want some lascivious details, don't you? But I never did that with Bruce. We barely got to second base. I was bad because I stole him from Katie. I had to be his girlfriend, and I did it by touching his chest and flashing my legs and letting him see my underwear, giving him the hint that he could have some of it. Which I wasn't going to do, though I wanted to. And I kept working him until he left Katie, one of my best friends, and he started calling me and coming over for dinner. And he took me to his house and showed me that owl and other birds and a rabbit he'd carved, and a possum with a tail—but that penis was never mentioned. And Katie was so pissed at me she took a pair of scissors to a jacket I'd worn to school and cut it into shreds. Which I deserved. Bruce and I didn't last a month, maybe because I felt so guilty. I *was* guilty. Ah, Miles, if you could tell stories I'd make you tell me about how bad you were. Because we all were, right? You were almost bad with my son. And when you were younger, were you bad then?"

Miles blinks, waits, and blinks again, twice.

"Very bad, right?"

He blinks again. They should have told these stories before, back when he could still speak. It's good now to tell him these tales she might never speak of to anyone else, but the imbalance of it wears on her. Nothing can be equal with Miles anymore. She stands, says she's going inside to make a cup of tea, and heads for the kitchen.

When she returns to the back yard, Miles has closed his eyes. He does sleep more these days, but Ginny sometimes wonders if he's faking it, to give her and Jamie a rest. No, he's asleep. His breaths have slowed and now come easier.

Miles isn't done. The next day, as they sit in the back yard, he has another request. BAD WTH COACH.

"You know all about him."

WHT YOU DID. He stares at her, his head perfectly still. She has told him about this forbidden passion before. Miles likes to hear about it, she thinks, because it parallels his own history with Jamie. Those two have been coupled for more than a decade now, but they had a delicate start at Darwin Academy when Jamie was a senior and Miles his art teacher, and all was forbidden.

Miles knows about her diving coach in high school, but she's never given him any details, other than to say that she never went all the way with him. Not that she didn't want to, but Mike Blake clung to some obscure loyalty to his wife, Lucille. Ginny was seventeen, and Mike ten years older. The heart of it, the delirious arousal, isn't something she's going to describe now. Miles will have to settle for the doughnut story.

Lucille hated doughnuts, she wouldn't let them in her house. In fact, her restrictions were wholesome. Lucille had the perfect figure, and her husband was both lean and muscled. Doughnuts and cupcakes were the enemy, along with cookies, pastries and biscuits baked with lard. So one day Ginny bought a pair of Boston cream doughnuts and took them in her tote to practice. Afterward, alone in the training room with Mr. Blake, she pulled them out. She was in her bathing suit, he as usual in his slacks. He was demanding as a coach and experienced as a lover. He was perfect, but married. Ginny tried always to hide her desire, but of course he saw through that, for she had throbbed under his hands a dozen times already. The doughnuts were a ploy, a way to corrupt him. He couldn't share in them because his wife would not approve. Ginny ate the first one slowly, wiping her mouth with a napkin as the custard squeezed out. After practice, she claimed, she got hungry. It wasn't true, she was only hungry for Mike Blake. But she picked up the second doughnut and told him if he didn't touch it he could have a bite. His hands had to stay clean for later. She fed the doughnut to him in smaller and smaller pieces. She'd never had the least power over him and never would, because her own desire was too great. But now a bite for him, then a bite for her, their faces close, until they wound up kissing through the last of the sweet slime.

"Damn," she tells Miles, "how jealous I was about his wife. Imagine, *me* jealous of *her*."

Miles stares at her. He wants to hear more, she knows. More of this story, or some other. But she's told him so many tales that she's running out. Close to them in the ungated back yard, a chicken struts by. It watches them, scratches, then wanders off. Ginny goes inside to pick up their latest book, *Madame Bovary*. It's long enough to last them forever. Though it's beautifully written, Emma Bovary is a wreck of a woman.

Miles closes his eyes. It's not a rejection of Flaubert's novel, she can see. He's just going to sleep again.

17

There's a gift to looking after Miles. Ginny's despair, her doubts and indecision have all lifted. Maybe they're hovering and will descend upon her later, but for now only one thing matters, that Miles is dying. The rest of the world runs on. Patty Hearst has been kidnapped and the war continues in Vietnam, but in this quiet house there are no quarrels. The moon and stars pass overhead, waves tumble onto the beach and Miles keeps breathing.

They give him lots of attention, and he can offer almost nothing in return. If this bothers him, Ginny can't see it. But that has long been the problem, how little he can show. He no longer signs PILW, no longer gives any muffled screams, rarely calls for the alphabet board. Of course, Ginny thinks, it's how people die. They move less, they stop speaking, they can't respond.

Over the years she watched a half dozen patients die on the operating table, or minutes later. But those were medical deaths, not the end of someone she knew. She was out of the country when her father died. Her mother died alone, in her sleep. With Miles she wants to be close when he stops breathing. Jamie, of course, will want the same. That coming day looms, and little else matters. They cook, they eat, they wash the dishes. Not a minute is meaningless. They still roll Miles to the sea in his chair, often the three of them go together. The sand grinds beneath the waves. They watch the bright slant of sails offshore, listen to the laughter from a party down the beach. She and Jamie don't say much themselves. They have all pulled back from the world.

They find a second hospital bed. Its frame is dinged and locked half-upright, but the mattress is clean and they set it up in the back yard. Most days, and most evenings, Miles lies there facing south. Though the sea is two hundred yards away past a half dozen houses, if the breeze is right they can sometimes smell it. Miles is silent. He's still. Does he want some water? Occasionally he sips through a straw. It's been a week since he signed, NO MRE FD. They move him once again to the wheelchair and strap him in, but his body slumps and his head lolls to one side. They ask if he's in pain, but he doesn't respond. They've taken their last roll through town.

Still, Ginny reads to him. Emma Bovary has had a child, a girl she names Berthe, but Emma shows little affection for her daughter. She's obsessed instead with jewels, stylish clothes and carriages. "Flaubert never had any children," Ginny explains. "I don't think he knew anything about them." Even so, the book is a powerful story. It's a good thing they'll never reach the mournful end.

One evening before dinner, Ginny goes out for a walk. When she gets back she finds Jamie in bed with Miles, an arm across his chest, their long legs spilling over the single mattress. Miles's eyes are closed. Jamie's are open but he doesn't move or say anything, or look at her.

She goes up to her room and sits on her bed, unhappy. She wanted to be close to Miles and hold him when he dies, but now knows she can't. She must give that time to Jamie for the two of them to share.

An hour later when she goes downstairs, Jamie is preparing dinner. They speak little, and after eating she asks him to walk with her to the beach, where they come to a stop beside the sea.

"I'm guessing that when Miles dies you'll want to have him to yourself, at least for a time. If that's so, I'll try to give you that. I'll try not to be in the house."

Jamie turns and takes her in his arms. She feels his slow breaths. It's a minute before he lets go and says, "You're the best mother."

No matter that she was right, it saddens her as they walk home. Before, everything pointed to a common goal. Now when the time comes she'll have to get out of the way. She loves Miles, but of course not the way Jamie does. That's what she knew, what she remembered, when she saw the two of them wrapped up together.

Among the few frangipanis still in bloom, she sits beside the hospital bed in the back yard. Miles lies beneath a white sheet they change every day. His face has grown smoother, and she wants to think his cares are lifting. There's no longer any hope, so perhaps no need to struggle. His breathing, though, comes harder and harder.

She tries to remember her drug and alcohol days, the many times she wished to be unconscious. But not dead. She had no vision of death, no conception of an afterlife in which she would walk around still herself, happy and aware. She only wanted her troubles to stop.

Miles has had enough. Why else would he have told them to stop feeding him? He's at the edge, but she cannot imagine him gone. How can someone be here, moving and talking or just lying in bed, and then no longer exist? Impossible. Every human of the past has disappeared, but surely it will be different with Miles.

He still opens his eyes, though not as often. He sleeps and sleeps. She has stopped asking him questions, stopped prodding him to respond. *Madame Bovary* lies on a chair. Chopin nocturnes play in her head, and Schubert's Trout Quintet. It's been a decade and more since she played the piano. Her mind wanders, and it must be the same with Miles when he's awake. It's what minds do. A rooster's cry floats in on an unsteady breeze, in the everyday Key West afternoon. Without warning, a convulsion wrenches her forward and tears spill from her eyes.

How little she knows about Miles's early life. He was born before the Depression and grew up deep in the closet, only taking his first steps out when teaching at a boarding school for teenage boys. It's a wonder no one made a fuss about him there—or ripped him to shreds. Of course there were some gay boys at the school, along with several effeminate masters who everyone guessed were homos underneath. But almost always, the masters behaved. Their example to the boys was clear: you might feel poofy, but don't act on it.

Softly, Ginny taps his lips with a straw, and Miles sucks up some ice water. A third of a gulp, barely that. His breaths are shallow and labored. Night is falling as she and Jamie sit on either side of the bed, each holding a hand. A hand that to Ginny feels nearly lifeless. Well, no more so than the plants and bushes all around them. And while no one wants to be a vegetable, they can be wonderfully alive. She stands up and goes outside, picks an heirloom Brandywine tomato from its trellis and places it in Miles's left hand, folding his fingers around it. He can't respond, but from what she's read he can still feel it. *There*, did his lips part as if at the start of a smile? She picks another tomato and gives it to Jamie, who touches it to Miles's lips.

"I think he likes it," she says.

"How can we know?"

"Look at his face. Don't you think he's almost smiling?"

"Mamá. I know he would have liked it, once upon a time. It's probably a good guess now."

The next day Ginny shops at the outdoor market for some vegetables and fruits that Jamie doesn't grow. She brings them home in a cloth sack, and during her hours with Miles she pulls them out one at a time and folds his fingers around them. At first a peach with its subtle fuzz, then an onion with its slippery shell. A red pepper almost ten inches long, gently creased and waxy. She holds each under his nose for a few seconds so he can breathe it in. After the pepper an avocado with its crinkly skin. Then an eggplant, round and firm and womanly, she thinks. Which leads her to a cucumber, as phallic as it gets. And suddenly she imagines Jamie placing his organ in Miles's hand, a callout to the old days. *No*, she can't think like that, not for two seconds. Though underneath, as she settles down, her guess is that Miles would like it. Better than a fat old eggplant, anyway.

That night, alone on her own bed, she wonders again what she'll do after Miles dies. As long as he's alive her days are ordained, but what will come next? Sobriety, first, but that's only a focus. She needs some project, some passion. She's glad to have her house in Sag Harbor, but that's a dwelling, not a life. She drifts along, far from sleep. Though she's going to outlive Miles, it's his life that seems more vital.

The next morning, as Miles fights to breathe, with his hands curled and his chest heaving, his death seems close. To follow her promise, she tells Jamie she's going for a drive. He understands and squeezes her hand. Miles is asleep.

Inside their house, someone is dying. Outside, you'd never know. The sea is blue, fishing boats weave back and forth, the sails in the distance are stabs of white. She drives from key to key, past stores and restaurants all going about their business. She stops at a bakery and buys a pair of croissants, wrapped in sweet-smelling paper. She has brought along a folding chair and a book by García Márquez, and sits on a beach at Big Pine Key with her back to the sun. *Macondo era entonces una aldea de veinte casas de barro y cañabrava.* She should stay away for hours, perhaps all day. She should have driven to Miami, gone to see a movie, eaten dinner at some restaurant. Here, she can't bring herself to take a bite from either croissant. It's an involuntary constraint, she thinks, an act of sympathy with Miles. NO MRE FD. He may have died already, which would be for the best. His struggles have gone on too long. Then she feels guilty for such a thought.

A dolphin breaks the surface not twenty yards from shore. It's a rare time of year for dolphins, and no others appear. Ginny goes back to her book. She'd like to read this Macondo story to Miles, if she could find a copy in English. She keeps imagining the things they could do together.

When she gets home that afternoon, he's still alive. Jamie looks exhausted. Miles looks peaceful except for his breaths. Jamie asks, in the kitchen, "How much can he stand?"

"We should ask for the morphine, don't you think?"

Jamie calls the doctor, but he has left the office. The receptionist says he could come by tomorrow. If only Ginny hadn't lost her license she could have prescribed and administered the drug herself. She'll never take another drink.

Jamie has put on a pair of long pants, as if on this day shorts would be too relaxed. Ginny now does the same. Her trousers feel heavy and awkward, but the sun is setting and the night will be cooler. The last direct rays slant into the room, lighting up Miles in his bed. His feet stick up and his chin lies on his chest. It's dinnertime but no one mentions food. Ginny has fasted all day and now, she thinks, eating would be a transgression. She and Jamie sit on chairs on opposite sides of the bed. Miles breathes, and breathes again. It grows dark and no one turns on a light. A cricket chirps from somewhere in the house. Ginny wants to find it and smash it.

Music, bike bells and the soft whirr of tires filter in through the door, through the open windows and uninsulated walls. Miles doesn't move but keeps breathing. Jamie sits like a Buddhist, silent and emptied. Ginny keeps her eyes to herself, staring at the floor's pine planks. She tries to still her mind, but that never works. This town, this house, this room will be the last that Miles knows. Better here than in some hospital, she thinks. Better here than anywhere, unless they could somehow cart him to the beach. She imagines what it would take to put Miles in the Hoyer lift, leave him hanging in it as they turned the bed on its side and carried it out, then wheeled everything to the sidewalk. No, it's a crazy idea. But if he's still thinking, she knows that's what he'd want. He hasn't moved since she came back.

Jamie rises quietly and goes into the kitchen. Ginny follows, and with a small wave of his head he leads her out the back door, where Miles's outdoor bed sits empty. The stars are softened by a nighttime haze. "It doesn't look good," Jamie says.

"I can't tell how much he's suffering."

Jamie takes her in his arms and holds her, which is just what she wants right now. After a minute or two they go back inside and pause beside Miles in his bed, to hear him breathe.

He doesn't. In those few minutes he has died.

Has he? She puts a hand on his chest. She keeps thinking he'll start again, that he's only taking a break. But no, he's spent. He's gone, but where? It feels as unreal as it always has: the impossible fact that he will no longer be one of them. She puts an ear to his chest, then realizes she's doing exactly what she shouldn't, getting in Jamie's way.

"I'm going out."

"Thank you Mamá. Let me have him for a while."

When she walks onto the pier at Higgs she can't remember how she got there. A couple stands at the end in each other's arms. She turns around and walks back to the shore, then inland down streets she can't remember, houses with lights, a growling dog, rocking chairs on porches, people who have no idea. She walks until she's exhausted, then stops and stands in the middle of a quiet street, watching for any movement anywhere. There is none. She walks home.

When she slips inside, Jamie is in bed with Miles, their four long legs entwined, his hand on Miles's heart as if still feeling for a beat. He turns that hand and stretches his fingers toward her. "There's room," he says. "Lie with us."

She lowers the side rail and climbs on. It's tight, and she has to hold onto Miles to stay with him. But this is what she wants. The whole time Miles was dying, this is what she wanted, and Miles might have wanted it himself. He probably did. What was she doing, just reading and talking? She should have climbed into bed with him. Now she rests her head against his cool cheek and the three of them lie still. She keeps imagining that he's about to take another breath.

They don't tell anyone. There is only the screen door between them and the world, but no one knocks. The phone rings and they don't pick it up. Late that night they go to sleep in their own beds, then get up early, eat breakfast and go back to their chairs beside Miles. They want more of him. They're not ready to turn him over to some authority and a crematorium. He looks as if he's asleep. No wonder people believe in ghosts.

That afternoon Jamie calls the coroner, then some of his friends, and Ginny calls Rob. Slowly they acknowledge that Miles is gone.

18

Though it's the peaceful off-season in Sag Harbor, Ginny has a hard time settling in. Her house is warm, but at the beach she's as sensitive to the cold as Jamie was a year ago. And while she thought that Miles's death might be a kind of release, as the days pass she only misses him more. Jamie reports that he's painting again and slowly rejoining the world. Ginny walks and writes letters on her typewriter. She sends one to Jamie every two or three days, at first with only trifling news, her lunches at the Paradise Grill, the clams she cooks for dinner, a visit she makes to Shelter Island. But then, a blowup.

> Dear Jamie,
> After ten days here I started back with my AA meetings. Not that I needed to, but I know few people in this town and I wanted to connect to my old group. Most of them were still there, and I was glad to see them—but in my turn around the circle, I was telling them what happened in Key West, how Miles had died, and I exaggerated a little, saying it almost drove me to drink again. People say that all the time, and I was trying to be part of the group. Mainly I talked about you and Miles and your gay community, how supportive they are. Then one of the old guys lifted his hand and said, "That kind of life is not what the Lord intended."

"Then *fuck* the Lord."

It poured out of me, I was so angry. There's a rule about it anyway, you're not supposed to crosstalk after someone speaks. Okay, I was a little extreme, but whenever someone says something about fags or queers I want to smack them. Mostly the group was quiet, but I could feel them turn against me. I'd insulted Jesus and they didn't like it. Three days later, when it was time for the next meeting, I didn't go back.

I've noticed before that I'm sad about Miles, but also angry at him for dying. That makes no sense, but I watch myself and it's how I feel. Or maybe I'm just angry at everything. The cold wind at the beach, or someone tailgaiting me, or just some litter on the sidewalk, anything can set me off.

Could you do another painting of Miles for me? His body, his face, you choose, and send it to me so I can frame it? I want to have him in my house.

Love,
Mamá

Rob writes from Ohio and invites her out. The twins are six months old and starting to crawl, or at least scoot around on the floor. Sleep for their parents is still a problem. "It hasn't been easy, but I know you'll love the little ones. Come if you can, Mamá."

Three days later she does. By getting up at three and passing through New York before the rush, she makes the trip in a day. She pulls into the commune in the late afternoon, and even before she shuts off her engine she hears the twins wailing inside. Both of them, it sounds like. She sits in her car, hoping to wait until they quiet down, but they don't.

Finally she takes her suitcase and goes to the door. She knocks and nothing happens. The babies could be steam engines. When she goes inside she finds Rob with one in his arms, and Lisa pacing with the other. Natalia sits in a padded chair, barechested, holding a hair brush. She looks at Ginny.

"What are you doing here? Oh, right, a visit. No one knows how hard this is." She passes the brush through her long dark hair, tosses it back, sets down the brush and says, "Okay, I'm ready for them."

Diapered but otherwise unclothed, the babies cry and gulp, then wriggle around on her lap and in her arms. She looks calm enough, Ginny thinks, as the wailing slowly subsides. One of the twins latches, this seems to persuade the other, and once they're both nursing everyone settles down.

Rob comes over and gives her a hug. "Mamá, we're glad you've come." Lisa and Flora also embrace her. It's a smaller group. Maybe some are still off at work.

Rob takes her elbow. "Let's go for a walk."

He leads her down the drive beside the creek. His shoulders are rounded, his hair longer. "When they both nurse at once," he says, "I get a break."

"How's Natalia doing?"

"She sleeps even less than I do. And she needs to be alone herself sometimes. All day she feeds the kids and carries them around and holds onto them. She wants them against her skin. Then, without a word, she walks out the door and we don't see her for an hour."

"Well, we get to walk out the door."

"You're right, it's only fair. People told us how hard this was going to be. Hell, you told us, and still we had no idea."

Above the creek a hawk pulses up over the sycamores, screeching repeatedly. It looks like the same hawk as last time, but they always look the same to Ginny. She wonders if humans all look the same to hawks. Probably not.

"It does get easier," she tells Rob. "They start crawling, then walking, and they won't cry as much. You know all this, I'm just trying to make you feel better."

They climb the hill. Halfway up she stops for a rest and turns to face him. "How are the two of you getting along?"

"Okay. Sometimes."

"And other times?"

Rob stares off into the trees, into the new leaves of maples, buckeyes, young ironwood. "All her attention goes to the twins. We don't talk much anymore, and it's not as if we're equals. I'm her helper now."

"Because she's doing the essential job."

"You always understand, Mamá."

She doesn't really. As they continue their climb she thinks of her own babies when they were young. She was never as devoted as Natalia seems to be, so ready to make a child her life. She envies Natalia's softened look as the two babies latched. It jars her to remember how that felt: the tug and pain, and the deep relief of her milk letting down. But she was busy and had a job to get back to. She should have been more motherly.

In Key West such painful thoughts were cushioned by the care she gave Miles. Jamie needed her help and it was a job she could handle. Here, if Natalia keeps fending her off, she won't be helping much with the twins.

They reach the high meadow and walk on through the new grass. Spring is a wave of green. Not all the leaves have unfurled on the trees, but all that have are perfect. No insects have fed on them, no blight or fungus has a hold. Every time she comes they take this peaceful walk.

She's given her old room. The commune is down to six people, and she's flanked at dinner by Flora and Lisa, who ask her questions about Key West, because they've both thought about living there. Natalia doesn't come to the table. She eats on the couch with one baby on her lap and the other asleep beside her. When the meal is done she points without a word to Rob and Lisa, who stand up, take a baby apiece and head for the door. Ginny tilts her head toward Rob, meaning *Should I come?* He gives her a miniature shake of his head and walks out.

At breakfast the next morning Natalia looks subdued. Rob is off at his half-time job, laying block for a house foundation. "They let him work mornings only," Natalia says. "Because that's what the world wants, another house. In the afternoons he helps out here."

One of the twins is at her breast. The other lies quiet in a crib, but probably not for long. Natalia guides the baby's mouth back to her nipple. "How long did you breastfeed Jamie and Rob?"

"Not long enough. After a month or two it was formula with a bottle. It doesn't sound right, but it's what most women did back then. I think your way is better."

"It is. Some women breastfeed for three or four years."

"Really?"

"The longer you do it, the smarter they get. That's how it works."

She looks both calm and serious. It's the delirium of motherhood, Ginny thinks, and she's not about to challenge her. "Is it all right that I've come for a visit?"

"I guess. If I don't like it I'll tell you."

"I thought I could work in the garden, like last year."

"Fine, just don't mix up the seeds."

How does Rob live with this? He's always been in thrall to Natalia, but before them lies this vast project, with Natalia making all the decisions.

The garden beds are tilled and the last frost has likely passed. There are beans to be seeded, sweet potato slips to be set, tomato and pepper starts to be moved to their garden beds. Ginny is glad to be out of the house and down on her knees. How rich the soil is here, dark and moist.

After a strangely quiet dinner, Rob talks to her in the garden. He and Natalia have had an argument. "Not really an argument, just a list of things that annoy her, that she wants me to change."

"Like what?"

"My tone of voice when I talk to Sophie and Chilo. It should never be childlike, she says. And a shirt I shouldn't wear around them, because it has an odd smell. And a song by Don McLean she doesn't think they should hear. It's all getting strange and she doesn't listen to me about any of it. She gives me a hundred fierce words, then it's over."

Ginny has no advice for him, no suggestions about how to respond. With Joe she never learned anything about arguing, because they didn't. But Joe wasn't filled with crazy notions. When she glances back toward the house, Natalia is standing on the back porch with one child at her hip, staring at them. The other starts to cry inside, but she doesn't move. She waits until they return to the house. Rob goes in to pick up the wailing twin, and Ginny goes to her room.

The twins wake her the next morning, both crying hard. She gets up, dresses, and finds that Natalia has left the house. She rose before everyone else and drove away. She didn't leave a note. Now the twins are hungry, they want their mother and her breasts.

"We've got to feed them," Rob says, "and there's not a bottle in the house. We have to go to town."

He and Ginny take off in the commune's old pickup, leaving the hard job to Lisa. The McArthur general store has bottles with nipples and rows of Similac formula. Rob doesn't know how much to buy. He settles on two bottles and four cans, and they hightail it back to the farm. The twins are still crying as they mix the powder and warm it up. It's a job that no one on the farm has ever done, and Ginny can hardly remember. A loud and frightful ten minutes pass before the first twin submits to the bulbous nipple being pushed between her lips. She starts and stops, and finally settles in. And as often happens, the first twin leads the second, and soon they're both slurping away.

Natalia comes back at noon and walks into the house as if she's done nothing strange. The twins are asleep and she wakes them both. "They have to take my milk. I've been leaking all morning and it hurts." Her breasts look swollen and two dark stains run down to her waist. She pulls off her shirt, bra-less beneath it, and Sophie and Chilo latch within seconds. They drink noisily, as focused as birds in flight. Rob asks, as they settle in, "Where did you go?"

"What do you care?"

"They were hungry and unhappy. We had to go to town and buy formula."

"*Formula.* They don't need that crap."

Ginny dares a comment. "They had to have something."

Natalia stares at her, hard. "What do you know about it?"

"We couldn't let them go hungry," Rob says. "If you up and disappear they have to drink something."

"Well here I am."

Ginny wants to step away from this hopeless quarrel. But sitting in silence seems less intrusive, and now it's quiet save for the gurgling of the twins. Chilo twists and unlatches, and Natalia struggles to keep him cradled. When he starts to slip out of her arm, Rob jumps up to help. He crouches beside Natalia's chair, guides the baby back to her breast, and the two infants keep on nursing. Ginny wonders if this crazy disappearance by Natalia was actually directed at her, to make her feel less welcome. In a few more days she'll be headed home.

19

Back in Sag Harbor, Ginny is sometimes at peace and sometimes bewildered. She considers her years with Joe, her affair with Rich, her time in Chile with the steadfast Alberto. Gone, all of it. She writes Carol but gets nothing back. On her typewriter, she starts to set down how Rich abandoned her in Miami, how lost she was, how that led to all her troubles. But she gets no further than a page and a half. It's too complex, and as soon as she writes a sentence she wants to revise it. She has spent all her discipline on never picking up another glass of wine, another benzo or barbiturate. This has been her victory, but it's not enough. What if she starts to forget everything, the way her mother did? No sign of that so far. She remembers her past, she just can't make sense of it.

All the same, it's a lovely time of year on the South Fork. A peaceful May, the potato fields lined with new green plants, the afternoon sun at her back as she heads east on the beach. When the crowds take over she'll have to come at dawn if she wants to be alone by the ocean. Today her worries blow away like the spume that flutters offshore.

The hours after dinner, when she used to drink, are still her difficult time. Will this quiet house be all she knows? Having left Jamie to work out his new life with friends, she won't be going back to Key West any time soon. She can't imagine returning to Vinton County either, with Natalia so cranky. She could visit her sister Lauren in New Brunswick, but the drive is too long. For now she'll venture no farther than Sagaponack.

After a quick dinner she picks up Durrell's *Justine* and reads the first chapters again. She's read the novel several times, and never tires of it. She's drawn to characters in books, to their dramatic lives and desires. And no wonder. People in novels don't spend time paying bills or washing dishes, or god forbid pissing or taking a shit. Day after day, no one in a novel ever uses the toilet. They're too wrapped up with one vital encounter after the next. Ginny, for her part, sits on a chair in her living room, immersed in Alexandria and Corfu.

She wants to go back to Connecticut to see her sister. Carol clearly isn't as interested in their mother's last days and years, but there's no one else Ginny can talk to about it. Whether Carol will join her or not, she wants to visit Gran's nursing home again, to soak up anything that touched her mother's life in her sad last years. She gives her sister a call and invites herself to spend the night, which is fine with Carol. "Though I will be having a cocktail or two. I don't have to give that up, do I?"

"No, I'm fine with that." Ginny promises a late-morning arrival, so they can eat again at the Red Barn. It has become a tradition.

She knows what Carol will think about another visit to their mother's nursing home, but at lunch she asks anyway.

"We did that," Carol says.

"I keep thinking about it. Thinking about her."

"All in all she was a pretty good mother."

"I can't get over that she spent her last days in a place like that. I want to go back so I can feel what it was like."

"Why this obsession? Why not remember her better days? We've got our own lives to live, and wouldn't it relax her to know we're having a good time?"

No, Ginny can't lean on her sister. She will visit the home by herself. For ten minutes she sits in the parking lot outside the columned front doors. It's a perfect June day. Bright cardinals skitter among the leafed-out dogwoods, brilliant clouds drift overhead, there are chairs outside the doors but no one in sight. There were plenty of aides the last time she came, and shouldn't they be guiding the residents on a walk, or pushing them around in their wheelchairs? A concrete walkway circles the building, but no one is on it.

She tells the woman at the reception desk about her earlier visit, and asks if she can sit for a while in the common room. The woman says "Just a minute," and goes back into an office. When she returns she says, "I'm sorry, not unless you have a friend or relative here, or have an appointment."

"My mother lived here. She died here."

"I'm sorry."

As simple as that, they boot her out. She goes back to her car and sits, letting her anger grow. Then she gets out and follows the surrounding walkway, looking into the windows. She waves at an old woman inside, then an old man as they stare out through the glass. Neither of them waves back.

Why did she move Gran from her New York apartment to this useless place? The idea was to have her closer to two of her daughters, but the more senile she grew, the less she and Carol came to see her.

Around the building and around again. How little she knew about dementia, back in the days when Gran first showed it. Once, Ginny took her to Gristedes in town to buy some groceries and there, as Ginny considered the lettuces, Gran walked off to find some special toothpaste. Were there special kinds? Off she went, and only a minute later Ginny couldn't find her. She looked in every aisle, she talked to the two cashiers, she left her groceries in the cart and stepped outside. The town's Main Street was a quiet two lanes, but Gran wasn't always attentive to cars. Finally, at the edge of panic, Ginny caught sight of her a block away, staring into a bookstore window. She ran to her, and Gran never moved.

"I read that book," she said, pointing through the glass. It was a book about frogs, which seemed unlikely. "And that one," Gran said, about a novel just released. "And that one," pointing to a book about Vietnam. Eventually they returned to the store, paid for the groceries and took them home. Ginny should have understood by then. This was more than senility, and it was undermining her mother's brain. Maybe there was nothing to be done about it, as now there's nothing to be done about Lou Gehrig's disease. But Miles, at least, was loved and taken care of. Ginny and her sisters all but abandoned their mother, in a building she now can't enter.

For the first time ever she spends the night at Carol's house. Over a dinner of shrimp, avocados and nothing more save for Carol's wine, Ginny describes her failed visit to the nursing home. Carol listens without a response. Ginny is annoyed but holds herself back. She doesn't know if she's angry at Carol, or at everything. Her sister has suffered the worst loss anyone can know, the death of her child. Every day forever, Janna won't be here, and if this is why Carol has retreated from their mother and from much of their shared past, Ginny will accept it. Carol starts in about a boyfriend she had in high school who now has Parkinson's. She smokes a pair of cigarettes and drinks another glass of wine. She's tipsy or more, but given her own history, Ginny's not going to chide her about it.

Later that night when she walks past her sister's door on the way to the bathroom, she smells cigarette smoke again. This is Carol's worst habit. She takes a sleeping pill every night—so she has admitted—then smokes in bed. Ginny stands still in the hallway. After the troubles she's made for others, how can she spout off about this? Still, the whole world knows this is wrong. *You don't smoke in bed.* She puts her hand on the knob and turns it, opens the door a couple of inches. Carol doesn't hear or see her, or at least she doesn't look over. She's propped up on a couple of pillows, staring at the ceiling. She takes a drag, then lowers her hand to the bedspread, the cigarette still glowing.

Ginny steps into the room. "Carol, this is dangerous."

Her sister's eyes wander over, unhurried. "You're going to tell *me* what to do?"

"For your own damn good I am." She walks to the bed, plucks the cigarette out of Carol's hand and stubs it out in an ashtray on the bedside table.

"Tomorrow night you won't be here," Carol says, "so I can do what I like."

She looks calm. Her two fingers which held the cigarette are still lifted into the air. Ginny wants to slap them with something. A shoe or a book, but there is no book. The table holds only the ashtray, a lighter, a reading light and a bottle of pills. Ginny picks up the orange prescription bottle with its Nembutals.

"Don't you remember? These things almost killed me."

"Because you took too many of them. You've never had any discipline. I take one pill and smoke one last cigarette. It's not a problem."

How to get through to her? Ginny holds up the bottle, stares at it, then flings it into a corner of the room. Carol doesn't move. Ginny wants to grab and shake her, pull her off the bed and make her see the danger. Carol blinks. She looks calm. Of course, Ginny thinks, because she's floating on a Nembutal.

June 30

Dear Jamie and Rob,

A typewriter has some advantages. One of you gets the original, the other a carbon copy. I'll flip a coin.

Now, Sag's quiet days are coming to an end. Sitting in my house I sometimes hear horns from Main Street, and what the hell can anyone honk at there? I'll walk up to see sometime. I need to walk more, so I'll walk past the church where I insulted the Lord. I'll walk through the Old Burying Ground, because I like cemeteries and how quiet they are. Though you can probably hear the horns from there, too.

I have a job of sorts. I wrote Richard Jackbin at Columbia Presbyterian and asked if he had any work editing medical studies. I used to do that for Virginia Apgar when I was a resident at CP. It's a plod, but as close to medicine as I can get now, and the first study is in the mail. Every one I ever read was in need of an editor.

The Brennans are coming for a long weekend over the 4th. There will be just the three of us for our picnics at the beach, which sounds a bit thin, but I'll be glad to see them. Don't worry about me drinking or downing some pills. I'm through with all that, I just need some focus.

I went to visit my sister Carol. She drinks and smokes in bed, which worries me. But she's still quite hopeful about things as she looks for a companion. I'm older, I grew up in charge, but now I'm the wobblier sister, trying to figure things out, obsessing about our mother's last years. I'm lucky to have the two of you.
Love,
Mamá

This admission of shakiness is new, but after lying to them about being immune to alcohol and drugs, she had to include it. She won't relapse, she won't be cradling a bottle of gin, but the struggle isn't over. It's with her every day, like breathing, as she imagines the smooth feel of a glass in her hand and the first drops touching her lips.By the time she and the Brennans get to the beach on the Fourth, it's already crowded. They walk past the many blankets and towels, the kites and beach balls and hula hoops, all the way to the inlet where it's quieter. They've brought with them, for the first time, some folding chairs. Chairs on the beach! It seems a travesty. Always in the past they merely stretched out on the sand. But in fact, the chairs make sitting a pleasure. The three of them face the sea with their bread and deviled eggs, their wine and ginger ale nestled on a towel in front of them.

Ginny asks about Tommy in the city, about his anxiety and his drugs. Patty demurs. "Let's talk about it later," she says. "It's hard on Bill, it makes *him* anxious."

"You two can get into it," he says. "After we eat I'll take a walk down the beach."

He never does, and Ginny holds back from spilling Rob's story, or Jamie's. She'll meet up with Patty later, when they can talk more freely. For now they watch the gulls and sandpipers and young couples in the briefest of bathing suits, holding hands as they walk beside the waves.

It was always like this. When she and Joe came for their Labor Day visits, the adults rarely shared any intimate talk. It was the husbands who held back. Ginny had to catch Patty alone to hear how she felt. Of course, in those early days they had children to look after and play with, they had sand castles to build and waves to tempt. When you had young kids, friends were less vital, at least at the beach with the kids laughing and shouting and demanding more lunch.

Bill might not talk that much, but he's considerate. He's the one who asked her, as they planned this picnic, if she was comfortable with them drinking around her. And now he asks how Joe is doing. "We miss him," he says. 'Never a fuss about anything—unless you've written something that doesn't flow."

If Joe were here, he and Bill would be talking about articles and books and *Life* magazine, back in the days when they worked together. Ginny wonders if she and another anesthesiologist would talk about halothane, cyclopropane and rates of inhalation. She's not even sure about the latest practices.

Patty and Bill will now come out to Sag almost every weekend. Ginny watches them, and wonders again about their marriage. It can't be the perfect relationship. Bill's eyes rest too long on other women, something Joe's did not. But the Brennans have their routines, they have a daughter and two sons, they're a comfort to each other. They both dress with care. Patty never wears trousers, it's always a dress or skirt. Bill often puts on a tie for dinner. They cut or style their hair every couple of months. Surely, Ginny thinks, they have sex on occasion—but she has never asked about that. Bill has never flirted with her, nor she with him. But how much can she know of what they share, as they lie with their heads on two pillows on the same bed? Because they always sleep in the same bed. She and Joe did not. They had twin beds, identical, narrow, ridiculous. No, the Brennans have made the eternal bond and will always be a pair. When the three of them get together, Ginny is a moon to their earth.

20

July 24

Shit fuck I knew it could happen. Carol's house burned down last night and she was in it. I should have stayed there and convinced her of the danger. Instead I came home and now she's gone. I'm a damn fool.

I never really knew how much she suffered after Janna died. She hid that. But now it feels like Janna's death has lead straight to this one. It led to drinking and sleeping pills and smoking in bed, and I should have seen it coming. I did see it coming and didn't do enough about it.

I've called Lauren up in New Brunswick, and Janna's husband out in Pennsylvania. Now I have to tell Jamie and Rob.

The funeral home depresses her all over again. She and Lauren should have known better after their mother's death, but they wind up in the same polished asylum with Carol's remains—what the coroner has given them—in a plain wooden box. They arrange for the cremation, a terrible irony, and choose an urn. They try to ignore the obsequious director, hovering in his pinstripe suit and glossy pointed shoes, and return the next day for a service led by no one, in a room lined with black velvet drapes, overseen by a pair of marble Christs. It isn't a service at all, they just talk about Carol. No one speaks of the fire or how it started.

Janna's sons are there, boys of nine and eleven, silent, sitting on either side of their father. He's a tall broad guy someone once dubbed, when he was courting Janna, as "a bartender out of work." But now Ginny sees how good he is with his boys. He sits with an arm around each as he tells stories about their grandmother. And later, beside a dark Long Island Sound, as Ginny and Lauren weep in each other's arms, he holds the two of them and cries along with them. For a moment he softens a bad day, but in the late afternoon he takes his boys and heads back to Pennsylvania.

July 28

People always say the same thing about the dead, that now they're at peace. If Carol is conscious in some other world, I suppose that could be. But I don't believe in that. Where she lives on is here, with all of us who knew her, and we're not that peaceful ourselves. Maybe this is now my job in life, to ease up and rest so Carol and Miles and my mother and Janna can all be at peace. haven't been doing well at it. Too often I'm annoyed. I'm pissed at Carol for being so stupid, and at myself for being so foolish. Or she was foolish and I'm stupid. There had to be something I could have said or done.

Now I have to deal with her lawyer, because she named me her executor. It feels more like executioner.

August 3

Back to Westport to sign some papers and find a tax attorney. Then I drove to what's left of Carol's house and parked next to the yellow tape surrounding the two blackened chimneys. I'll have to find someone to clean it all up, then the property can be sold—if anyone wants to touch it. In a wide circle around the house, every tree is scorched to a sickening black. As I walked around the lawn, the ashes were up to my ankles.

August 10
I sit at my kitchen table, eating my granola as the sun pours
in though the east window. The morning is cool and the
village quiet. I hurt all over. My neck hurts, my knees and the
bottom of my feet. I want to blame it on grief, but Miles's
death didn't beat me up like this. The difference is, with
Miles I knew it was coming. Carol's death should never have
happened.

Jamie writes from Key West.

Dear Mamá,
What a blow. I wasn't good with Aunt Carol recently, hadn't
written or called her in a couple of years. I regret that now,
as one grief compounds another. She was great when I was
young. She taught me how to play Solitaire and Pounce.
She snuck me Junior Mints when you weren't looking, and
always gave me presents on my half birthday. When I got
my learner's permit she let me drive her all the way to Dan-
bury for the demolition derby. The rest of you thought we
shouldn't watch such chaos. I'm sorry Mamá, I know this
can't be easy for you.
    I'm painting and taking bike rides every day and keeping
pretty quiet. I drink a little but keep it sane. Aunt Carol is
yet another lesson. She and Uncle Milton always drank too
much, and even as kids we knew that was so. I'll forever be
grateful for all you did with Miles.
Love,
Jamie

Rob writes from Ohio.

Mamá,

I'm sorry I couldn't make it to the gathering at the funeral home. Not much advance notice, and things are hectic
around here. The twins can almost stand up by themselves,
but Natalia has some crazy notions. She thinks, with this
warm weather, that they shouldn't wear any clothes at all.
No shirts, no pants, no diapers. She says they should be one
with the natural world.

In a way, I don't argue with it. What kid wants to
sit around in a wet diaper, or one squishy with poop? But
Natalia, of course, is extreme. I come home from work and
find all three of them lying out under the peach trees on
a blanket, stark naked. No clothes in sight, and certainly
no diapers. If they start to pee or crap, she lifts them off
the blanket, but she doesn't always catch them in time and
cleans up with a towel. And it's not just outside. Half the
time she keeps their diapers off in the house. "They have to
live free," she says. Before they go down at night I always
diaper them, but in the morning they're usually naked. I do
a lot of laundry.

It's hard on everyone. Lisa and Flora, who used to
be such a help, are pulling back. Lisa refuses to hold either
one of them if not in a diaper. She's been pissed on enough,
and I can't blame her. It's easier to train a dog than kids
this young. Sometimes I come in and find some small round
poops on the floor. The couch is now stained with both piss
and shit. When Natalia isn't looking, Flora puts her finger
to her temple and twirls it.

If I put up a fight or even give her a hard look, Natalia ignores me. Yesterday when I came home and found her in the orchard, I asked if she needed another towel, because the one she had was all stained with shit. She stood up and marched to the truck and got in. I thought she was going to drive off with no clothes on. But she wasn't quite that crazy. She stopped and went inside, came out in shorts and a tank top and drove away, and didn't come home for two hours. I have no idea where she went. She won't talk about it. She's still devoted to the twins, she holds them and plays with them endlessly, but I never know when she's going to bolt. She puts on her shoes and takes a hike. Sometimes she goes up to the meadow, the one you love so much. She just has to get away. And I understand it. After two or three Chilo and Sophie hours, I'm desperate for a break myself.

I'm sorry Mamá, you tell me the news about Aunt Carol and I write you back about all my troubles. I wish I could have made it to the service. I hope things will settle down here with Natalia, and that I won't feel so frazzled. Whenever I talk to Jamie he tells me how great you were with Miles. We helped you out some when you left Silver Hill, and you've been helping us ever since. I'm glad you were nowhere near Aunt Carol's house when it burned.

Love,

Rob

Ginny has spent many Labor Days on the South Fork, so the crowds are no surprise when she and the Brennans walk onto the beach at Sagaponack. They go a quarter mile west, past almost everyone, and nestle their chairs in a triangle above the waves. "Pretty busy these days," Patty says.

"Still," her husband says, "out here it's my favorite day of the year."

"Why so?" Ginny asks.

"Because starting today, every time we come there will be fewer people. It's kind of how Joe saw the winter solstice, a turning of the tide."

Patty laughs. "What makes us dislike other people so much?"

"They make too much noise," Bill says. "I like an empty beach and open water, not a cluster of buzzing humans."

"Who probably feel the same way about us."

Silence, save for a faint song from some radio, the crash of the waves and cries from the gulls.

"We have so much history here," Ginny says. "I only wish our kids were with us. It's hard when they live so far away and they've got troubles."

"Bill and I haven't missed a Labor Day here in twenty-five years," Patty says.

Bill takes a handful of sand and tosses it onto her toes. "My dear, Ginny wants to talk about her sons."

What a surprise, for Bill to be the more attentive listener. "Go ahead," he says. "We know Miles's death was a hard one."

Ginny explains how Jamie has coped, with friends and painting. But it's Rob she wants to talk about, and Natalia's strange ways. She describes her campaign against diapers, and her occasional disappearances. "She just gets in a car and drives off, while Rob stays and handles the twins. It only makes him love them more, he says, but he and Natalia can hardly talk about it."

"Couplehood," Bill says. "It isn't really natural among humans."

"What are you talking about?" Patty is offended. "We've been coupled for thirty-six years."

"Sometimes I think we're more like a pair of rivers flowing side by side."

"That's because you hold back when you should help." Patty stands up and faces her husband. "I keep asking you to go into the city with me to see Tommy, who's so anxious he can't leave his apartment. I want you to come with me next time."

"All right. We could have gone to see him today, I'd have done that."

"Easy to say when it's too late. Stand up so I can talk to you."

"Sit down so I can talk to *you*."

She picks up her own handful of sand and rains it down on his legs. He stands up and Ginny does too, stepping between them. She's heard them argue many times, but always lightly and laced with affection. What has she been missing?

"Let's go for a walk," Patty says. "Ginny, excuse us."

They march off in silence across the sand. What's it like, Ginny wonders, at night in their house when no one else is around? Soon they are dots far down the beach. She watches until she can't see them anymore, then runs into the water and dives under a wave. She has always been a diver.

The village is quiet as she lies in bed. The Brennans have left Sag early, not waiting until their usual Tuesday morning. They were cordial enough after returning from their walk, but spoke of nothing serious. They dropped her at her house, each gave her a hug and off they went. Now in bed, Ginny's glad she doesn't share it with anyone.

She likes being alone, she wants that every day. The Brennans won't be back until next weekend, if then. She'll be here on her own, with plenty of time to edit her latest paper, on fibromyalgia and encephalograms. But a couple of hours a day on that is all she can bear. Fall is coming and it's going to be quiet. A drink now, just a small one, would take care of all her troubles.

How can she still think this? In the end, as always, it will be sleep that relieves her.

21

Rob calls one late afternoon. He says, "She left."

"What do you mean?"

"She took off in the car two days ago. I don't think she's coming back."

"She didn't say where she was going?"

"She left a note. Just one line, *I can't do this anymore.* So now I have the twins full time. I feed them and dress them and change them and carry them around. It's unreal how much work it is."

"Does anyone help?"

"Flora is gone and Lisa's freaked out. I'm kind of desperate or I wouldn't have called you."

"I see."

She wants a minute to think it over. She wants an hour, she wants a long solitary walk. Can she do this?

"Mamá?"

"All right, I'll come."

She'll ask the Brennans to check on her house. She'll deal with Carol's estate by phone. She'll pack her clothes and books and typewriter and fibromyalgia study, her purse and checkbook and all the cash in her house, her toothbrush and shampoo and some food from her fridge. She starts to write out a list. Instead, she lays out her suitcase and a pair of duffels, starts to fill them and is done in thirty minutes. It's dark outside. She'll leave early in the morning.

Crazily, just like the last time, when she pulls up and gets out of her car she can hear the babies crying inside. One stops, the other starts, then it's a duet. She's tired, she's been twelve hours on the road. The last twenty miles were on a restful wooded two-lane, but as she neared the farm she imagined walking into the house to find the twins napping. A hopeless dream. She walks empty-handed to the door. She taps, no one responds, she goes in.

Rob and Lisa stand at the far end of the room, each holding a baby. "Mamá!" he says, and she crosses the room to join their huddle with the two little howlers. Rob laughs. "Oh yeah, you remember what it's like." As smoothly as if long planned, Lisa hands over her baby. Ginny stares down at him, or her. She still can't tell them apart. The three adults sway left and right in an age-old rhythm of comfort, and only a minute or two later both kids stop crying.

"Chilo," Rob says, holding his baby upright with legs dangling, "This is your grandmother."

"They're beautiful," Ginny says, still cradling Sophie.

"We hoped you were coming soon," Lisa says. "But we didn't know what magic you could work."

"I haven't done anything."

"But look at them," Rob says. "They're entranced." And indeed, they stare at Ginny as if her face held the secrets of the world.

Lisa smiles, then laughs. "Better live it up now," she says, and two minutes later she's out the door.

"Where's she going?"

"I've leaned on her hard these last few days. She's been great, but she does have another life." He drops a blanket on the floor and spreads it out with his feet, then sets down the first of the twins. "They're fed, so let's see if they'll play."

Moments ago Ginny was exhausted. Now she's wide awake, because every move the little ones make charms her. They can both stand up on their own, but after a step or two they plop back onto the ground. Rob goes into the next room and brings back a crate full of smooth wooden blocks. "I cut them from a sugar maple that came down this spring." They're sanded and varnished and the kids love them, building tiny towers two or three blocks high. Their true genius is knocking down what Rob and

Ginny build for them. They send the blocks tumbling and laugh every time. Ginny crouches, then stretches out on the floor. *I can do this*, she thinks.

After dinner, with the twins down, she and Rob talk at the big round table. No one else lives here now, save for Lisa when she's not at her boyfriend's. Natalia is gone, Flora is gone, the other couple left months ago, the Six is ancient history. The commune's many plates and glasses sit untouched in a cabinet. Outside, as the last light fades over the garden, the green hills embrace the house.

"Have you heard anything from Natalia?"

"Not a word."

"Did you talk to the police?"

"I don't think vanishing is illegal."

"They could put out a missing person alert."

Rob stares out the window. "No, I don't want to talk to the cops."

"She could be in some danger. Don't you worry about that?"

"The real danger was to these two." He lifts a hand toward the sleeping children laid out on the couch, their beige coverlet faintly rising and falling. "She was too loose with them. It got worse and worse."

Ginny waits.

"The way she carried them around. When she took them out to the orchard she picked them up by the ankle, one in each hand, and swung them as she went. Not that they didn't love it. They laughed and screamed, it was like Moon and the football only upside down and doubled. She never dropped them, but I was always afraid. I was afraid when she drove to town with the two of them plunked down in back. Forget car seats with Natalia. And they crawl so well now, it can be trouble. A couple of weeks ago I found them next to the creek, half in and half out of the water. It was hardly flowing, but Natalia wasn't even looking at them, she was hunting for feathers under the trees. When I ran over and scooped them up she got angry. I should have let them be, she said, they had to figure out life on their own. I tell you, Mamá, it was getting scary."

He's half glad Natalia has gone, Ginny can see. "Good thing she didn't take them with her."

"That would have been a disaster." He stands up, checks on them, and sits back down at the table. "I'm glad you've come, but I don't know how much to ask of you."

"Ask for whatever you want, and I'll set my limits. You don't think she'll come back?"

"I have no idea. I don't know her anymore."

In this room Ginny has seen parties, dancing, drinking, a festive dozen people who joined their lives. It feels sad and empty now.

"Natalia is twenty-six, right? And this odd behavior of hers—when would you say that started?"

"She was always different. I loved that about her. What are you getting at?"

Ginny finds herself stumbling onto another diagnosis she knows little about. But she remembers reading that the early and mid-twenties are the most common age for the onset of schizophrenia, and she repeats this to Rob. "Is there any mental illness in her family?"

"Something, for sure. Her father shot himself when he was thirty-seven, and there was an uncle who was kind of odd."

"It can run in families. It's just a guess, but it might explain some of her behavior."

Rob stares out into the dark. "I'd be glad to blame it on a disease. I'm tired of blaming her."

Rob wants to go back to work, but takes another day off to show Ginny his routines. They've agreed on a schedule in which he'll go off to lay bricks in the morning and return for the afternoon shift at home. He brings Ginny up to date on feedings, formula, laundry and naps. And games. He has a closetful of old pots and pans and wooden spoons to bang them with, rows of stackable cups, a badly inflated four-square ball, crayons and sheets of paper, balloons to blow up and four rolls of toilet paper ready for an exciting mess. Also, a dozen kids' books sit on tables and windowsills around the living room.

On their first scheduled day Rob is up and gone by 6:30, eager to satisfy his boss, who would prefer he laid bricks full-time but is also a father of four, and sympathetic. The twins sleep in Rob's room, often in his bed, and today, well before the sun slants down into the hollow, Ginny finds them both awake. Miraculously, they lie there in silence. Of course it doesn't last. Chilo is the first to bleat. Sophie watches for a time, then joins in. Ginny has already warmed their bottles on the stove.

An hour, a single hour with them and she's drained. They're bent on her attention, they want it every minute. When they finally go down for a nap at ten, she lies back on the sofa beside them. Within minutes she's asleep herself.

Wild Sophie and willful Chilo. She's starting to tell them apart, but has pinned a bit of red cloth to the back of Sophie's shirt just to be sure. She feeds them again, then pulls out some pots and drums for them to bang on. Rob is due back at one, and well before that she's listening for the sound of his truck. Her own children never wore her out so much, though of course she only had one at a time. Two alluring urchins shouldn't be so hard, but by the time Rob gets back she's completely played out.

Every day after lunch, with Rob and the twins carrying on, it would be hopeless to lie in her room and try to relax. First she walks up to her meadow, grown over with goldenrod and iron weed, the first maples showing hints of yellow, the vultures hovering above. Then off to the library in McArthur, which has become her refuge. A quiet main room with solid tables and chairs, other rooms stacked full of books, magazines and newspapers, and light pouring in through the elegant windows. She finds a quiet table.

Sept. 29

I miss my house in Sag, but there's no time to mope over it. Every morning I look after the beasts, as Rob sometimes calls them. I imagine them grown to full size but acting as they do now. Scary! Whatever they can reach they grab and shake and throw around. They stand up, walk a couple of steps and collapse.

I thought maybe I'd get used to this job, but not yet. Looking after Miles wasn't a tenth this much work. Of course, when Miles didn't like something he didn't start bawling.

These two are so beautiful. It's a hard path, but how can Natalia have left them?

22

Lisa sometimes sleeps at the farm, and for a day on most weekends they pay her to look after the twins. Rob and Ginny get to take a hike through the Hocking Hills, eat a peaceful lunch together, float down Raccoon Creek in a borrowed canoe. Any calm time feels like showered peace. Sometimes they work the garden together, harvesting the butternut squash and sweet potatoes, the Brussels sprouts and Jerusalem artichokes.

In October a postcard comes from Natalia. On one side, a Santa Fe cathedral. On the other, scrawled opposite Rob's name and address, "I'm on the road in New Mex. I miss those two, Nitilia."

"*Nitilia?*"

"Sometimes she plays around with her name."

"Is there anything we should do?"

"I don't think there's anything we can do. She's far away and she's a catastrophe. One of these days she'll walk in the door. Or maybe not. I never know what's coming next."

A Connecticut lawyer handles Carol's estate, and hires a crew to clean up the burned property. Though it's a jumbled mess of foundation block and residue from the fire, a realtor lists the half-acre and sells it in ten days. The price was probably too low. But the estate also includes cash from three mutual funds, bought years ago when Uncle Milton was doing well at Macy's. The will leaves half of everything to Janna's husband and their boys, with the other half split between the surviving sisters. Eighty thousand dollars goes into Ginny's Sag Harbor bank, and she writes a check to Rob for half of it. It's a sad but welcome cushion. Ginny thinks of it as a kind of salary for her job with the twins. When the work saps her she likes to pretend she's getting paid to do it. No matter where it comes from, money is a comfort.

Her own house sits vacant in another world. Here the old farmhouse often sets her on edge. Cobwebs gather under the ceilings, mice are in the walls, Rob's marriage has crumbled and the commune is a failure.

There is much they don't talk about. She wonders about Rob's interest in other women. In a couple of years he's gone from three partners to none. She guesses that he's still half in love with Natalia, that if she came back he'd try to take care of her. She wonders about his job. In another month it will be too cold for masonry. But by then the current house will be dried-in, and they'll move on to insulation, floors, windows and drywall. Rob is handy with all of it.

He doesn't complain about taking care of the babies. She does sometimes, and wonders how long she can keep at it every morning. Chilo and Sophie can be friendly together, a tumult of charm and laughter, and a minute later she thinks that one of them, if they had a knife, would plunge it into the other.

Rob buckles down whenever they need him, pouring out his attention and affection. He's a genius at changing their diapers, he can do one in a minute, complete with the dangerous pins. He cooks fast as well, it tires Ginny just to watch him. He's given up much else. He used to play soccer and ultimate frisbee, but now has no time. He reads for twenty minutes before sleep.

It grows dark early now, and soon after dinner the twins go down. Ginny and Rob talk in front of the woodstove. They now share some history. Rob's marriage has failed, as did both of hers. He asks about her first husband, Justin Tidwell.

"I was too young. Maybe we all think that after a marriage falls apart. I gave myself to him in the back of a bakery truck, on a pad on the steel floor. I should have figured out that night what a selfish guy he was. He didn't give a thought to my pleasure, it was all his. What a world that was, back when no one ever talked about sex or how it felt. If someone had come along and invited us to join a six-marriage, I bet he'd have done it. But then, when he saw me having fun with someone else, he'd have blown a gasket."

"Natalia was all in from day one."

"She was always ahead of the game, wasn't she?"

"She was always ahead of me."

Though absent, Natalia looms over the house and everything they do. They see her daily in the faces of the twins, and there's always the chance that one day she'll appear at the door. What chaos that would bring. There has been no word from her since the postcard from New Mexico.

Rob tells about the day they met, in Panajachel on Lake Atitlán in Guatemala. He was on a break with a couple of Peace Corps friends. She was beautiful, and her English as native as his. They sat on a bench in front of the lake and talked about Guatemala City where she grew up, and San Francisco where she went to high school. Then she asked him if he wanted to walk around the lake. That sounded crazy. It was a huge lake surrounded by mountains, it would take days to walk around. But Rob said sure, and they started. There was a quiet road near the water. Women carried baskets on their heads and men hoed the fields. Natalia said she'd like to be an Indian, that she *was* a quarter Indian and someday she would learn to speak Quiché. It would be easy, she'd just go live with a family. It sounded as if she'd thought it all through, that she might actually do it. They walked and talked for two hours. Then she was hungry, so they turned around and caught a ride back in a *colectivo* and went out to dinner. "She made everything seem easy," Rob says.

"I did like Natalia. I'm sorry she didn't like me."

"She did at first, pretty much. A lot changed after she got pregnant. And then the twins whacked her. She had two younger siblings and thought she knew about babies, but this was something else."

"It whacks me sometimes."

"Mom, I've asked too much of you."

"Don't worry, I'm not ready to quit. I'm glad we have help from Lisa, and maybe we could get some more. If I could get off by eleven or twelve some days, that would be good."

"Done, I'll double her pay and ask if she can do it."

"Isn't money great? Thank you, sister Carol."

The library in McArthur has come to seem cramped. People walk by her table, often talking too loud, and the sound of traffic floats in from the street. The town is small but noisy. She likes Ohio, she grew up here, she's soothed by the hillside woods that surround the fields at the bottom of the hollows. But sometimes it seems a narrow world. It's not that she hasn't lived this way before. Her Peace Corps years in Chile were far more primitive—but all that was an adventure, one scheduled to end after a couple of years.

One afternoon she drives the half hour to Athens, the home of Ohio University. There, behind the College Green, she finds Alden Library. A paradise, she thinks, as soon as she steps inside. She roams the stacks to see what she can find about Alzheimer's, reading again about the man and the disease named after him. She sits in a carrel on the sixth floor and looks out over the railroad tracks, the Hocking River and the last of the year's foliage. It's a perfect place to work. She writes a letter to Richard Jackbin and tells him that what she'd most like to edit are research papers dealing with neurological diseases: Parkinson's, cerebral palsy, Myasthenia Gravis, Alzheimer's or ALS.

Day by day she still struggles with the twins. The many members of the commune would have been a help, but the commune is finished. The twins might have been too much for them anyway. Everyone loved Moon, but no one had to take care of her for more than thirty minutes. Now, for hours at a time, Ginny's the one who cradles the toddlers, feeds them puréed beans and chicken and wipes their bums. She's glad to have this time with Rob, as she did with Jamie, but this is a harder trial.

How long, she wonders, will Rob hold on to this isolated farm? How long will she live here? At night she lies in bed reminding herself, after all her selfish years, of how much she owes her children. She didn't spend enough time with them when they were young. She and Joe hired a full-time nanny so she could keep working at her magazines. Then she wanted a job that felt more vital. She read about Louis Pasteur, who had five children and lost three of them. She read about Jonas Salk, who saved the lives of millions. The value of their work was clear, and at the age of thirty-five she went back to college, already headed for a career in medicine. She and Joe sent the boys off to prep school and didn't see them for months at a time. She hadn't even met Rich Villamano then, but she was making room for him, and he came.

Now she's the nanny herself for half of every day. She'll get up tomorrow and clean the babies' slobbering chins, change their smelly diapers and toss the fouled cloths into Rob's old wringer washer. With all that money in the bank he could buy a new one, but for now food must be served and butts cleaned.

Lisa is a steady help, though her days are tinged with regret. She wanted to get pregnant with her boyfriend and they did, but then she lost the baby. After arguments, a split-up and another try, now they're friends and occasional lovers. Lisa's still great with Chilo and Sophie, still looks after them for a day on most weekends. Like Ginny, she's grown thinner. Looking after twins is a job that can slim you down.

Three or four afternoons a week Ginny makes the drive to Alden Library. She's been given a study on epilepsy. It's both technical and arcane, but her interest is stirred. It's remarkable how much scientists can learn from mouse brains, and buried in the convoluted prose are some vital human dilemmas. How to deal with this disease, whose grand mal seizures grip its patients as if with a giant fist?

23

Her mother's nursing home in Connecticut is far away, and Ginny wasn't welcome there the last time she went. So now she makes a visit to The Wellspring, the only memory care unit in Athens. She mentions her mother's dementia to the receptionist and is promptly given a tour.

At the very start, the coded lock on the door disturbs her. "This is for their safety?"

"Without it some of them would walk right out. They'd head for the woods, or maybe worse, the road."

The patients hardly seem to notice her, until a well-dressed elderly woman approaches. "Don't listen to what they tell you," she says, "the food isn't all that bad. Not as good as when I cooked, but they don't have the right pots. What was your name again?"

"Virginia, I'm glad to meet you. And you?"

"I have—a young girl's name. A pretty name. I'll get it in a minute. Are you going to stay with us?"

"For a while, I hope."

"I'll be right back. I just have to.... One moment."

She walks off and is soon talking to someone at the far end of the room. Ginny meets another woman and a man, but neither seems easy with speech. The man sits in front of a chessboard and picks up his pieces at apparent random. He's focused and precise, but moves his pawns like a rook. The unit seems clean and well organized, though chaos hovers. When escorted back to the front desk, Ginny asks to talk to someone in charge.

She's led to a woman sitting at a desk piled with papers, to whom she explains that she's a doctor, though retired. Her mother died with dementia some years ago, and she wonders if they welcome volunteers here, to spend time with the patients.

The director, or whoever she is, stands right up. "We'd be so glad to have you!" she says, and promptly schedules Ginny in for Tuesday afternoons.

Her sixtieth birthday hangs above her like a weighted pendulum. So far it has only grazed her, but she fears how something—most likely dementia—could overcome her. The Wellspring will teach her more about it. She's given the door code, and each Tuesday lets herself into the locked unit. Again she talks to the well-dressed woman, whose name is Marissa. She grew up in northern Vermont, a rural homeland she abandoned for Scranton, Pennsylvania and the man she married. "I don't remember much about him," she says. Her clothes are orderly and clean. She rests a hand briefly on Ginny's shoulder, and Ginny doesn't know if she should return the gesture. She'll ask if there's a policy.

She plays with the silent gentleman, moving her own pawns as he does, like a rook. He clearly likes the feel of his old-fashioned ebony pieces. He plays for hours, but Ginny only for some minutes, as she tries to spread her attention. Not equally—there are sixteen residents of the wing—but she doesn't want to make favorites. She makes some anyway, and Marissa is the most engaging of the lot. She has held onto language better than the rest, and she can still serve up a surprise. One day, as her eyes follow a young man who has come in to mop the floor, she touches Ginny's arm and says, "Quite a piece of ass that one, don't you think?"

"Marissa! Did I hear you right?"

"You bet."

"That doesn't sound like you."

"I'm no cowbell, I tell it like it is. Do you know about the thieves in here? They want your jewelry and come down at night from the attic."

"There is no...." Ginny stops herself. Her first rule is not to contradict the patients, no matter what they say or believe. She holds out her ringless hands. "I don't have much they'd want."

"Have you spent the night here?" Marissa asks.

"Not yet."

"You could help me look for my bracelet. I think they took it. Or maybe I dropped it over here." She leads Ginny to a table with paper and crayons, where she sits down and starts drawing freehand circles, some wavering, some almost perfect. She says, "My son comes here sometimes and we talk. Do you know him?"

"No, I haven't met him."

"He likes gardens. And books." She turns away, folding and unfolding her hands.

Was it like this with Ginny's mother? She'd know, if only she'd gone more often to see her.

One dark winter night, sleep is elusive. Ginny's lying on the same bed where Moon slithered into the world—and now, strangely, without being touched at all, Ginny's body wakes up. Her buttocks, the inside of her thighs, then her breasts. Goddamn, she's aroused! Gently, she touches herself *there*. Then the feeling is gone.

Where did it come from? Maybe it's the Henry Miller and D.H . Lawrence she's been reading—but no, because she's been on those for a month and never had a response like this. More likely, she thinks, it's the twins and how they crawl all over her. They brush against her, they take hold of her hair, her ears, her fingers. They're sixteen months old now and talking, but touch still comes first. And how Ginny loves the skin-on-skin. Other than her sons and Miles, for years she has rarely touched anyone.

In truth, there are days when she's had too much of the holding and grasping, and by the time Rob gets home she's glad to pass the twins on. But come the next morning she's happy to pick them up again, to dress them and carry them around the house. She loves it when they hook their arms around her neck, sometimes both at once.

What, she asks herself, has become of the sensual rush that ruled her from the age of twelve? The longing she later spurred, then drowned with alcohol. She knows some women lose it after menopause, but not all. In spite of the trouble it gave her, she wants it back.

March 11

I listen to Marissa's wandering talk. She forgets so much, but I think she still has some idea about how a conversation should run. She'll have something to say, then forget part of it, often a name, and fill the gap with something that bears no relation to what came before. All our minds jump around, but most of us hold onto the thread. When too many nouns go, the whole system falls apart.

Sometimes when I talk to others on that wing, Marissa hovers as if waiting for me to listen to her. Sometimes she stands by the door as if hoping it will open. I've been warned that twice she has slipped by and made it out of the building before they corralled her. She stood there today, wringing her hands the way she does, saying to no one, "They don't know. You could bring some if you knew. He can't come today. He told me about the flowers. They're right outside. It isn't far and they're big. I don't know where I am."

Okay, I made up half of that. I can't remember exactly what she said. My own memory's not that good.

She planned on ignoring her birthday, but Rob has remembered and emerges from the pantry after dinner with a small cake and six lit candles. Sixty is supposed to be a milestone, whatever that means. A stone by the side of a highway doesn't sound too momentous, but Ginny is touched by Rob's attention. With the twins already down, they eat the cake in peace.

"No word from Natalia?" she asks.

Of course there isn't, or Rob would have told her.

"If she comes back, will she let you know beforehand?"

"Mom, you know she won't."

"She's an impulsive woman," Ginny says. "Sometimes I've wondered about you and me and our mates. I think we both have an inclination to yield, to submit."

"You weren't that way with Dad."

"No, I was thinking of Rich Villamano."

Rob gets up, as he does every thirty minutes, and checks on the twins, then comes back and sits down. "I remember what you told me about him, that time you visited me in the Peace Corps in Guatemala."

"What was that?"

"You said, 'He dominated me completely, and I loved it.'"

"Now I'm embarrassed. Though it's true."

"It wasn't quite that way with Natalia. She just decided things and I went along."

Yes, Ginny thinks, it was always Natalia leading the way. They got pregnant when she chose, and raised the kids according to her convictions. Ginny wonders if that dominance was ever played out in bed, as hers was. She won't be asking that.

"What if she recovered some and wanted to start over? Would you take her back?"

"Probably. Though I doubt if it would last. Would you take Rich back?"

"I couldn't. Too many years have passed."

"Would you, or not?"

"Now that I don't drink," Ginny says, "I think I can say no. Because it would only lead to trouble."

She doesn't know if she believes this herself. She wants to, and they let the topic rest. Outside, from a nearby marsh, the spring peepers have begun their calls.

"I do worry," Rob says, "about how much I've asked of you. To come and live this hectic life, month after month and when will it end?"

"It won't end. But it has been getting easier. Don't worry about me, I look after myself."

Don't worry, she thinks. What kind of useless counsel is that? She might as well have told him to stuff it. "I want to help with the twins," she says, "and I need to. It's good for me to be busy. I wonder less about the rest of life."

"Maybe I should pay you."

"So you won't feel guilty? You can repay me when I'm ninety-five and my mind is shot. Or when physically I'm a platypus. When that happens, you'll have to come visit me every week."

"Twice a week," he says with a grin.

24

A note comes from Natalia's mother in Guatemala. Natalia has returned home, and after some bizarre behavior Meches has sent her to an institute for ten days, "*para dar a su mente un descanso.*" To give her mind a rest.

"They're probably just subduing her with drugs," Rob says. "That's what they did with her father when he went off the tracks. But Meches would like me to come for a visit."

"With the twins?"

"I think that would be too hard."

"Do you want to go?"

"I'm glad Natalia's there. She used to say she'd never go back."

Love dies hard, and it's no surprise to Ginny when a few days later he plans his visit and books Lisa to help look after the twins.

He leaves early one morning, trying not to make a fuss over Sophie and Chilo. But they pick up on it when he steps outside with his backpack, and only a minute later turn desperate. *My daddy* they keep wailing. On that first day Lisa is there to help, and she and Ginny mount the two in their carriers, where they can ride up high on their walk. Spring has come. The daffodils have been up for a month and the first redbuds are flowering at the edge of the woods. The twins' calls for their daddy don't resume until they get back home.

Lisa is wildly fond of them, and she and Ginny never have the least spat over running the household. Neither of them runs anything, they just get the jobs done. Rob is gone for two weeks, and when he walks back into the house, tanned and eager, four scabbed wounds stand out on his cheeks.

May 17

When Rob landed in Guatemala City, Meches had her car in the repair shop. Natalia, after her ten days in rehab, had borrowed it and driven up to Nebaj in search of some Buddhist mystic she'd heard about. She drove around all day but never found him, and on the way home she got two flat tires and kept driving on them, which destroyed the rims. Rob bought them new ones.

Natalia is an endless surprise. Who could have guessed that she would want another baby? She hardly talked about the two she has, but tried to get Rob to couple and make another. When he wouldn't do it she raked his face hard, and the scratches are still healing.

Meches knows what Rob has taken on. "You look after your children," she told him, "and I'll look after this one."

She also advised him not to give a bunch of money to Natalia, she'd just spend it wildly. He left what he had with Meches, to dole out a bit at a time.

At the end of June Rob works it out with Lisa so Ginny as well can have a break. "Take two weeks," he says. "Take three."

She wonders briefly if he's looking for some time alone with Lisa. But it isn't that, they're old friends. They reminisce about the glory days of the commune, back when the Six was in play, back when Moon was a child with half a dozen parents and as many aunties and uncles.

Ginny times her trip to arrive in Sag Harbor after the Fourth has passed. The Brennans, on their weekend visits, have been looking after her house. No leaks, they report, no termites, no trees leaning onto the roof. But when she pulls into her drive in the early afternoon the place looks hunched and empty. The weeds poking up on the gravel drive are a foot tall, and the shingled roof shows streaks of moss. Ginny unlocks the door and steps inside the kitchen. She's forgotten how low the ceiling is and how small the rooms. All is still and cool. She turns the water on, then the furnace blower, and still the house feels lifeless.

She leaves her bags inside, gets back in her car and drives to the beach. The waves at Sagaponack will calm her.

They break beside her as she tramps over the sand. There are other walkers but they pass with a quiet nod. Every minute of every day she's been gone, the waves have been building and breaking, the wet sand has gleamed, the seaweed has washed up onto the shore. As long as she's at the beach, the rest of life vanishes.

Back in her house she opens some windows and takes a duster to the cobwebs. The fridge is empty but she has cans of soup. She opens one and warms it, then eats it with a sandwich she brought from Ohio. She'll buy some food at Schiavoni's tomorrow. Her mother's silverware lies in a drawer. She has water, she has a toilet, she has four plates and bowls. At dusk she steps outside to stand before the misty blooms of the smoke bush. She's no longer afraid of the house, as she was after her stay at Silver Hill when she feared every pill and bottle. She has proved herself ever since.

Jamie will join her in a week. She wonders whether he's gone back to the hot tub parties in Key West. There's been no mention of a steady lover or partner. Will there ever be anyone for him like Miles? He won't know himself until one day it happens, and it might not.

She no longer imagines a mate for herself. Yet as the mourning doves coo outside, she takes off her clothes and lies down in bed. Several times since that night last winter her body has responded in a faintly sexual way. It's been only a slender link to the old days, but now, as she trails her fingertips over hips and thighs, there's a welcome flicker.

A day later she sits with the Brennans outside their house, the three of them telling stories of their children and grandchildren. She sees no trace of last summer's distance. They both seem at ease, and give each other room to talk.

In the afternoon she and Patty stroll the back streets of town, down to the bay. Patty's been putting together a book about lighthouses. Mainly her photos, but also some stories about the keepers. She's driven up and down the east coast to talk to them, from West Quoddy Head in Maine to the Carolina Outer Banks. She goes on her own, giving Bill some days alone at home.

"I think it's good for both of us," she says. "How about you? Is there a man in your life?"

"My sister used to ask me that. She was on the look until the very end. But no, I still can't imagine it. The last boyfriend I had was five years ago when I was in the Peace Corps."

"I remember your stories. Don Alberto, right?"

"He was great, but Chile's too far away."

They're walking down a narrow street with water on either side, the bay full of sails and boats at their moorings, their halyards tapping in the breeze. Ginny watches as Patty bends down to pick up a scallop shell.

"You're so thin," Ginny says.

"You too, pretty much."

"One forty and I can't drop another pound. You remember what I weighed before."

"A hundred and eighteen," Patty says, "forever."

"I did gloat about it, didn't I?"

"You know what works for me? Bill watching when I undress at night. He pretends not to but I see him do it. It's a little ritual we have. He comes in to give me a kiss and tuck me in before he goes off to write, and I often worry about how I look. I wish I could ignore what he thinks, but I can't."

Seen from behind, in her dark blue dress with her hair spilling over her shoulders, Patty looks like a twenty-year-old. As far as Ginny knows, she has never let anyone like Rich Villamano into her life. Her loyalty to Bill lights up Ginny's infidelity to Joe. Her treason. She will never shake free of that crime. Joe was such a decent man—if only he could have given in to some emotion.

Patty has her own troubles, of course. She talks about Tommy, who still can't hold down a job, or a job of any worth. She tells stories about her two young granddaughters, one of whom keeps biting the other. But Patty is well-grounded, both eager and content. Ginny's too busy to be content. That isn't what you get with year-and-a-half-old twins.

Sometimes, of course, she's ecstatic. What else can she call it when the two of them toddle across the floor to her crying out "*Mamá! Mamá!*" That's what Rob calls her, so the kids do too. What else but joyful when she reads to them at night and they fall asleep at almost the same time, leaning into her chest.

25

Ginny picks Jamie up at LaGuardia. Having booked the cheapest flight he arrives at the worst hour, late in the afternoon. The highway is stop-and-go, the two-lane after Riverhead is just as clogged, and they don't reach Sag Harbor until eight at night.

After a quick dinner they sit in the living room, as they did so many times with Miles. They place his chair between them, the one he sat on backwards. Those were troubled times after the neurologist's assessment, but a far different world from this one. Then, Miles was alive.

"This is what it's like for me every day," Jamie says. "He should be here and he's not."

"Isn't he? Right now with the two of us thinking and talking about him?"

"That's way too thin for me."

The house is still in the windless night. Ginny waits.

"What I can't understand," Jamie says, "is how the rest of the world just slides along without him. I can't even get people to talk about him, or not enough. I had a little pin made, a silver pin that said *Miles*, and I wore it as a prod. But all I heard was some bland shit like *Yeah, he was a great guy*. I couldn't stand it, so I'd contradict them. I'd talk about something wild or stupid he'd done, like the time he got into an argument with the mayor and dumped a key lime pie onto the hood of the guy's Buick. And then some jerk would tell me that Miles is in a better place and everything will pass. Screw that. I put the pin in a drawer."

Ginny leans in. "Remember how afraid of him I was when the two of you went off to Provincetown? I was sure he was going to steal you from me."

"And he did. It's what happens, Mamá. Kids grow up and go off in the world."

"And come back years later to remind you of how life works. Tell me some story about Miles, something I don't know. Tell me about that year in Provincetown."

"It was a wild first summer. We couldn't have gone to a better place. We'd walk down the street at night holding hands and people just said *Hi, how're you doing?* I couldn't believe it. Miles could talk to anyone, and he loved to show me off."

"You were kind of a prize."

"And I was legal by then, I was nineteen. Miles started dressing me up in silk shirts and satin pants. We were close enough to the same size that he could wear my clothes and I could wear his, so we did away with his and mine. We had one dresser and one closet and wore whatever we liked. We had lots of blouses for shirts. It was all a trip for Miles as well, because back when he was teaching he never wore anything fancy. Now he could buy whatever he liked. He loved our first Speedos, which felt like panties."

"He was still coming out, right?"

"He'd never held hands with a guy, or not on the street. He'd never really had a boyfriend. He'd fooled around, but he'd never been part of a couple. Of course he was older, but we learned everything together."

"I wonder what I'd have thought, if I'd seen all that."

"I might have made you laugh sometimes. Miles knew more about the world, and sometimes I was a bit of a fool."

"No."

"Oh yes. Here's one I never told you. We almost always cooked dinner at home, but one night we ordered a pizza and I walked across town to pick it up. I didn't know about pizzas. When I was growing up we hardly ever ordered one, and if we did it was Dad who picked it up. So this was a first for me. I went into the shop and paid for the order and carried out the box.

Fine, except I was listening to the birds and saying hello to people on the street and I never thought about it, just tucked the box under my arm as if it were a little briefcase. When I got home and opened it, the pizza was a lump at the bottom. Miles just laughed. He said 'Hey, it's still warm,' and scooped it into two bowls and we ate it."

"You were lucky to have him," Ginny says.

"Now you. You talk about him."

She tries to come up with something. "I think you know all my stories. You were always around when I was there."

"So tell one I already know."

"All right," Ginny says. "You remember that time in Key West when he stopped to give a quarter to a beat-out guy on the street?"

"Oh yeah."

"A quarter wasn't enough. The guy wanted a dollar so he could buy a bottle of wine."

"He was probably already drunk. He threw the quarter on the sidewalk."

"And Miles picked it up. He added another quarter and held them out, but the guy wouldn't take them. *Damn queers* he said, and Miles just laughed. He told the guy it was the new thing and he ought to give it a try. The guy wanted to get up and fight, but he could hardly stand. He started yelling, and somebody called the cops and eventually they took him away. So what does Miles do? He starts picking up the drunk's backpack and bedding, and we carry it all to the police station so when they release him he'll still have all his things. And the whole time I'm thinking, *he's an old drunk, why are you so worried about him?* But you know, Jamie, over the years I've come to think that Miles was looking after *me* that night. Because *I* had been that drunk who wanted some wine. I think Miles was trying to show that he'd always take care of *me*."

"Mamá...." But Jamie starts crying and can't speak.

They get up at six the next morning to catch an empty beach, but other walkers have beaten them to it. This doesn't ruin everything, but Ginny is disappointed. It's absurd, she knows. Behind or on top of the dunes there are several houses in sight, and all the way to Montauk there's hardly a pristine stretch. There are always humans somewhere. Still, the following morning she wakes Jamie at four-thirty and they set out in the dark, and make it to the shore as a first pale radiance gathers on the eastern horizon. No fishermen yet, and not another walker in sight.

Another afternoon, sitting on the beach on their chairs, Jamie tells a story. A month ago he got a call from Miles's father. He was in Key West, had come a couple of weeks earlier. "It took him that long to let me know, because he was afraid I'd hate him. Which I did, really, after all the stories Miles had told. But over a couple of calls I figured out something I never knew, that the guy had always been a heavy drinker. Miles must have known that, but as he saw it, his father's problem was how much he hated gays."

An alcoholic for forty years was how Ron Greer described himself to Jamie. But six months after his son died, with help from AA, he quit cold turkey. And after a while he took on the most difficult of the twelve steps, making amends to those he'd done wrong.

Miles was dead and no amends could be made with him. But looking back at how he'd treated him, Ron was unhappy. His homophobia had indeed been a fear, one that hemmed him in. He went to his library and read some gay and lesbian writers, and they seemed like decent people.

He made a visit to Key West and found it a beautiful world: the bright streets and colorful houses, the sea shining at either end of Duval. He gathered his courage and went out to bars and drag shows. Much of it seemed bizarre, but it was a friendly scene.

"People thought he was some old lonely gay guy," Jamie says.

"You never ran into him?"

"I don't go out as much as I used to."

Finally Ron called him, hesitant and apologetic. What softened Jamie was how much the man had suffered. They agreed to a walk on the beach, after which Jamie invited him home. There, where his son had lived for ten years, where he himself had never once come to visit, Ron lingered over every detail.

"I think we both softened each other. I could see Miles in his face and gestures. He came over again, and a third time. Now he's back in Delaware, but he's sent me a couple of letters."

"If only he could have done all that when Miles was alive."

"That's what he feels himself."

Out past their chairs the waves roll in. They've never stopped, of course, Ginny just forgot them for a while.

At the end of the week she drives Jamie back to LaGuardia, sees him off and returns to sit in her house. She takes a walk through the village, out onto Long Wharf and back along Main Street. She tries to soak it all up, because who knows when she'll come here again. She's headed back to Rob, the twins and Ohio.

26

When she walks into the room, Chilo and Sophie barely look up. They're busy with their blocks. It doesn't look like they've missed her at all, but when she sits down on the floor beside them they're soon in her lap. They crawl over her knees, laughing and holding things up for her to see: a kitchen spoon, a rubber ball, a banana peel. They're enchanted by it all. Chilo pries off his socks and flings them onto a chair, and Sophie rolls onto her back, making the sounds of what might be a truck or a goat. Lisa, who's about to take off on a trip of her own, joins them on the floor.

Rob asks, "What do you think, Mom? Have they grown?"

"It's only been three weeks."

"Really? I thought maybe a couple of years had gone by."

Lisa laughs at the joke. She's often the most patient of the three adults. "They are the sweetest of beings," she says, "and with any luck they won't tear you to pieces."

"All it takes as they grow older," Ginny says, "is for me to grow younger. How hard can it be?"

"That was my plan," Rob says, "when I asked you to help out."

One afternoon she drives up to Columbus to look at 822 North High, where her family lived when she was in high school. Their country house is gone, and the orchard behind it. Instead, a two-story brick building built flush to the sidewalk holds a flower shop, a bakery and a clothing store. Nothing here stirs any memories, and the block feels almost like downtown. This doesn't appeal to Ginny, and in the late afternoon, forgoing a restaurant dinner, she drives back to Rob's farm.

The next afternoon she stops by a real estate office in Athens. Larry Conrath gives her plenty of attention, but she makes it clear that she's only browsing. On paper, Larry shows her some homes in the country and some small-acreage plots. She has only started to think about what she wants. A small wooden house, perhaps. A cottage might do.

Through the perfect early days of fall she settles in. Her job is exhausting but will not go on forever. The twins will never again be twenty-two months old. She wonders if kids need to cry a certain number of minutes per day, if it's part of some basic code. In the mornings, as the two possums turn into tigers and back again, she learns to pause in the midst of the bedlam. She doesn't have to leave the room for this, she just stops responding to cries and demands. She takes her time, she breathes, she pulls her attention down into her chest the way the gurus tell her to. Even as the twins wail, if they aren't hurt she can retreat. She calms herself, and ten minutes later comes around to their tears or ecstatic play.

Four afternoons a week she goes to the library, and once to The Wellspring. There she listens to patients whose language is hopelessly fractured. Marissa is still the most verbal of the group, though she's often confused. "Who was that guy," she says, "he was a pilot, he flew to Paris or somewhere." And then, "I like to fly planes." Or, "This works best. I write on cards and keep them in this box so I know what's happened."

Her three-by-five cards are indeed in a box, but in no apparent order. They say, "The meat is ham," and "I come from Vermont," and "I brushed my teeth."

Ginny has tried to befriend another resident, Dolores, whose only interest is birds, who stands at the window and stares outside for hours. Ginny has asked about taking her for a walk, but no, she must stay locked inside, the attendants wouldn't want to chase her if she bolted. This seems unlikely, as she's one of the slowest walkers on the wing. Everyone needs more attention, and don't they all want to walk or get rolled in the open air? Ginny keeps a list in her mind of everything wrong with this place. She wonders about a harness and cord for Dolores, then gives it up.

One day she opens the door and sees Marissa at the far end of the room talking with someone she doesn't know, a spare attractive man. When she walks up, Marissa announces, "My son."

"Lyle Demaris," he says, and holds out his hand, palm up.

She considers shaking it, but instead turns her own palm-down and lays it on his. She tells him her name. Not Ginny, but Virginia Thorndike.

"*Enchanté*," he says.

How ridiculous, she thinks. "You speak French?"

"Just a few words. My mother talks about you. It's why I came in today instead of yesterday. I usually come on Mondays. Marissa tells me how helpful you've been."

He says this with a smile, and not a lot of smiling goes on in this room. His teeth are good, his hair is turning gray, he might be her age or younger. Marissa watches over them like a stork, her neck long and eyes steady.

"Do you live here in Athens?" he asks.

"No, I'm out in Vinton County."

"Ahh...." He trails off.

Vinton County and hillbillies are often conflated, but she's not going to set this guy straight. He can figure it out for himself, and soon he does. He asks if she was born there, how long she has lived there, how much land does her son have, how old are his twins, how hard is it to take care of them? Each question leads to another. Then he pauses and brings the attention back to his mother, and the three of them wander about the room together, briefly engaging with others. It's Marissa who pulls them out of the main hall and down to her room, where she perches on the bed. Lyle gives Ginny the only chair and they talk, trying to follow his mother's lead. She doesn't hang on to anything for long.

"Do you ever read to her?" Ginny asks, remembering how much that meant to Miles.

"I've tried, but she's not very fond of it. Mom, I'd always be glad to read to you."

Marissa looks around the room as if she's never seen it before.

Lyle explains, "At night my father used to read out loud from the newspaper. My father," he repeats, touching her shoulder. "Your husband."

He tries steadily to keep her involved, but he doesn't ask her many questions, as he did of Ginny. It's Just as well, since questions are often hard on Marissa. Light pours in through the window, into the gaps in their conversation. The first maples outside are tinged with red.

"I've asked about taking patients for a walk," Ginny says, "but they won't let me."

"If you're family you can do it. After you sign a dozen waivers, of course. I've gone out with Mom any number of times. You could come with us next Monday. She likes to go to the College Green."

They decide it. The three of them will go together next week.

Ginny lies in bed at the farm, the crickets growing quieter outside. The twins now sleep through the night, and Ginny will wake before they do in the morning, if she doesn't stay up too late thinking. She liked Lyle, and was drawn in by his many questions. She was moved, too, by his devotion to Marissa. She wonders, and now wants to ask, if her dementia ever overwhelms him. That hasn't happened to Ginny, but it's not the same. At The Wellspring she can always move on to someone else. She watches the disease, she studies it, but she's only there three hours a week.

The Green is surveilled by giant sycamores with their broad leaves and white bark rising into the tallest branches. The lawn and trees are ringed by brick buildings, and a Union Civil War soldier on a pedestal stares into the foliage fifty feet up. The Green is just down from the library and Ginny has walked here many times, though never with anyone else. How much more beautiful it is, she explains to Lyle, than the campus at Barnard where she finished college, or the stark high-rises at NYU where she attended medical school.

Outside, they haven't had much luck getting Marissa to speak, to listen and engage. Lyle turns to her again. "Sometimes you like to just watch, don't you Mom?"

She nods but says nothing. They sit on a bench, then move to another. Shortly before two, students pour by on their way to class. Lyle drapes his arm around his mother's shoulders. She doesn't move toward him or away.

After the Green is quiet again, Ginny asks Lyle that delicate question, "What do you do?"

"You mean my job?

"Yes."

"I'm head of the dance department."

"There's a dance department?"

"There certainly is!"

How little she knows about this town and the university.

"We're quite famous," he says. "Maybe not across the nation, but here in Ohio. At the top there's us and Ohio State, and to be honest I think we're better. We offer ballet, but our focus is on modern."

A dance teacher. Can he be gay? She has a pretty good eye after her time in Key West, and she's seen no hint of it in Lyle. Gay men often disguise themselves, out in the wide world—but that would seem unlikely with the head of a dance department.

"I used to dance," Marissa says. "It was all ballet. I had lots of shoes."

"That's right, Mom, you're the one who got me started. I'll dig up some photos and show them to you."

"You have photos? Why didn't you tell me?" She stands abruptly and walks off across the Green. Lyle and Ginny soon catch up to her, but she shakes off their hands. They walk on either side of her until she calms down.

"It's good there are two of us," Lyle says, quietly, and later they agree to an outing next week, a visit to a café without Marissa.

After their first palmed contact, he hasn't touched her. Nor does he now as he holds the door open and she passes beside him. They sit in Another Fool's Café, looking out on the sidewalk, and he explains his history with dance. It's been a dozen years since he capered across a stage, because the last time he did he ripped his ACL in two. "I had it replaced with part of my patella tendon, but it's never been the same."

Talk of the anterior cruciate ligament and its repair unsettles her. The ACL has nothing to do with ALS and the brain, but the faint similarity of the letters is enough to give her pause. And Lyle notices. He seems to notice everything. "Yes," he says, "enough talk about the body falling apart. You'd almost think we were getting older."

"How old *are* you?"

"I turned sixty in April."

"Did you really? When?"

"April ninth."

"Lord love a duck. You're one day younger than I am."

She doesn't tell him what she thought, that he was half a decade younger. Across the table he smiles steadily. There's no sense pretending any longer that he's only attentive because of her interest in his mother. He likes her, and soon starts asking questions again. He asks about her first marriage, about her twenty-two years with Joe and what that was like. "Did one of you hold the upper hand?"

That's not how she likes to think about it, but yes, that would be her.

He asks what broke up the marriage. He asks about Rich and she tells him the basics. He asks about Jamie and Rob. He asks about the twins' mother. He asks about Ginny's drinking. He asks easy questions and hard ones and in the end, as she drives home, she's ashamed of herself because she asked him so little. After talking for two hours she doesn't even know if he's been married or has children. He's head of the School of Dance and has a mother at The Wellspring. Ginny just sat there and responded to his questions, absorbed by her own stories. She'll do better next time.

27

The trouble is, she isn't ready for Lyle or anyone else.

He's ready, she thinks—though for what? A date? An affair? A coupling? He wants to know her. He'll talk about anything that interests her. He barely touches her, just a hug when they meet and when they part. Carnally, he seems no more daring than a boy of fifteen—or perhaps he's simply smarter than that. She isn't ready, and if he comes on too hard she'll run.

What unnerves her is the thought of a boyfriend with expectations. So far, Lyle doesn't seem the demanding type. They have coffee, they have dinner, they walk under the autumn trees. Ginny invites him to the farm to meet Rob and the twins, and within minutes he's down on the floor playing with them. He has indeed been married and has a single son, Jed, who lives by himself in Chicago, who dates women but has never settled down. "He doesn't want kids. He says the earth is in too much trouble."

Lyle invites her out to dinner at the Casa Que Pasa, the town's Mexican restaurant run by a bunch of hippies. When she sits down in the booth he slides in beside her instead of across the table. "This is how I like it," he says. She edges farther in to give him room. They order enchiladas and talk about their mothers and dementia. Waiters move through the room, and from the nearby kitchen comes the sound of pans on the stove and knives on cutting boards. After a pause in their talk, Lyle drops his hand below the table and rests it on her leg.

She pokes him with her elbow. "Stand up, please."

When he does, she gets up and sits down across the table from him.

His gaze is steady. "Was that so bad?"

"Lyle, I'm sorry."

"Are you?"

She thinks about it. "No, I'm not sorry, I'm afraid."

"Of me."

"Of what you might want. I feel like some old grandmother. Hell, I *am* an old grandmother. I'm stiff and unsure and not the woman I used to be. I'm going to make you unhappy."

"I don't think so." Over a quiet minute, each time she looks up at him his eyes are on hers. "You're kind of making me happy right now," he says.

"What are you talking about?"

"You're telling me the truth. I like that."

"But it's a pretty sad truth."

"No, it's fine."

"It is? Okay, now you tell *me* the truth. Would it be fine with you if all we ever did was talk? If any time you touched my leg I jumped? Would you be satisfied with that kind of connection?"

"I guess not."

Relieving them, a waitress in a blue caftan sets down their sizzling meals, and they begin to eat. But Lyle isn't half way through his first enchilada when he puts down his fork.

"What if we make a rule about touching? What if I can only touch you after you touch me? If you touch my wrist, I can touch yours. If you touch my shoulder, I can touch yours. And nothing has to lead to anything else."

She likes the sound of it. "Though we do know that the foot bone's connected to the ankle bone, and the ankle bone's connected to the leg bone."

How easy it is to make him laugh. And what a cagey rule it is, she thinks, because without it he might never get anywhere.

He says, "Do you want to give it a try?"

"Done. I now consider it the law."

They go back to their meals and talk. It's only after he's paid the bill that she reaches across the table and grazes the back of his hand with her finger.

Outside, as they head up Court Street, he takes her hand in his and they walk up to the Green. And there, as they stroll under the trees, he lets go of her.

Another day, out on the farm, his feet get wet on a walk up to her meadow. Back in the house and fully aware, she brings him a pair of alpaca socks and unrolls them over his toes. He makes no immediate move, but a day later, at his house in town, he pulls a massage table out of a closet, spreads a soft gray sheet over it and invites her to climb on to it barefoot. She hesitates, but slips out of her shoes and socks and lies face down on the table. It's a rich smell and lovely feel as he dribbles coconut oil over her insteps and heels, and rubs it in. She worries at first that he'll move on to her calves, but he doesn't break the rule.

He doesn't talk or ask questions while massaging her. "Drift away," he says. Still it's awkward, because she's certain he wants more than he's getting. She feels more hesitant now, more damaged by her solitary years than she did when she wasn't being touched by anyone.

After his session with her feet, they sit at his kitchen table with bowls of tomato and red pepper soup, both from his garden last summer. The floor is waxed, the windows clean, the house still. His plates, bowls, oils and herbs sit exposed on open shelves. He baked the bread as well, dark as a turtle, filled with raisins and walnuts. They lean forward over their bowls, dipping their bread into the soup. And now, of course, he wants to talk. How odd, that she's the one who holds back. So often in her marriage it was Joe who wasn't eager.

"This is working out pretty well," he says, "don't you think? How we touch and don't."

"I guess it is. Your massage did feel great, and I could do your feet next."

"Let's forget about reciprocity. Though if you'd like to do something for me, how about listening to another plan I have?"

"Oh dear."

"No, I think you might like it. Really, the idea came from you, when you were so honest about your fears. Just admitting that set me thinking."

"Which makes me afraid all over again."

Lyle spreads his hands on the table. "What if we create a world in which we tell each other everything? Minute by minute, instead of hiding what we think and feel, what if we just come out and say it all?"

"*Chaos*," Ginny says with a laugh. Because it's a mad dream. "We could try it for a few minutes, but then we'd go back to what we always do. What everyone does."

"Don't you think it would be fun? I lay in bed last night thinking about it, and I was so convinced."

"You weren't stoned last night, were you?"

"No, no, I don't smoke dope and I hardly care about alcohol. But doesn't it sound like a great exploration? What good are secrets when everything gets played out anyway? If I'm upset about something and try to hide it, you're still going to feel it."

"Upset about what?"

"I don't know."

"I think you do. You know it and you're hiding it."

"Look at that!" he says. "You're already better at this than I am. Okay. It makes me sad when you keep holding back." He lifts his hands as if cradling the topic. "This could all go smoother, and we could be much closer."

His hands are almost a young man's hands. His legs are a dancing master's. And after thinking that, is she supposed to report it along with everything else that crosses her mind? All right, she'll try. "I don't look as young as you do, Lyle, and it worries me."

"You look great. That's what I thought the first minute I saw you."

Is he telling the truth? He's supposed to, if they're to follow this crazy game.

He keeps at it. "I like you and I want to hear everything. How about a little session the next time you come over? Just thirty minutes of telling the truth. How hard could that be?"

Worse than hard, impossible. But to please him she agrees to the plan.

They talk on the phone. He reports on some of his dance students, he asks for news about Sophie and Chilo. There is no news, of course, just the endless round of care. The weekend comes and nothing changes for Ginny, she's on call the same as every other morning of the week. But Saturday is a free day for Lyle, and he invites her over for the afternoon.

His house is up by Sells Park at the top edge of town, on a curving drive with nothing but woods behind it. Lyle greets her at the door, takes her hand and leads her straight upstairs. What the deuce is he up to? He walks her to a small room down the hall that looks recently painted, its walls, ceiling and trim all eggshell white. There's a single dormer window, and nothing inside save for two chairs and a lamp.

"I thought this room could be great for talks. I cleaned it out and painted it." He sits down on one of the chairs and extends his hand to the other. "Here we can say what we think and not hide anything."

She sits on her rigid wooden chair. With no shelves or books or pictures on the wall, there's nothing that grabs her attention. What a clean contrast to her room at the farmhouse, where the ceiling has begun to flake. She remembers the ceiling work she did in Sag Harbor with Jamie and Miles, the mess they made sawing the boards in the kitchen, and how good the cedar looked after they nailed and oiled it.

No, her run of small thoughts is hopeless and doesn't bear reporting.

Lyle watches her from a few feet away. "Maybe we could ask questions," he says. "Is there anything about me you'd like to know?"

Now that she thinks about it, "Who else have you had on that massage table?"

"These days it's just for me, with a therapist who comes over twice a month. A couple of women were on it years ago, after my wife left. And—what's your response to that?"

"If it was that far back, I won't worry about it." She admits, but only to herself, that she's glad there's been no one recently. "Go ahead," she says, "ask me what you like."

Without the least pause, "Is there anything that arouses you sexually?"

"Goddamn Lyle, that's blunt."

"It's what I most want to know."

"This was supposed to be fun, but I've already had enough."

"Bravo," he says with a smile. "That's a little nugget of truth right there."

She's never going to win an argument here—but maybe there is no argument. Because underneath, as unlikely as it seems, his fantasy still draws her. "Go ahead," she says. "Tell me some intimate secret and we'll see if I can handle it. Tell me something that arouses *you*."

He tells her, as smoothly as if he'd rehearsed it, about a time he watched his wife, back in their early days, make out with another man. "She expected me to get upset, and instead it just turned me on. I was always like that about her and other men. I guess it's one of my perversions."

"How many are there?"

He shrugs his shoulders.

"You're supposed to tell me."

"I don't know. Maybe four or five."

He's playing with her, which doesn't sound like part of the game. "Maybe that's why you find Rob's six-marriage so interesting."

"I think it's anything that arouses me that's not supposed to. Perversions are exciting. It's a pretty good guess that you have some yourself."

"Lyle, slow down."

"You can be the boss here any time. You were the boss with Joe, right? Were you the boss in bed?"

"*Stop it*. I just asked you to slow down."

"We still have twenty minutes. You agreed to a thirty-minute session, and you came of your own free will."

"This isn't like you, Lyle. You used to be so considerate."

"It's just talk. I'm not grabbing you or anything. I just had this idea."

"You're pushing too hard."

"Hey, the door is open, I haven't locked you in. You can walk out any time."

And she does. She stands up, goes down the stairs and out the door. She's afraid to pause or look back. Then, driving home, she's sure it was a mistake to leave.

28

Lyle doesn't give up. He calls the next day and apologizes for making her feel uncomfortable, and tells her he has another idea.

She's glad. She has felt fragile ever since leaving. "Let's meet at the Hocking," she says, "and you can tell me about it."

They meet at the river and head down the bike path. The river is swollen from recent rains, the foliage on the hillsides is turning, the red maples stand out from the other trees.

"Okay," she says, "tell me your latest plan."

"It's just an idea. I thought maybe we could be milder about it, and instead of demanding complete truth, the rule could be *No lies*. No deceptions, no matter how small. But no demands, either. If there's something we don't want to admit or talk about, we can look away and say nothing."

"That's probably what I do already."

"But also, don't you sometimes lie a little? I do. We could stop that. It would be a fun experiment, don't you think?"

"Is it fun you're after?"

"Well, I guess not."

"What is it?"

"I want to know you better."

"What if someone else is with us? Can I lie then? What if I want to tell Rob I had an easy time with the twins when in fact they were driving me crazy? What if Lisa makes one of her sodden apple pies and I want to tell her it tastes great?"

"No problem. This is only a deal between you and me."

"Which I haven't agreed to yet."

Lyle pulls back. Even as they walk she can feel it. This softens her. "Let's give it a test," she says. "I'll ask the first question, and you can answer if you dare."

"Okay, shoot."

"Do you sometimes think about dropping me?"

He looks at the river and says nothing. But half a minute later the hint of a smile creeps onto his face.

"What does that mean?" she says.

"I'm just showing you how easy it is to take advantage of the rules. And if we sit down again in that room at my house, I'll be much more polite."

What with the hullabaloo of the twins, his house is always more peaceful than hers. They walk the nearby trails under trees still full of leaves, and after dinner he leads her up to what he calls the Simple Room. When they go in he asks, "Can I turn out the light?"

She's not afraid of him, and he has only once overstepped. It's a cloudy night, and with the lamp off the room is completely black. She finds this oddly comforting, and she's the first to speak. "Tell me about your wife."

"Doris. After twenty-five years, she left. One day she told me it was over, and a week later she drove away."

Ginny waits, glad to have the dark hide her posture, her face, her expression.

"It caught me by surprise," Lyle says, "and she wouldn't talk about it. She just said we were done and that was it."

"Was there another man?"

"I think it was a woman. Or women. I could probably figure out the details if I started digging, but Doris won't say a word about it. And my son says let her be, let her tell us what she wants to."

"The gay world keeps growing," Ginny says.

"But after twenty-five years? Was she sitting on that the whole time?"

"If you could talk to her like this, in a Simple Room, maybe she'd tell you."

"No chance of that. I haven't seen her since the day she drove off."

"And how unhappy were you then?"

Silence. Following their latest rule, of course, he doesn't have to say anything. She waits in the dark, thinking of their parallel histories. How Lyle's wife left him, and how she left Joe. How unhappy, she wonders now, was Joe that day? The silence continues, broken only by the caws of the crows outside.

"It hurt," Lyle says. "And I felt like a fool because I didn't see it coming. We had drifted away from most sex, but I thought it was just that we were getting older. Of course, that hadn't settled *me* down. Anyway, I wasn't paying enough attention."

"That doesn't sound like you at all."

"In a long marriage you can build up some ruts. I'm sure you know. And I was distracted by my mother's troubles."

How clever he is, she thinks, to have prepared this liberating cell, and then to turn out the light. There's nothing here but Lyle's voice and her own, the chair beneath her and the crows' talk growing fainter. "Tell me about her dementia."

Early on, he says, no one understood. The first thing to go was her proper nouns, the names of people and places she knew perfectly well. She was living in Scranton still, in the house his father built when they were still together. Lyle made several confused visits, once with his brother, once with his sister-of-little-help. Then the police began to call him. They told him his mother had gotten lost, had driven all the way to Tunkhannock and had to be escorted home. Her sink was piled with dishes, her clothes lay on the floor, her aide could not keep up. Her autonomous life was coming to a close.

Lyle had always been the favored son, and she agreed to move in with him. He filled his car with some of her clothes and books, her letters and photos and silverware, and drove her to Athens. She was barely eighty and moved around easily, but she had some odd habits. She stashed his toaster inside a cupboard and wanted to use it there. Everything had to be kept where she placed it, but she often couldn't remember where that was. No one could touch her hair. She cut it herself and made a mess of it. And she had no friends in Ohio. On some days Lyle hired a woman to visit with her for a couple of hours while he was off at Putnam Hall running the dance department. Months passed. A doctor, asked for a consultation, gave a diagnosis of senile dementia. And then she began to wander. She walked down to State Street with its stores and restaurants and gas stations, then couldn't find her way back.

"She lived with me here for three years. She ran off everyone I hired to look after her during the day. After rescuing her a dozen times, the cops were fed up. And she started to escape at night. I put hasps and padlocks on both doors to keep her in. A dangerous practice if there should ever be a fire, and it didn't work anyway. She learned to escape through a low window, feet first, dropping to the lawn like a teenager. In the end I gave up. I talked to The Wellspring, and one afternoon I took her there. Just to have a look, I said. She had nothing with her, not even her purse. They let us into the locked unit and we sat around for a while. Then she wanted to leave and I had to tell her the truth, that The Wellspring was her new home. Damn, it was a scene. After a while I came back here and packed up her suitcases, and when I returned a couple of attendants were still looking after her. She'd thrown a hell of a fit, screaming and collapsing onto the floor. She was laid out on a cot when I got back, and I'm sure they'd drugged her, though they're not supposed to."

"What else could you have done?"

"Hire people around the clock, I guess. But no one could handle her. She had a hard first year at that place, but now she's pretty much adjusted to it. She kind of has friends there, and you're one of them. These days of course, every time I forget someone's name I wonder if dementia is closing in on me. Do you know if it runs in families?"

"It's not something they taught us in med school, but from what I've read, genetic links are rare."

"Can you see one of us," Lyle says, with a smile she can hear in the dark, "twenty years from now and headed for The Wellspring?"

"Damned if I'd let that happen. We know what it's like in there."

"But that's the problem. Bit by bit we *wouldn't* know. The dementia would creep up on us and we'd have no idea."

"Maybe we'd wind up in there together," Ginny says.

"Except there we'd be, and we'd have forgotten each other."

One evening as Lyle stands at his kitchen stove, braising some halibut and collard greens, Ginny comes up behind him and folds her arms around his waist, holding him as he works. She has sanctioned another level. But Lyle restrains himself, he doesn't take her in his arms until her next visit. They eat dinner and clean up, but all that is merely a prelude. Lyle guides her to the couch and stretches out beside her, his arm around her, their feet on the coffee table and their heads close.

As they lie there together she wonders, *Is this sex?*

She remembers talking to her boys when they were young teenagers, awkward talks they didn't want to hear. But the world was so messed up about sex that she had to straighten them out a little. Sex can be something you do, she told them, but it's also what you feel. You could sit down with a girlfriend—she said girlfriend to Jamie as well as Rob, though already she had her doubts—and sit on the couch with your arm around her and never touch her breast, perhaps only kiss her cheek. But if you were aroused, that was sex.

First base, second base, third base, a false and inadequate guide. Sex could be lying in bed at night and thinking about it. For Ginny in the seventh grade, it had sometimes been the wind lifting her skirts as she thought about a boy she liked.

She could go no closer than that with Jamie and Rob. Already it was too much and she backed away. How much her sons took in she had no idea, because they showed no response. But now, each time she goes to Lyle's house she wonders about it. Is it sex when he comes up behind her and lifts her hair, so as to give her neck a kiss? It is for him. That's clear from the occasional touch of his erection against her hip. And it must be sex for her, as well, for the quivers have been growing. Sometimes he takes her up to his bedroom and spoons her, and the flag of his erection—something they've never said a word about—either holds steady or subsides. He spoons her but lets her breathe.

Rob plans a trip to Key West to spend Thanksgiving with Jamie. The spoken motive for the visit is that the two haven't seen each other since Miles's funeral, but to Ginny it's clear that Rob needs a break. Life with the twins is demanding, and whenever he's home they eat up his every hour. When he's gone, everything will fall on Ginny, so they contract again with Lisa to come over in the afternoons.

Rob leaves on Sunday, and the next three days roll by smoothly. But Lisa wants to spend Thanksgiving with her family, so the meal is up to Ginny. She buys a pumpkin pie from the farmers market, and she'll make all else at home. An arugula salad from the garden, sweet potatoes laced with maple syrup and a turkey baked in an oiled paper bag. Lyle will help with Chilo and Sophie, so she can focus in the kitchen.

He has always been good with the twins. He hops around the room like a frog, then moos like a cow or bleats like a sheep and has them guess what animal he is. They figure out cat and horse and pig, but owl and coyote stump them. He helps with their perpetual wooden block castle, then entices them out for a walk. They barely make it two hundred yards before a cold wind turns them around. He makes them hot chocolate, he bangs on a drum with them, he even changes their diapers. "I remember all this," he says. But long before the five o'clock meal he starts to pull back. "Aren't they old enough to be finished with diapers?"

"Clearly not," Ginny says. "We're still working on it."

The kids have withdrawn to the toy corner, where they're arguing over a Slinky. "*It's mine*," they both claim. It's kind of a miracle, how few outbursts they've had all day, but now they pitch into it. Ginny tries to console them, and Lyle announces that he's going for a walk.

It's almost dark when he gets back, just as she's taking the turkey from the oven. She offers him a knife. "Want to carve the bird?"

"I'll try. But Ginny, how do you do this every day?"

"I don't. I haven't cooked a turkey in years. The paper bag was my mother's trick."

"No, I mean the kids."

"Supply and demand," she says. "They demand attention, and someone has to supply it."

The meal draws them together, the twins soon happy with the food and their adults. Later, bedtime is not so easy, because they want their daddy to read to them. No one else will do, and they drown the room in tears. Finally they settle down to *Horton Hears a Who!*, and they're asleep by seven thirty.

For Ginny this is always the loveliest time of day, but Lyle isn't ready to relax. He insists on cleaning the kitchen, down to the last detail. Dishes washed, spice shelf in order, compost removed to its bin by the garden.

"Any chance," he says, "that we could turn off the lights and have a talk?"

After working all day, Ginny would like to just lie still in his arms and let the peaceful night flow over them. But talks in the dark are his quest, so she agrees to it. When he clicks off the lights, only a slice of moonglow on the floor beneath a window lets her see anything.

"I know it's your life not mine," he says. "But I have to wonder at this devotion of yours. First, how much you did for Jamie's partner. For months, for a year, looking after him every day."

"Jamie needed help, he couldn't handle it on his own. And I loved Miles."

"And now the twins. Who are Rob's obligation, not yours. Of course you want to help, but do you have to make it your whole life?"

This stings, because it's the question she has asked herself a hundred times. This must not become her whole life—but what else does she have? She tries to explain it. "It makes me feel safe, to be needed every day. I guess it's a defense against addiction. The twins are my structure, and the more time I spend with them the less I think about taking a drink."

"Yet with me, you're afraid of getting too involved."

"That's different. The twins are more—inevitable."

"How long do you think you'll keep living like this?"

He's probably right, and arguing with him feels useless. Now she wants to see his face, but can barely make it out. "This isn't like you," she says, "to be telling me what I ought to do."

"Yes, I'm being selfish. I want more of you and you're too wrapped up."

"What more do you want?"

Silence.

"Do you want to sleep with me?"

"Of course."

"I'm going as fast as I can."

"Who knows what you could do if you set your mind to it."

"Lyle, you're pushing me again. What if I never want to?"

"Never? What do you mean?"

"What if I never want to, what would you do?"

He looks stiff, she can see that much.

"I guess I'd move on to someone else. We could still be friends."

"Except we'd probably avoid each other and hardly talk, because that's what people do. If I want you to stay, which I do, I better start putting out."

"That would never work. Because if you do something you don't want to do, I won't like it. It's why I try not to get too excited myself. I don't want us to get out of balance."

"You're too good for me Lyle."

"I keep thinking you'll come around. Because you're so perceptive about everything that happens."

"But half the time I can't relax, and I don't like myself because of it."

They sit in the near dark. Maybe, because he's helped so much with the twins, she owes him her body. No, he'd never say that. He'd never even think it. They wait on their chairs. They haven't resolved anything, and Ginny no longer hopes to be held. She's going to fail with Lyle as she has with every other man.

Only a minute later she knows it's true. "Maybe these talks in the dark are too dangerous," he says, "and we shouldn't have them. Ginny, I'll call you later. For now, I'm off."

He finds his coat, puts it on and leaves her house, as she left his.

He calls a few days later, but he's busy with a Senior Dance Concert, a week's residency with Alvin Ailey and interviews of a dozen potential students for next year's incoming class. After a couple of weeks they manage a short walk by the Hocking River, but Lyle doesn't take her hand. The river is gray and laced with ice. She wonders if they're done. For Christmas and New Year's, he tells her, he's going up to Wisconsin to spend time with his son Jed in a borrowed cabin by a lake. He'll call when he gets back.

In the evenings Rob talks about Jamie's life in Key West. He's edging back into the party scene, but more often, during Rob's visit, they just sat around and talked about Miles. "He drinks," Rob says, "but I wouldn't say he's drowning his grief. We have an unhappy bond. He lost Miles and I've lost Natalia."

Ginny wants to point out that she's in the same boat, having lost Rich. But enough of that old story, which her sons are surely fed up with. Even less can she claim that she lost Joe, or that now she's afraid of losing Lyle.

On Christmas Eve after the twins go down, she and Rob give his brother a call. No luck, they can't raise him. Likely he's out with friends, and they're glad he has them. Here they must dress the tree, wrap presents and bake cookies. They've set this Christmas up to be mostly a surprise to Sophie and Chilo, who have only been told that Santa will come in a sleigh.

In the morning, when the twins skip into the living room, they find the tree covered with glittering bulbs, garlands and tinsel. They jump up and down at the sight of the presents beneath it, and at Santa's glass of half-finished milk and the gingerbread cookie he didn't finish eating. They're delirious, as long as the presents and stories last.

29

Finally a call from Lyle, who sounds quite cheerful. After a few minutes of generic talk he says, "I want to see you. Can you come over tomorrow night? I'll cook you dinner."

She goes, and after the meal they sit in his quiet living room. He's been attentive over the meal, but not affectionate. He hasn't once touched her, and she can't read him. She crosses her legs, her winter skirt hanging almost to the floor. His house is still and she imagines a lovely solitude when no one else is here. Maybe he's given up on her.

He never mentions the Simple Room, but explains that he has something to tell her and he wants to do it here, downstairs. "This way, if something I say upsets you and you want to leave, it won't be hard."

There's another woman, she thinks. "Go ahead, tell me."

He describes his time with Jed in a northern cabin beside a frozen lake. It was the simplest life. They walked and read and cooked and talked. They fished on the lake but didn't catch anything. Jed read Doctorow's *Ragtime*, Lyle read Salter's *Light Years*, and when they finished they traded books. They talked about Jed's mother, who lives in Tucson and wants nothing to do with the Midwest.

These details must lead somewhere, Ginny thinks, and lets him ramble. He mentions three times how well he and Jed got along, and finally he comes to it.

"The morning I left, he gave me a little capsule of white powder, one of two he had in a jar. At first I thought *cocaine*, but it was nothing illegal and nothing you could buy. It was MDMA, an experimental drug made by Merck. Psychiatrists are doing trials with it. They make it in a lab in Chicago, and one of Jed's friends works there."

He speaks the full name slowly: "Methylenedioxymethamphetamine."

"A pep pill," Ginny says.

"Not really, though there must be some speed to it. I wasn't interested in some random drug, but Jed kept talking about it. He said it had made him feel alive like nothing else, and I could see he was offering me something precious. He wouldn't be getting any more of it, and he was giving up half of what he had so I could take it. I tucked the capsule into my suitcase and brought it home. It may not have been illegal, but felt like it. I had no prescription for it, and the University could fry me for any drug activity. But I kept remembering Jed's zeal about it, and after a few days I pulled out the pill."

He pauses.

"I want to tell you about it. but I know you might not want to hear a drug story. And there's a lot about my body in it."

She waves off his warning. "You think I'm going to say *don't tell me?*"

"You could."

"But I'd keep thinking about it, and in the end I'd have to hear it."

"I'm sorry, Ginny. I take it back."

"You can't. And I don't want you to."

"I'm lost," he says.

Good, because she is too. *There's a lot about his body in it.* What the hell does that mean? "Go ahead," she says, "tell me what happened."

He starts slowly. Here in his house he unplugged the phone, locked the door, turned all the lights off downstairs and went up to his bedroom. Jed had assured him that he wouldn't want to be interrupted. He swallowed the capsule, took off his shoes and lay down on his bed. He told himself to think positive thoughts, then stopped worrying about it. His ears were ringing faintly, but that was his usual tinnitus. He wanted to open a window, to feel the night outside, but it was too cold. After thirty minutes he felt a first tremor, and soon he knew it was coming on.

"I lay there, and all I wanted to do was touch myself. It was some kind of arousal, something like sex but not, because I never got an erection. Sorry, some things I have to say. My whole body felt alive. I took off all my clothes. I had to touch myself all over and keep doing it."

From her years of drug use she doesn't remember anything like this. The closest she came was with some Valium a few times, soaking in her bathtub and feeling her pores open up.

"It was arousing," he says again, "but somehow beyond sex."

Is he trying to relax her with this? Fat chance. Even now he looks excited.

"I know it doesn't sound like much. A movie of it would bore anyone. Lying in bed for two hours and caressing myself? But what came next was a revelation. The whole focus shifted to you and me, and I felt as at ease with us as I did with my body. Everything about us looked great."

"Clearly it's not."

"Okay, I probably knew that, but I didn't have to worry about it. I was sure we were going to get closer. We have our upsets, but that's not going to stop us. And I saw that I don't have to keep holding back with you. I don't mean physically, I mean that I can relax and tell you anything. I lay there in bed for another hour, consumed by that vision. It was like Jed said, I'd never felt so alive and sure."

"But Lyle, you were stoned."

He nods, calming down. "It's true."

"This is why people take drugs, to make everything look better. It's why I took them. But afterward here we are. You have to deal with me, not some notion of what I'm like. And you know that in ways I'm still a mess."

"I don't think you are. Or it's not so bad that I can't handle it."

"You had a great time, and I'm glad. But you were right to worry about me and a story like that. I still can't hear it and relax. It's not as bad as walking into a bar full of drunks, but I'm still too delicate for drug stories. I don't trust anything about them."

He says no more about it.

There is no other woman, but that doesn't help. If she doesn't quicken herself and let him get closer, she's going to fail him. A pep pill would help. *She* should have taken the MDMA.

Of course she thinks that. A hundred paths lead back to the drugs she must never touch.

She has pissed all over his story, his glorious trip with this new drug. His face glowed as he described it, and now he's pulling back. She better rescue something from this night. She stands before him and holds out a hand. "If you'd invite me, I'd sleep in your bed tonight. We could think of it as an experiment in affection."

In the week that follows she comes up with her own plan. She needs to tell him her whole painful history, her failures, why she keeps her distance. Sitting in the university library she makes notes, because having it all written down will make it easier. It's crazy, how much she hasn't told him.

She calls and asks for a session in the Simple Room. "But with the light on. I have some things to tell you."

"I'm glad," he says.

She takes the notes but never unfolds them. They drink a cup of coffee after dinner, a crazy suggestion of Lyle's but one she welcomes. She'll have trouble going to sleep later, but now she needs a push to get her started. She has her first lines down, having repeated them to herself a dozen times.

"I owe my kids. I hurt them and failed them and I've been trying to make up for that."

Lyle knows that she was unfaithful to Joe, but she must tell him more about how it happened.

"It's terrible now to think of how blind I was to what it would do to my family. I was so wrapped up with Rich, I thought I could let everything else go and it wouldn't matter. I don't know what Joe suspected. Maybe he knew all along, but he never said anything. That's how he was, he hated all confrontation. He could never stand a squabble, much less something serious, and other men were never a topic. There you were, Lyle, fantasizing about your wife getting it on with another guy and ready to watch it. You're quite the specimen. Joe was out on another limb, like his New England parents. He was honorable to the core, but allergic to trouble or talking about how he felt. So when he saw how I was pulling back from him, instead of challenging me on it he decamped. He started sleeping on the other side of the house, up the other staircase. He told the kids it was because he snored and that kept me awake. He even told *me* that. But I was glad he went off to sleep somewhere else, because then I could call Rich at night and talk to him, and as I lay in bed he guided me, telling me how I should touch myself. He always took charge, and I loved it. I used to pretend that none of it was my fault, because he'd bewitched me and I had to obey him. My boys were twelve and sixteen when it started. Not little kids anymore, but we were still a family. I tore us apart and now I owe them. These days, when Natalia takes off and leaves the twins with Rob, I think *That's what I did*. I was unfaithful to Joe, but the treason to my kids was worse."

They sit in the empty room, face to face. Lyle's a genius, she thinks again, to have come up with this space, this retreat where everything is easier to say.

"When I was growing up, I was sure that no one on earth got more aroused than I did. Rich saw that in me and played with it. He'd stir me up and then deny me. Instead of touching me he'd lie down for a nap and tell me I had to sit beside him to wave off any flies that might land on him. I'd soak up his body that I couldn't have, then he'd sit up and tell me what to wear, how my hair should be cut, when I could take a pee and when I couldn't. He liked to be in charge of me and everything else. A typical surgeon, you could say—but he was never arrogant. He was too crafty for that. He used to claim that *he* was serving *me*, that he was the devoted one. And in a way it was true. He spent hours turning me on. Lyle, do you want to hear all this?"

"Yes."

She watches him, studies his face. In all their time together she has never caught him in a lie. And she believes him, because he has always wanted to hear everything.

"I'm trying to explain something about sex and drinking and drugs. I had four voluptuous years with Rich, and from one day to the next it was over. Then it was only pills and alcohol that made me feel okay. I want to be sexual again but it scares me. I don't want it to feel like getting high. What if I come to love sex again, and then you leave me and my only way to survive is through the bottle? Sex was a thrill, and thrills are dangerous. What if sex feels too good and turns into another kind of addiction, a hunger that can't be stopped?"

She waits. For a long minute he doesn't speak. Finally, "I guess it's my job to reassure you, but I don't know if I can, or if that would be fair. Because it might just be my own hunger talking. Of course I'm going to tell you that sex is lovely, that there's no danger and it can't hurt you. But we both know that isn't true."

She sits up straight in her chair. Outside, a winter wind is blowing. Inside, the room is warm and still. "Go ahead and reassure me. I doubt if there's anything you'll say that I haven't been telling myself."

"To begin with," he says, "if you don't want me to, I don't have to get inside you. There's so much else we can do. I had a girlfriend once who didn't want that. We were together for months and never did it, never copulated. We had a hot time anyway, it was fine with me."

"Don't talk about other women. Not now."

"I'm sorry Ginny, I know I shouldn't. I'm an idiot."

"Not often, but from time to time."

"Then just you and me. We can do whatever you like and no more. Sometimes I think we're lucky to be sixty. No parents looking over us, no offspring taking care of us, no youthful image to keep up. We can try something, then talk about it. It's not like a drug that's going to string us out. We can explore what we like and no more. All right, is that enough?"

"Keep going. Why isn't it like booze and drugs? You already said it can hurt you. It sure hurt me with Rich Villamano."

"I'm not like him. I wouldn't leave you."

"How can you know that?"

"I guess I can't. But it's how I feel."

"There are always other women. I've seen you watch them on the street."

"I glance at them."

"If I weren't around, would you stare?"

"No, because that makes people nervous."

"What if you and I were a couple? How faithful would you be?"

"Completely, if that's what you want. I can't say I'd stop watching. I can't say all my thoughts would be pure."

"How impure would you be?"

"Okay, Ginny, now I ask *you*. Do you really want to hear this?'

She pushes her chair a few inches back. "Yes."

"I'm a man. I look at women and girls. I'm never blind to them. When I was married I fantasized sometimes, but I never put the cruise on anyone. Still, Doris knew. And when she asked me about it I told her, just like I'm telling you. We talked about it a couple of times, and I think it was a poison. I hope I'm not poisoning things with you. But when you ask me something, I'm going to tell you."

"Tell me about your fantasies."

"Hey! They don't grab me the way they used to. Maybe age has taken care of it. Maybe all that will melt away. But if it came back, if I were my old self, the scariest would be something like that marriage your son had. Okay, that didn't work out. Plenty of things don't work out. But my fantasies were along that line. Having a number of partners. Sex with threesomes. Not that I ever did it, but it always turned me on."

"And still would?"

"I guess. I haven't been with anyone for a while, so it's not something I've been thinking about."

"What about slipping off with someone else?"

"I wouldn't. I'd never want to leave you out."

"You're so considerate."

"Okay, I've pissed you off with the truth. I'm a randy guy, or I used to be. But none of that works and it all leads to trouble. And I don't want trouble with you, I just want you closer. Like every other guy on the street, I'm a horndog. Evolution or God or something gave me those urges, but they're milder now and easier to live with. You know what I want. I want to hold and touch you. And I'm convinced it wouldn't be like your addictions. Hell, if you got addicted, if you wanted it twice a day, I'm too old for that. Okay, I've said enough."

They sit in silence in the quiet room.

After a time she asks him to make her a cup of tea, she needs to step outside for a minute. "Don't worry, I'm not going anywhere."

He stands up when she does. He's gracious that way, old-fashioned, he bends toward her. Outside, she stands under the branches of a swaying willow. She wants to feel the night against her skin, the ground beneath her feet as the cold air passes over her. It takes her a while to understand it herself. She only came out to prove that she can leave and return.

Back inside, in the living room, she sips a cup of lemon ginger. She thinks, but doesn't say, that she likes it when he touches her, but cannot imagine a time when she'd welcome him inside her. He did make it clear that he wouldn't insist on that. But won't it always be the endgame? They both know it. She wants to respond the way she used to. She wants those quivers and more, but fears her history of inebriated, enticing nights. Too much pleasure still feels dangerous.

30

Sophie and Chilo love games of all kinds: hide and seek, imitate-the-beast and howling contests in the orchard. Also, a dress-up game that Ginny helps them with. "Dress me like a boy," Chilo says, and Sophie chimes in, "Dress me like a girl."

Ginny does her best to exaggerate it. A white shirt for Chilo with a pin-on bow tie, long pants, black socks, his only pair of leather shoes and a small plastic fedora. For Sophie it's a pink blouse, a flouncy skirt and a pair of ballet slippers. The two of them are abnormally patient, then tell Ginny to go wait in the living room.

Ten minutes later they appear, each wearing the other's clothes. Ginny goes along with the deception. She looks at Sophie and says, "Chilo, let me straighten out your tie, it's half undone." She looks at Chilo and says, "Sophie, have you been dancing?"

They stifle their laughter. What could be more fun than fooling an adult? And clearly they already have a grip on the stereotypes. Sophie puts her thumbs in her belt and swells out her little chest. She picks up a plastic hammer and swaggers around the room with it, nailing the air. Chilo gives a dance twirl, then grabs a Raggedy Ann doll and curls up with it on the sofa.

Where do these moves come from? There's no television in the house, Rob doesn't swagger, and Natalia—whatever they remember of her—was never dainty. Such clichés must be in the air they breathe.

Another day, Ginny invents the tossing game. The kids love to throw anything anywhere and today, she tells them, they can go into their room and throw anything they like: clothes, toys, balls, blocks, only books are forbidden. But they must remember what comes later, when everything must be put back where it belongs. Instant acceptance by the two, and in ten seconds they're twirling, laughing and throwing things all over their room, then picking them up and tossing them again.

Then the cleanup. It was Ginny's idea to teach them, through the game, a little discipline. Was she out of her mind? No matter that Rob always urges them to be responsible, that if they drop something on the floor they're supposed to pick it up, that if they need to use the bathroom they should tell him, that if he has something important to say they have to listen. They're used to rules, but Ginny has opted for a giant clumsy lesson, and now they won't touch anything. The room is one big clutter and they wail in misery. Yes, she was out of her mind. Though they did love it for a while.

Only a couple of nights later Rob ropes her into supervising the kids' bedtime so he can go off on a date he doesn't want to talk about. He's been reading them *Where the Wild Things Are*, and that's what they want to hear. To Ginny they seem too young for the book, but they're insistent. "Start at the start," Chilo says.

Only a few pages in, everything turns scary. Ginny stops reading half way through, because both of them have shrunk under their covers. Even then they want her to go on. When she says no, she'll finish another night, they wail and thrash as if possessed. Did her own boys ever cry so hard? She considers leaving and letting them cry it out, but Sophie's too clever for that. She chokes and gasps as if something has hold of her throat. Ginny kneels between their beds. She covers them with light blankets, which they fling aside. She tries to read them *Goodnight Moon*, but they won't listen. She brings them a pair of popsicles, but they're so committed to their misery that they knock the treats aside with flailing hands and feet.

She's still looking for her own place to live. Somewhere near Athens with its university library, its restaurants and movie theater. But not in town. She wants, still, the quiet of the woods, with the hawks, crows and vultures overhead. If she finds a piece of land she likes, Rob will build her a house.

A wooden house, she thinks, but he has other ideas. "Brick," he says, so it never rots. "A woodstove, a backup furnace, some good windows and doors. Mamá, it's going to be fun."

They design it together, a thousand square feet with one small and two tiny bedrooms, a single bathroom and the kitchen part of the living room. One afternoon she goes back to Larry Conrath's office. He's a friendly guy and drives her out to have a look at a couple of listings, but neither plot appeals to Ginny. One is too far from town, and the other a narrow slice of bottomland between two ridges.

"I'll keep my eye out," Larry says. "We'll find you something."

Every week she's invited back to Lyle's. He still wraps her up in his arms, and she spends several nights in his bed, though she has to hustle home before daylight to look after the twins when Rob goes off to work.

Sometimes she plays with Lyle. It's easy, because at any moment she knows she can stir him up. One night after he complains about his knees, how they're falling apart, she pulls down the covers, inspects them, and announces that they need a small massage. Which she proceeds to give him, straying some from the knee cap in front and the meniscus in back.

He refrains until her next visit, then caresses her in return, his touch somewhat lighter than hers.

Even so there are days when he disappears, when his work absorbs him, when he's buried in the Winter Dance Concert, when he worries about one of his dancers who is Catholic and averse to abortion, but now pregnant. He dives into a campaign to recruit more males into the program. He rants to Ginny, almost as if they've been arguing about it: "Male dancers aren't all gay, not even half of them. Nureyev, sure. But Baryshnikov's as straight as I am and Ballanchine married four of his dancers. I want to choreograph for a mixed company. I want more equilibrium."

Winter has passed but the fields are still gray, the trees without leaves. Days of rain and clouds, days of brilliant sun. The first daffodils have flowered, exposing their blooms to the dormant land. She used to think, when young, that she was the daffodil of humans, the one who grew up too fast. Now she revels in their promise, and invites Lyle to take a spring break trip to Sag Harbor.

"I love it," he says. They stand outside the door to her house. It's late March, the smoke bush is bare and the sycamores leafless above them. "When was it built?"

"At the end of the seventeen hundreds."

She'd hoped for this, that he would like the house with its low and welcoming windows, its uneven shingles and wide brick chimney. Inside, she turns on the water and the furnace, and they let the house warm up as they walk to the village.

From the wharf, the last light of day is a curtain of red to the west. Though she lobbied for Lyle to join her on this trip, she's not sure even now what she wanted to show him. Walking back along Main Street, she assembles her past like a kid with blocks.

"I grew up in Ohio," she says. "I never imagined going back. I spent years in New York and Connecticut, then moved to Sag. I drank here and recovered here. Then down to Key West for a year with Jamie, and out to Ohio with Rob—and after all that moving around, this still feels most like home."

"Will you live here again?"

"I don't think so. Not with Rob and my grandkids in Ohio." And *you*, she thinks.

Main Street is lined with naked trees, spring still a promise. Ginny slides an arm around Lyle's waist and they walk on in their sneakers. It's all he ever wears, there's not a leather shoe in his closet. He waits a block before he circles *her* waist. His timing is often perfect.

Back home, Ginny turns down the covers of her bed so the sheets can warm up along with the rest of the house. They drink some juice and eat the burritos they've brought with them. Then she leads him into the living room and stands in front of him. "In all this time, she says, I've never seen your naked chest."

"It awaits you. It will be happy."

She unbuttons his shirt and pulls up his T-shirt. She runs her hand through his hair, circling, slowly settling on his nipples, brushing them, pulling on them, holding them in a light pinch.

"Can I assume you're giving me permission?" he says.

"You know the rules. You made them up." But then, as he's about to get her bra off, she stops him. "Before we go on, I need to tell you what happened in this room."

He doesn't want to stop, she can see. But he does. It's unfair, after she led him on. She hardly knows what she's doing, but has to tell her story.

"I almost died here from an overdose. I woke up on the floor, right there." She points. "I called the hospital and they sent an ambulance. After the hospital and rehab I came back, and with Rob and Jamie's help I never relapsed."

And just like that, she understands.

"This is where everything changed, where my new life started."

Which is why Lyle must hear this. Because all is about to change again, when she sleeps with him. She knows now that she's going to, and this is where it will happen, far from Rob and the twins, far from Lyle's house and their tangled courtship of the last six months.

But not tonight, after their long day of travel. Better tomorrow. Tonight she'll just give him longer and slower kisses, and let him play with her breasts. She's ready to lead him on, so he can take over.

At the beach the next day the waves have built up under an offshore wind. Seaweed, driftwood and bits of balsa are drying out in the meandering wrack line that heads toward Montauk. Gulls sweep past, surveying waves and people, and an occasional dead skate flops back and forth in the shallows.

Lyle, in the bright morning sun, is clearly no young man. His face and neck are creased—like hers, of course. They are an older couple. It's just as well that it's too early in the season to think of a swim. If she were wearing a bathing suit her belly would be on display, and she's not as trim as she used to be. What is it with humans, anyway? Fish never swell with age, and seagulls don't get pudgy. They flare with timeworn grace and settle on the sand, then strut around the more bizarre species, *Homo sapiens*. Maybe terns notice when one of their kind grows stiff, when it can no longer scoot across the sand and lift into the air in a tenth of a second. But if there are birds impaired by aging, Ginny has never seen one.

That night they eat dinner at the kitchen table. Soft white flounder, spinach, and sweet potatoes laced with butter, raisins, vanilla and cinnamon.

"Delicious," Lyle says.

She's come along from the days she rarely prepared a meal. She tells him about her first years in the house, when the only range was an old kitchen wood stove with a massive burnished top. "If I wanted a couple of fried eggs, or even a cup of tea, I had to build a fire. I thought somehow that would purify me, that it would put me in touch with the first dwellers here. But it was way too much work. For a while I cooked on a little hot plate. Finally I got rid of the stove and had a range installed. Now I cook the modern way, by pressing a button."

"So up to date," he says, lightly mocking.

She wants to tell him a story, to describe a scene. Though she doesn't want to hear about sex between him and some other woman, the perverted Lyle will be excited about her and another man. "Let me show you something," she says, "from my pool days with Mike Blake."

Lyle knows about her coach, knows she did everything with him except the act itself. From a back shelf in her closet she pulls out a pale blue diving suit, still shiny, still silky.

"I can see you in it," Lyle says.

"Poor Coach, as I always called him. He kept clinging to some kind of loyalty to his wife and refused to go all the way. Instead, he lingered over this suit as if it were the relic of a saint. He could take an hour removing it, slowly stroking and—you know, as he went."

"I don't know."

"You do, you just want to hear me say it."

"Yes."

"Licking me. You'd have thought I was made of chocolate."

"And you were happy with that?"

"I wanted more."

She steps in front of him. She has given him the clue and now takes his hand, to lead him into her bedroom.

31

Rob has taken up with Celeste, a slender young woman who helps run the Farmacy, the Athens health food store. And Celeste, who's divorced or perhaps was never married, has a seven-year-old daughter. Willow loves to play with the twins and no one, older or younger, can keep up with her.

"When I jump," she tells Chilo and Sophie, "you have to jump. Now higher."

Long-limbed Willow is their goddess, but of course they can't keep up, they're half her age. "Now let's jump off the couch!"

Rob is fine with that. Ten minutes before Willow came, Sophie was moaning that they *had* to get a television, life was boring without it. Chilo agreed, "It isn't *fair*," he cried. Now the three of them jump and roll across the floor, then spill outside onto the grass. They do shoulder rolls and half-baked cartwheels as the adults watch from the porch.

"Sometime," Rob tells Celeste, "you could take the twins for a week. Think of what fun you'd have."

"You could take Willow for two weeks. In fact that would only be fair, since it's two to one."

Then they turn to Ginny, as if the thought has just come to them both. "Once we build your house," Rob says, "with several little bedrooms, you could take all three of them for a month or two."

Ginny laughs. It *is* a joke. But behind every joke there's always some germ of truth. When she has her own place the kids can spend the night and their parents will get a break. But damn, not for a month.

Ginny and Lyle have a new game themselves. When they get together they talk things over and choose to be, for that night, either lovers or old friends. Or one night she decides and the next time it's up to him. Or they flip a coin. It relaxes Ginny to know what's in store. She doesn't have to guess if he'll be soothing or arousing her.

He does disappear sometimes. The week of the Senior Dance Concert she doesn't see him at all—or only from the back row of a final rehearsal, at his invitation. The choreography isn't his, but he's immersed in every piece, moving about the stage and making suggestions. The students are attentive as he talks, spins, flares his arms or shows how long a pause might be held. He's so far away, and so wrapped up in his world, that she can barely think of him as her lover.

She's found a piece of land, ten acres of woods and meadow. There's a level building site, a creek, and at the foot of a hill in back, a pond. Rob has already cleared some ground and poured a concrete footer, but for now she still shares his farmhouse with him, along with their endless care of the twins.

One late spring afternoon they're out in the garden, weeding around the sweet potato vines and keeping track of Chilo and Sophie, when the phone rings inside. Rob runs in to pick it up—hoping, Ginny guesses, that it's a call from Celeste—and only a minute later steps back outside.

"That was Natalia. She's at the Columbus airport."

Christ on a crutch. In the last year they've heard almost nothing from her, only that she's been living with her mother in Guatemala and that she has another child. A son, by an unknown father. Meches must be headed for sainthood, Ginny thinks, to be taking care of both Natalia and an infant.

"Did she come alone?"

"I don't know. I have to go pick her up."

After all these years, he and Natalia are still legally married. But that has little to do with it, Ginny thinks. When she calls, he jumps. He waves to the twins, gets into his pickup and takes off down the road.

Ginny tries to prepare the children. She tells them their mother is coming to visit, but they pay that no attention. She cleans up their room with them, tossing their dirty clothes into the laundry basket. She takes them for a walk in the woods, where they spot and collect a dozen morels. She cooks and feeds them dinner, including a couple of the fried mushrooms. They sniff them and leave them on their plates.

Just at dusk Rob's truck pulls into the drive. The twins jump up and so does Ginny, but no one is ready for this. Clinging to Natalia's neck as she walks to the house is her small, dark-haired, wide-eyed son—whose name is Chilo.

"I've already told her," Rob says, "this can't be."

"That's his name," Natalia says. "Chilo Moreno Betancourt. *Así es en su certificado de nacimiento.*" That's what's on his birth certificate.

She sets the boy down. The twins hover as he stares up at them. Chilo—the original Chilo—doesn't look happy. "Why does he have *my* name?"

"You don't own that name," Natalia says. "You're lucky to have it. I gave it to you and I can take it back."

"No you can't."

"Of course I can. I'm your mother. You wouldn't be here without me."

Two minutes in and all is havoc. Both twins shrink back. Natalia wears a purple skirt and a long white sash draped from one shoulder to the other. After the chaos of her disappearance, how abruptly she has returned. A plane flight, a telephone call, and here she is.

"*No importa nada de eso,*" she says about young Chilo's name. She pulls a pair of blue shorts out of her suitcase and tosses them to Rob. She has barely looked at Ginny. "He could change into these and I think he's hungry, what have you got for dinner?"

"Shouldn't we be changing his diaper, too?"

"If you want." She digs around in her bag, finds one and tosses that as well.

Chilo junior can walk, but holds out his hands to the twins. They let him grab on, as Ginny heads for the kitchen to heat up what's left of their dinner, roasted tofu and slices of fried red pepper. She skips the morels. Chilo seems too young for all of it, and after it cools all he does is suck on a pepper. Then he turns to his mother. She pulls up her braless shirt and begins to feed him. "He's getting too old for this," she says.

"How old is he?" Ginny asks.

"Fourteen months."

"Didn't the twins breastfeed until they were a year and a half?"

"I've been training him. And what do you know about it?"

Her antagonism hasn't changed. Natalia is the one who abandoned her kids, and Ginny the one who has helped out with them ever since. But arguing with Natalia has always been futile.

Rob puts off his work on Ginny's house the next day. Chilo junior keeps crying because he wants his mother's breast, and she wants him to eat solid foods. Ginny makes a run to the store and returns with bananas, avocados and jars of pureed carrots.

Natalia, Ginny thinks, is strangely distant from Sophie and Chilo senior. She doesn't call them by name, just says *you* or sometimes *tu*. She doesn't take them in her arms or seem inclined to, which Ginny finds bizarre, because no two creatures on earth are as darling as the twins. Though it's true just now that they seem a bit hesitant. They're not sure what to do around Chilo junior, and when he cries they turn away. Natalia watches them all in silence. Ginny takes it as an inspection of her and Rob, perhaps a judgment on the job they've been doing.

When Natalia leaves Chilo with them and goes off for an afternoon walk, Rob and Ginny step outside. "What's she after?" Ginny asks. "Does she want her children back?"

"Sure doesn't look like it."

"How long does she plan to stay?"

"I've asked, but you know how she is. She doesn't commit to much."

"I'm sure she needs help. But Rob, I have to ask. How much will you do for her?"

"I wonder that myself. She asked for money and I gave her some. Not too much, because I can see what a calamity she is. One thing for sure, we can't leave her alone with the kids. I don't trust her for a minute."

Ginny wonders how long will this go on. "Have you told Celeste?"

"We canceled a dinner. She understands, because her ex is kind of crazy himself."

The Six was a rare kind of family, Ginny thinks, but this one is stranger still. A pair of twins, once half-abandoned, are united with a toddler who needs more attention than they do. Their mother, whom they don't seem to remember, is quiet and insistent. Their father is enmeshed with another woman. Their grandmother is helpful, but sometimes steps back, exhausted. And there's a step grandfather, who's fun but who comes and goes. Ginny's trying to see life as the twins do, and it looks confusing.

Dinner, breakfast, another day with Natalia wandering through the house, looking at everything. Chilo junior, at least, is quiet at night, sleeping in his mother's bed—until he wakes at 5:30 and his hungry cries wake everyone else. Rob, early on, takes Ginny out to the vehicles in the drive. They usually keep the keys under the front seats, but he passes the car keys to Ginny and pockets the truck keys himself. "Don't let her see them. You remember how she drove off last time and disappeared."

Still, Natalia seems milder today, at least with Chilo junior. He wants to sit on her lap, and she lets him. He wants to be picked up, and she carries him around. She doesn't talk much, but keeps inspecting the house, opening the oven and the freezer, picking out paperbacks and hardcovers from the living room bookcase, standing inside the tool closet for twenty minutes as she fingers wrenches and pliers and packs of sandpaper. She lifts the sofa cushions and turns up a few coins and a pen. As she nurses Chilo junior she glances around the room and taps her foot. It's exhausting just to watch her.

Ginny offers to take the twins to town and buy them some ice cream. Really, it's to leave Rob and Natalia alone with Chilo junior. The twins are excited by the promise of ice cream, along with playtime on the swings and slides of the town park. And of course, everything will be simpler without the younger Chilo.

After dinner, Ginny asks Natalia how her mother is doing.

"All right. But she's not that good a grandmother. She's always telling me what to do."

"She has a new house, I hear."

"Yes, I liked that house."

She *liked* the house? Is that all in the past? Neither Ginny nor Rob has asked her the vital question: what comes next for her, and how is she going to take care of this child? But that's how it is with Natalia, how it has always been. Talks with her are curtailed by the threat of her vexation.

After the twins go to bed, she doesn't go in to say goodnight to them. Chilo junior is asleep, but still in her arms. She rocks him for thirty minutes, as if he's in constant danger of waking up.

Rob asks, "Why did you come back?"

"What do you care?"

"Your kids are here and you barely pay them any attention."

"Because you stole them."

"Natalia, you left them."

"Because you wanted them to love you and not me." She stands up and plops Chilo on the sofa. One of the twins would have woken instantly, but Chilo junior merely curls up. Rob brings a blanket to cover him, and Natalia wanders around the room, stopping and starting. "You and my mother are just alike. You think you know everything."

She never gives Ginny a look. Ginny wants out, but won't abandon Rob. Natalia takes some bills out of her pocket and holds them in the air, shaking them.

"Go ahead, take it back, I don't need this crap."

He folds his hands and doesn't touch the money. "Let's go outside," he says, "and take a look at the sky."

"You and your stars. What are you going to learn from them? They don't know anything."

"They don't have to," Rob says. "They're beautiful."

"That's all you think about, isn't it?"

"No, I think a lot about our children and what they need."

"You're full of shit and don't even know it. It's like you're asleep. And then you want to tell *me* what to do." She picks up Chilo and marches off to their bedroom.

Rob and Ginny step outside. They stand on the grass, dark and moist.

"What are you going to do with her?"

"I have no idea. I'll call Meches tomorrow, but it doesn't sound like Natalia's headed back to Guatemala."

"Is she fit to be a mother at all?"

"Probably not. But she is one."

"You could call Children Services."

"Are you kidding? I know what they'd do. First an interview, then they take the kid away and put him in some group home and no one gets to see him. No, I'm not calling anyone. Let's see what we can work out tomorrow."

The next morning, Natalia's not in the house. Her suitcase sits on the living room floor, and Chilo is still asleep in bed. She must have gone out for a walk, but an hour later there's still no sign of her. Chilo has been crying. He wants his mother's breast, of course. He pushes aside a mashed-up banana and a soft piece of bread, and ten minutes later Ginny takes off for the McArthur general store, where she buys some formula and more baby food. After she gets back, the famished Chilo drinks and eats.

There are no hints inside Natalia's suitcase, though Chilo's birth certificate is there, nestled among his clothes. Just as she said, *Chilo Moreno Betancourt.*

They've been down this road before. Rob calls the police, who haven't seen or heard anything. They promise to keep their eyes open.

"How much money did you give her?" Ginny asks.

"Two hundred."

"How far can she get on that?"

"Pretty damn far. Or she did last time."

"But if she doesn't come back," Ginny says, "what are you going to do with this Chilo?"

"I don't know."

She's pretty sure he does. He's not going to let some agency take the boy and farm him out. He's not going to let some couple with three foster kids add to their income by taking in a fourth. Ginny sees or imagines all this in his face. He's been put to the test before, and she has watched him with the twins. Over the years his bond to Natalia has been battered, but something remains, and the biology doesn't matter.

Maybe she's only gone out for a hike and will return. But she doesn't. Chilo junior cries half the day, starting up over and over. The twins don't want to hear it. Chilo senior says, "What's the matter with him?" and Sophie says, "*Quit* it."

Month by month, taking care of the twins has gotten easier. Now, with a one-year-old the chaos takes a leap. There are quiet moments when the twins relent, when they guide Chilo junior as he walks and explores. But then, through the long afternoon, he starts wailing again. Rob digs out an old carrier, and they all go up to the high meadow.

Another day off work. Rob sits everyone in a circle on the floor and says, "Little Chilo needs another name. What do you think we should we call him?"

Quick as a wink, big Chilo says "Froggie."

Sophie shakes her head. "That's silly."

"What do you think, Ginny?"

"I think we should think about it."

"No," says big Chilo. "*Now*."

"How about some other suggestions?"

Sophie offers Danny. *No*, says her brother. All four of them must agree on it, and they run through Timmy, Ben and Tony. Little Chilo has no opinion, though he seems to know they're talking about him. Bobby. Jimmy. Derek. And finally the one that sticks, Jesse.

"Good," says Rob. "We can handle this. We found one we like and now his name is Jesse."

How much they can handle is on trial in the days that follow. Jesse eats, sleeps, plays and craps his diapers, and he also wails. When he's calm, he's fine with any of them picking him up. Even the twins can carry him for a few steps. But he keeps staring at the door. They don't mention Natalia's name around him, which seems misguided to Ginny. What do they think, that he's going to forget her? They try to fill in for his mother, but it can't be done. Ginny rocks and feeds him, lets him grab onto her breasts, lies down with him at night and sleeps with him. But in the morning, he knows he's been abandoned.

32

From Natalia not a word. Rob calls her mother in Guatemala and tells her what happened. He asks Meches if she wants to have her grandson back.

"*Dios guarde, m'ijo, soy muy vieja para eso.*" She's too old for that, she says. She loves Chilo but she can't take care of him on her own.

"*Ya no se llama Chilo,*" Rob says. That's not his name anymore, because two Chilos was far too confusing. "*Ahora se llama Jesse.*"

"*Djesse? Que es eso?*"

That's his new name, Rob explains.

"*Ay, Roberto. Que tristeza nos lleva, esta debilidad de Natalia.*"

What sorrow it brings them, this weakness of Natalia's. That's what she calls it, a debility that runs through her husband's side of the family. Neither Meches nor Rob uses the word *esquisofrenia*, though they've spoken of this before. Over the years, even as Natalia has come undone, the two of them have maintained their friendship and a mutual respect. Rob tells her that he now has help from his own mother, who's been living with him and the twins. And you

never know, he says, Natalia might reappear.

"*Ojalá que sea,*" Meches says. May it be so. There's always a chance.

When Lyle hears the news about the abandoned one-year-old Jesse, he sounds oddly enthusiastic. Ginny hasn't conveyed to him the boy's desperation, but he'll see it himself tonight, because he's coming for dinner. He asks if he can pick up Willow and bring her along, because she's so great with the twins.

"We're still getting used to this," Ginny says. "Let's keep it to the three we've got here now."

Ten minutes after Lyle shows up, he's absorbed with the kids. He laughs with them and invents little games. He says, "Hey Jesse, come over here," and lays his palm on the floor. "Can you step over my hand?"

Jesse has almost no English, but he follows Lyle's gestures. He's hesitant at first, but after making the step once he wants to do it again and again. Lyle never tires, but Jesse does and plunks himself down on the floor. Dinner calms him, and by the time Rob reads *Make Way for Ducklings*, he's nestled in Ginny's arms and half asleep. What a change in this house from the old days. Now there are as many children as adults. With the kids in their beds, the grownups sit in the living room.

"If his mother doesn't come back," Lyle says, "what are you going to do with him?"

Neither Rob nor Ginny answers.

"I take it there's no father involved?"

"No one we know of," says Rob.

In the dusk outside, the first cicadas are whirring. Ginny too has wondered what they're going to do with Jesse. She knows that Rob, with the twins in his arms every day, is still bound to Natalia, and she doubts that he'll pass the boy on to some state authority. Perhaps they could have done that the first day. They could have wrapped him up and unloaded him at Children Services. But even then Rob wasn't willing, and now they've had him for a week. They've held him and calmed him and kissed his hands, his face and naked belly. They've renamed him, and now he's theirs.

Lyle, it seems to Ginny, is great with every kid, and in his bedroom a few nights later she asks how this came to be.

"Early training," he says. He tells her how, after their mother left them, he looked after his sister and brother. Ginny hasn't heard this story. Again, she hasn't asked enough questions. She keeps telling herself she will, then she doesn't. Lyle explains that when he was twelve he and his siblings woke one morning to find their mother gone. They asked their father why, but he was evasive. Slowly the truth came out, that she'd run off with another man. "From then on it was a closed topic. If we talked about Mom, Dad left the room."

Three years later she came back, his father took her in and they resumed the marriage. But in those painful absent years it was Lyle who cared for and comforted his brother and sister.

"So," says Ginny, "here are two women who both ran off, your mother and I. I have to wonder, was that something that drew you to me?"

"I don't think so."

"They say that when choosing a mate, people often seek out echoes of their own past."

"Maybe unconsciously."

"I can't believe you wouldn't be aware of it," Ginny says. "You're aware of everything."

"Believe me, I don't need to replace my mother. Especially that part of her."

"Yet like her you have—what shall we call it? The non-monogamous urge.'"

Lyle hunches himself against the headboard and stares across the room for half a minute. "Let's make this an old friends night," he says. "Okay?"

She nods.

"I always wanted to know what was happening with my parents. But even living in the same house with them I could only guess. The way I saw it, my father wasn't enough for my mother. She had set her eyes on some larger life. That didn't work out, and you'd think it would have soured me completely, how she skipped out on the family. Instead, I've always wanted to know what drove her. She stayed away from the topic, and I think that was the worst part, that none of us could talk about it. I'm glad you and I are talking now."

"Would I bore you if I turned out to be a faithful lover?"

"Ginny, no! Let's both be faithful. I've said it before, that other stuff never works. It's something I study, but I don't want to do it. Besides, we're older now and monogamy must be easier. I look around at other women but that's all, I just look."

"And talk about it."

"We don't have to," he says.

"We do. We should always talk."

On a weekday night Ginny invites Celeste and her daughter for a dinner at the Casa. Once seated, Celeste gives the menu a close audit. "Half the food here comes from our store," she says, "and most of it's organic."

Willow reads out loud from the menu. She reads well, but stumbles over some words in Spanish. Still, she's ready to order when the waitress comes. "For me," she says, "a Casa burrito with everything."

"That's a good one. But you don't want the hot sauce, do you?"

"What's that?"

"It can burn your mouth."

"Okay, the cold sauce."

"The mild," says the waitress. "You don't want the *picante*."

"The what?"

"Kids don't usually like it."

"Fine," Willow says, annoyed, She sets her menu on the table. "Whatever you say."

Until corrected by the waitress she had everything figured out. As her mother and Ginny order, she picks up her knife and fork and holds them straight up, as if the meal is about to be delivered, or as if it should have been delivered already.

Ginny watches Celeste and her daughter. She invited them out to get to know them better, but now feels like some matriarch appraising a possible match for her son. This is silly, because the match has already been made and she has nothing to say about it. She'll be lucky if Celeste approves of *her*. Or if Willow does. And in fact it's Willow she's courting, because she's the one who entertains Sophie and Chilo, who delights them, who's better than ten televisions.

"Willow," Ginny says, "I want to thank you for being so good with the twins. And now, you know, we've got one-year-old Jesse, who's kind of the twins' brother. I don't know if you can have as much fun with him, but I think you'll like him."

"I can teach him things."

"Yes, you're great at that."

"It's what I'm going to do when I grow up. I'm going to be a teacher."

"Well," says her mother, "there's just one problem with that."

"Oh, Mom."

Celeste explains it. "I'm not so big on this growing up idea. I think it would be better if she stayed the way she is now. You can see how perfect she is, so why would I want her to change? I've been looking into a program that might help. If she eats the right foods and goes to bed at the right time and follows all the rules, she won't have to change and I'll have her like this forever."

"You're crazy, Mom. You probably want to freeze me like some TV dinner."

"Well, I never thought about that."

"Because you don't think too well."

By now they're both smiling away. It's clearly an old joke between them.

After dinner they walk to the College Green. It's almost empty over summer break and Willow skips around, climbs a little dogwood near Galbreath Chapel and perches there as if invisible.

"Can I ask about Willow's father?"

"Not a bad guy at the start, but in the end a dog and long gone."

They lived for a time on a commune in Pennsylvania. It was one reason she connected with Rob, that they shared that history. When she married Eric he wanted to be a father, or so he said, but after Willow was born he bailed on it every day. That was easy, because there were so many others in the commune who were eager to help out.

"He didn't carry her around or play little games, or read to her at night or anything else. He was a worthless guy and then he took off. Eventually the commune fell apart, and two years ago I moved here with Willow. And look, here she comes. You see, she *is* perfect!"

Ginny has to agree. The girl has woven a dozen dogwood flowers into her hair and now wears a crown of flowing white blossoms.

One night at The Wellspring, Lyle's mother falls in the shower, smacks the side of her head and winds up in the ICU. When Ginny goes to see her she can hardly speak. Her pulse rate and blood pressure keep declining, and the doctors struggle with medications. They put her on a ventilator to help her breathing, and three weeks later she dies. The speed of it is stunning, and Lyle feels as much guilt as grief. He should have noticed there was only one handrail in the shower and made a fuss about it. He should have made sure they didn't let her shower by herself. He should have gone to see her more often.

Ginny reminds him of how much he did for her over the years. This doesn't soothe him. And she feels strangely rattled herself. It used to be births that hallmarked the years, and now it's all deaths. Her mother, Miles, her sister Carol and now Melissa.

A memory comes back to her from early in her life with Joe, on the day they walked out of the hospital in New York with newborn Jamie. Out on the street the flow of human faces seemed a revelation. It wasn't just Jamie who'd been born, but everyone she saw. Everyone who now walked the city streets, alive to the air and the sunlight and each other, had all passed through the same portal. Nowadays, instead, she watches the end of life. Everyone she sees will disappear from the face of the earth. I seems impossible, but they will all join Marissa and die.

33

March 3

Lyle has come apart. He berates himself, he bailed out of a class he was teaching, he keeps reading his mother's old letters. He hasn't had me over in two weeks. When we talk on the phone it's all stories and laments about Marissa.

Now that he needs more time to himself, now that I can't have him, of course I want him more. Ovid knew all about this: "She who follows me I fly from, and she who flies from me I follow." How much easier it was when Lyle was pursuing me. Well, sometimes it wasn't, sometimes it made me nervous. But now that it's me pursuing him, I worry that he could fly away or drift off.

Rob has been working on my house. He and a friend did the framing last fall, then the roof, exterior brickwork, windows and doors. Now they've moved on to the plumbing, electric and heating. Rob knows everything, and if he doesn't he learns it.

He and Celeste are moving into a three-story Athens house, an antiquated place some would say should be torn down. He bought it cheap and he'll fix it up, and he'll sell the commune's farm out in Vinton County. Which again makes me wonder if I should sell my house in Sag Harbor.

If I'm not going to live there, what's the point of keeping it?
The ocean, of course, and my years close to it.

Each day Ginny drops the twins off at pre-school, in a room filled with paper, crayons, books, play dough, a sandbox and giant beanbags. Then, for the rest of the morning, she looks after Jesse in Rob and Celeste's new house—a creaking gothic tower, as Ginny thinks of it. Rob now works construction full time, having hired a woman to care for Jesse in the afternoons, and to pick up the twins and Willow after school.

In June, Ginny moves into her own new house. She does her medical editing there, and in the afternoon takes a walk to her pond, half surrounded by last year's cattails. When rubbed, their brown catkins spill thousands of seeds over her hand, an eruption like tender lava. Often she strips and wades into the pond, then swims across and back a few times.

Once or twice a week, a newly-attentive Lyle comes to visit her plain and orderly house. Her bed and chairs came from Rob's farmhouse, and she's added a table and some lamps. In her bedroom, off to the side of the living room and kitchen, her clothes hang in a cedar-lined closet. Lyle notices the simplicity of it, and talks of ordering his own house.

"I should get rid of half the stuff I have in there," he says. "All my mother's things. Sometimes it's confusing. There are times when I walk into a room and get these half-second glimpses of her, as if she's standing there."

"You see her?"

"I imagine her."

"Perhaps because in your mind she's still with you."

"But all I get of her is a sliver."

"Nurse it," Ginny says.

Things have changed for them in bed, now that Ginny has welcomed him inside her. He doesn't hurry but slips into her gently, then lies still. Penetration has extended their foreplay. His goal is not to come too quickly, because after that it's all over for him. He alerted her to the problem early on with a repeated warning. *I come, you lose.* He'd still be considerate, he assures her, but the spark would be gone. So they don't let that happen, they save it for later. She still hasn't come with Lyle, but she can feel it building.

Other nights they only lie side by side on her bed and play a game, a variation on an old theme. If one of them announces "Time for a secret," both must confess to something they've never admitted to the other. And the secrets are given a cushion: at least on that night, they can't be explored.

Lyle. "You know how I told you my wife went off and slept with someone before she left, and I did not? So my secret is, before she ever did it I was on the edge of an affair myself. I never went through with it, so I was the guiltless party. But I wasn't."

Ginny. "That Jesse is an adorable kid, but sometimes he drives me crazy. He'll play with me for five or ten minutes, then he wants his mother. I think I make him unhappy sometimes, and this tortures me."

Lyle: "I like Chilo more than Sophie. I try to give them equal attention, but then I overdo it and spend more time with Sophie. Sometimes I wish I could snap my fingers and put her to sleep, so Chilo and I could do something together, just the two of us."

Ginny. "I eat less and less and it does no good. I want to drop another ten pounds but they won't come off."

Lyle: "I think the Ohio State dance department did better this year than we did. Their senior concert was better choreographed. I hate being second and I want them to fail, and us to be number one again."

Ginny: "The Probation Board has denied my physician's license for another six months, and they want to test me every week for drugs. *Every week*."

Lyle. "I wrote a recommendation yesterday for one of my seniors. She's a good dancer and can handle anything on the floor. But backstage she's a nightmare, she could tear a company apart. So I lied by omission and said nothing about that. I'm supposed to give a true report, and I didn't."

Ginny: "No matter what good times we have, I still think you're going to get tired of me. Which is not how I used to feel when I was young. I never thought anyone would get tired of me. Now, no matter what you say, I still worry."

Lyle: "The last time I spent the night I woke up early and lay there watching you. Every care on your face was gone. You looked thirty years old. Don't forget, you're not allowed to respond."

That summer she gets Rob to install a dock at her pond, using six slender locust trunks and some treated 2x6s, all designed for a one-meter springboard. A truck delivers the board, and a day later Rob bolts it to the dock.

"It does seem kind of dangerous," he says. "What if you bang your head on a dive out here and there's no one around?"

"A one-meter board is a picnic. I dove for years off a three-meter. I was an Ohio champion, if you remember."

"How about taking a few dives now, while I'm here?"

She goes back to her house, changes into her bathing suit and returns to stand on the board. The bounce feels perfect. She practices some lifts, then steps back and calculates the pacing. She takes a step, comes down near the end of the board, gives a preliminary spring and comes down again with her toes on the outer edge. She lifts both arms, rises, arcs and plunges, then surfaces with a smile. "I haven't forgotten anything!"

Almost every day after that, after walking across the meadow and peeling off her clothes, she swims across the pond and back, then works on her dives. A forward pike, a reverse, a swan. The pond is in its summer glory, the water clear after weeks of no rain, the far bank lined with deep green spruces. A couple of times in her life she has swum naked in the ocean at night, but diving naked in the daytime is a new thrill.

On several Friday nights Rob asks Ginny to look after all four kids so he and Celeste can take in a show in Columbus, or stay overnight in a cabin at the Serpent Mound. Fine, Ginny likes an overnight with the children. But after spending her mornings with them all summer, she's reaching the end of her compliance. When the older kids go off to school in the fall, she doesn't want to keep looking after Jesse.

She has to tell Rob but keeps putting it off, hating to feel disloyal. In the middle of August, after a salmon dinner at Rob and Celeste's, she helps put the children to bed. Celeste reads to Willow in her room, and Ginny lies down with the younger kids in the master bedroom. They surround her and go still as she opens the book she's brought. "Once upon a time there were four little Rabbits, and their names were – Flopsy, Mopsy, Cotton-tail, and Peter." At times like this, nothing can be sweeter than these children. Sophie wedges her forehead against Ginny's waist. Chilo holds a slip of her hair in his mouth, as if better to imbibe the story. Jesse sucks his thumb and sometimes a toe. How can she think of pulling away from him?

But later that evening, as she sits in the back yard with Rob, she remembers her resolution. She tells him that when school starts she doesn't want to keep looking after Jesse every morning.

"*No*," Rob says, "I need you." He's immediately desperate. "Jesse needs you, you're practically one of his mothers. I didn't know it was wearing you out, Mom. I'll start paying you. I should have paid you all along."

"No, I'm done. I'll still do Friday nights and Lyle will sometimes join me. But no more weekday mornings. You'll have to find someone else."

Rob stands up, walks out onto the lawn, comes back and sits down. "Jesse's delicate. He's already been abandoned once."

"I'm not going to abandon him. I'll see him every week. Sometimes he can sleep at my house. But no, I'm finished with every morning."

"Mom, please."

"No."

He rocks back and forth. "I never thought you had it in you. I knew Natalia could do something like this, but not you."

"You're equating me to Natalia?"

"You *are* a leaver. You left me and Jamie and Dad for that Villamano guy."

All these years and he's never said it. Hasn't she made up for it since, looking after the twins, then Willow, then Jesse? And before that it was Miles. She gave up everything to be with him and Jamie.

No she didn't. She didn't give up anything because she didn't have anything. She left Sag Harbor, where she had no job, no family and only the Brennans as friends, and moved to Key West to live with two people she loved. How much sacrifice was that?

All this she thinks in twenty seconds, seated beside Rob under the trees behind his house. "I'm sorry," she says, "but once school starts I'm done with morning childcare."

She stands, and so does Rob. He tries to take her hand but she pulls away. He has gutted her and she's not going to talk about it.

34

Jamie comes up for Christmas, and to help look after the kids. Rob and Celeste have planned a ten-day vacation in Belize, and even during the Christmas rituals their excitement about the trip is clear. They stir each other up with a few quiet words. Celeste wears a hip-clinging dress and rolls her shoulders at Rob's touch. When Ginny drops them off at the airport they fairly dance into the building, only turning at the door for a quick wave goodbye.

Ginny is happy for them, but sometimes they unsettle her. When it comes to sex she'd like to be fifteen again, and she's not.

Over the next few days the kids have a good time with both Jamie and Lyle, playing in their old house with all kinds of balls. They bounce ping pong balls into bowls of water, roll croquet balls into their wooden blocks and play volleyball indoors. For its tactile leather softness, this is Jamie's favorite ball. He ducks into town to buy one, then shows the kids how to spread their fingers over it, as if about to set it. When he closes his eyes and holds it to his cheek, they do the same. Then they stand in a circle and toss it back and forth. Even Jesse can sometimes catch the thing. Lyle makes a net for them out of a clothesline and some shirts strung low across the living room, and the ball flies back and forth. They knock a few things to the floor, but only break one plate.

After dinner they gather in Willow's room for their Dr. Seuss, with the three adults taking turns reading. After Jesse drops off they carry him and the twins to their beds, then pad into the living room to sit by the wood-stove and speak of Christmases past, of their childhoods, of the years they

clung to their belief in Santa Claus. Both the men were more credulous
than Ginny. They didn't want to let Santa go, even when they knew.

"For Miles," Jamie says, "it never really ended. Even with no kids in our
house we always set out milk and cookies for Santa. And for his elves too,
in case they came along in the sleigh. Not for Mrs. Claus of course, because
there is no Mrs. Claus. There can't be, because Santa is gay. He's a gay chub,
prancing around with his reindeer."

"I can see it," Lyle says with a laugh. "You could say he's always in drag.
How long has it been since Miles died?"

"Almost six years." Jamie stares across at Lyle. "You know he saved my
life."

"I've heard he was a great guy."

"No, I mean I'd have been dead without him. I would have killed myself,
back when I was at Dartmouth and it was impossible to be gay. I was going
to walk up into the mountains as a blizzard swept in and let myself be
frozen. Miles figured out how to make it just look that way, so everyone
would *think* I was dead. I left my car by the side of the road below Mt.
Adams, and Miles drove me down to his cabin in the Berkshires. Fooling
everyone was enough to keep me alive."

"You can see why I was so devoted to him," Ginny says.

"And these days I keep thinking that he never really died. That some day,
tomorrow, he's going to walk back in the door smiling and healthy. I know
it's ridiculous, but that's what I imagine."

"I've thought the same about my mother," Lyle says.

The three of them sit in silence. Until the kids wake in the morning they
are free of all duty. Ginny wonders if Joe had died, or Rich, or now Lyle, if
she'd hold onto them as tightly as Jamie holds onto Miles. Would his grief
be less if he had children? She imagines him adopting a child. She fancies,
briefly, that he could adopt Jesse. But that would be wrong, because Jesse is
now bound to his half-siblings. If only Jamie lived nearby—but that can't
be, because his world is gay Key West.

Kids bind you to life, Ginny thinks, even as hour by hour they separate
you from it, demanding so much of your time. Maybe years later you get

another round as a grandparent, which should be easier because there's less going on in your life. But no, it's harder, because you're older and stiffer and no smarter. With age is supposed to come knowledge, but where is it? She knows less about raising kids than Rob and Celeste, less about passion, less about devotion. They say there are places—India, Japan, China, Greece—where elders are honored, even revered. But those cultures are far from this world, where the elderly are put in homes. She did that to her own mother, as Lyle did to his.

"I'm glad the two of you are here," she says. "Imagine me here alone, trying to hold down the fort."

"All I ask," says Jamie, "is that tomorrow you cook breakfast, lunch and dinner, and soothe every child that cries, and exchange the presents that didn't work out, and keep giving me good
advice."

"And you, Lyle, what do you need from me?"

"All of the above and a kiss before bedtime."

"I don't know. I might have to go full women's lib here and abandon those old-fashioned duties so I can have a good time."

"We're with you," Lyle says.

"In theory," Jamie says.

35

She's glad to have her license back, and with it, in a day, she gets a job at Shagbark Urgent Care. They're always short of doctors, and happy to have her for twenty hours a week. Now she sews up wounds, treats strains and sprains, dog bites and minor fractures. Starting in med school, she was always good with sutures. Her clinic years in Chile, where she was the only doctor in a small town, gave her steady practice, and it all flows back to her now. She coaxes a buried splinter out of a teenager's eyebrow, digs out another from under a child's fingernail, stitches up a gash on a logger's thigh, calms with antihistamines a woman stung two dozen times by bees.

The trouble is, it's all a step down from her years as an anesthesiologist. Then she was part of a team saving peoples' lives, opening up their bodies to treat heart and liver, lungs and brain. Sewing up flesh wounds and diagnosing fevers and diseases is a worthy calling, but not at the same level. This grates on her. Peace, as well as knowledge, is supposed to come with age, but she's looking for something more. And she isn't even that old. If she feels deceived at sixty-three, what will it be like later?

All this, she thinks, she should be telling Lyle. When he's unhappy about something—his bad knee, or the negligence of one of his instructors—he tells her. But apart from his mother, the past doesn't club Lyle the way it does Ginny. She wants to be the woman she used to be, vibrant and filled with projects, with a list of books she wants to read and plays she wants to see. She does still read. She reads *On the Road* again. She reads *Lonesome Dove*, but has soon had enough of Texas. Steered by Lyle, she goes to dance concerts and enjoys them. But she doesn't want to enjoy a performance, she wants to be enthralled by it. So little moves her the way it did when she was young. She wonders if this is the toll of her abuse, her decade of alcohol and drugs, when every night she turned to gin and Valium to soothe her.

Though in fact, her detachment comes and goes. There are moments, taking care of the kids, when she's fully engaged. When Sophie or Chilo or Jesse or Willow—any one of them—comes into her arms, she asks for nothing more. Not long ago the childcare overwhelmed her and she backed away from it. Now Friday nights are the essence of her week. The kids exhaust her every time, but she loves them.

Does she love Lyle? Yes, she thinks, because whenever he appears both her body and mind seem to lift. He makes her smile. She never tires of watching him. Playing with the kids, or walking in the woods or lying beside him at night, she marvels at his limbs, sometimes entangled with hers. She doesn't know what it means or where they're going, but doesn't want to be without him.

Jamie has a ton of friends in Key West, but Christmas with them feels like just another party, so a year later he returns for a second Noel in Ohio. He's great, once again, at making up games for the kids. They're a year bigger and stronger, and ready to play more ball in the house. Rob clears some old furniture from a room on the third floor, staples up a double plastic screen to protect the window and turns the room over to Jamie. The kids start by kicking the volleyball around, laughing every time it hits a wall, the door, the ceiling. Willow is nine now and she can blast it. They tape a target on the back of the door and attack it. They yelp and howl. When Willow breaks the overhead bulb they all help clean it up, and Jamie screws in a new one. No problem, for Rob has seen this coming and set a broom and some bulbs in the closet.

It's clear that Jamie also loves to have the kids in his arms. He doesn't reach out and grab them, but when one of them cozies up he's apt to close his eyes and go still. Ginny watches him and thinks, *We're the same.*

On Christmas Eve they set out the milk and cookies on a table beside the tree. With the kids gathered in front of him on the floor, draped in blankets and sleeping bags, Rob reads them *The Night Before Christmas.* As soon as it's done they're eager to go to bed, because the sooner they go to sleep the sooner Santa will come. Once they're upstairs, out come the presents to be wrapped and laid under the tree. Steeped in old customs, it's an endlessly repeated evening. It could be a Christmas out of her childhood, Ginny thinks. Indeed, save for a pair of lamps on the wall and the tree's electric lights, it could be Christmas a hundred years ago.

For the adults, Ginny has brought her copy of Dylan Thomas's *A Child's Christmas in Wales*. She never tires of it, but this time as she reads it she's surprised by something she never thought about before: how little goes on between the boy and his parents. In fact, nothing. He has a home, but his mother and father are never mentioned. Auntie Bessie appears, and Auntie Hannah and an uncle who plays the fiddle and several young friends and a postman, but never a word about his parents. What kind of Christmas was that? On the final page, the boy goes up to bed on his own.

How impoverished this now seems to Ginny, and not at all what Christmas is like for the kids in this house. All day the five adults have been with them, telling tales of Santa and his workshop full of elves, icing gingerbread cookies, weaving lights through the tree and passing out gobs of silver tinsel to adorn it.

Not everything goes smoothly, of course. The kids usually get along, but sometimes they bicker. Willow has been annoyed recently at how much time her mother spends with Jesse, at how she jumps when he cries or complains. Yet Willow loves him as well. Her Christmas present to him is a big foam bat so he can wallop the older kids and they can laugh at it.

The twins, Ginny thinks, are in the golden zone. They have Willow above, whom they revere, and Jesse below, whom they mock and tease and hold close.

In the gleam of the stove's embers, Ginny asks Celeste if she misses last year's trip.

Celeste says it was a great one. "Caye Caulker was beautiful and we had a lovely break. But this year we wanted the full Christmas."

"I wonder sometimes, how is it for you to care for so many kids?"

The circle shrinks minutely as the others lean in to hear. Celeste smooths her skirt. "It *is* more than I planned on. Rob and I had talks about it at the start. Then little Jesse showed up, and I have to say I thought about running. But you know how it is with kids. You take care of them and then you love them. Hey, Rob."

"Yeah?"

"Want to get me pregnant and maybe we'd have twins, and then we'd have a half dozen of the little monkeys?"

"I don't know...."

"Rob, I'm kidding! What fun, that I can still tease you and you don't catch on. You're crazy enough to actually consider it."

Rob smiles. "Mamá, Jamie and Lyle, I present Madame Celeste. She's only so-so as a cook, and she'll rarely clean a bathroom sink, but she's way smarter than I am about everything that matters. Kids, money, jokes—everything."

"And *I* present," says Celeste, "our very own Robin Hood. He doesn't steal anything, but gives all he can to those of us who get lost in the woods."

What a blessing, Ginny thinks. A mother can't choose a mate for her son, she's just lucky when things work out well.

After Lyle goes home and Rob and Celeste go up to bed, Ginny sits by the tree with her firstborn. Jamie has seemed cheerful for the past three days, and Miles's death is another year distant. Still, she wonders.

"How are you doing for friends these days?"

"Plenty of friends," he says. "In Key West that's always easy."

"Good friends?"

"Mamá, what are you asking?"

"Okay, I always wonder about other—partners."

"They come and go, but I have some. I'm doing fine, I'm painting and selling and Key West is great. You've got your hands full here Mamá, you don't need to worry about me."

"Mothers worry."

"When I really needed you, when Miles was dying, you were there for me."

"Same as when I needed you, when I got out of rehab."

In the morning, she thinks, with kids and presents, there will be no time for such talk. Now they have a quiet house, but there are still things they can't discuss. Jamie and his lovers, clearly, and her own sex with Lyle, as vital as that has become to her. Why this barrier between parent and child, mother and son? Why not smash through it and talk about everything?

"I'm lucky to have found Lyle," she says.

"You are. He's great."

"And you're so young, with so much ahead of you. You might find someone."

"Mamá! Didn't you get the hint? Guys come and go. But my eyes are open and if someone seems just right I'll give him a try. And if it works out I'll let you know. If action turns to passion, to a blazing romance, to lifelong love and commitment, you'll hear about it."

"Now you're making fun of it."

"You had years when you stumbled around, so now let me breathe. It's Christmas, and right now I'm just glad to have this family."

36

In October, Ginny and Lyle drive down to Key West for a party, the third annual Fantasy Fest. That's the pretext, though in fact they're going to visit Jamie, who has sounded uneasy on recent calls. But Fantasy Fest, he has assured them, is a blast. "Whatever your cares, they'll go out the window."

They break the drive in St. Augustine, pass through Miami the next morning and roll down the Overseas Highway, a hundred miles of bridges and low-lying keys surrounded by an azure sea, ending at Mile Zero. Jamie's languid house is in need of a paint job, Ginny thinks, but otherwise little has changed. And even as they park, Jamie steps out to greet them. Hugs all around and he leads them inside, where Winslow Homer's "Undertow" still graces the foot of the stairs, and paintings by both Jamie and Miles hang from the wall studs. In the kitchen, the same teapot sits on the stove, the same toaster on the counter, the same blue towel hangs from its hook.

"Just the way it was when I left," Ginny says.

"Except for the hospital bed in the living room. I gave that away."

Maybe keeping his house the same is a way to hold on to Miles. She imagines stepping back into the Westport house she shared with Joe, into Rich's West Side apartment or Don Alberto's farmhouse in Chile, but none of those has a grip on her.

The three of them take a walk and tell stories, and at six Jamie bikes downtown to pick up some Pad Thai and conch fritters. Odd, because in the past he was a steady cook. While he's gone, Ginny takes a look through his kitchen. Indeed she snoops, checking for booze. She finds a half dozen bottles, both round and square, plus a six-pack of Rolling Rock beer.

Nothing out of the ordinary, she thinks. What's odd are the half-empty cabinets and the refrigerator, emptier still, holding little more than stick cheese, butter, a loaf of bread and some salad dressing. It looks like a fridge in Manhattan. When Jamie comes back he explains that he goes out for almost every meal. "Why bother cooking, when this takeout food is so easy and good?"

He opens a beer over dinner and offers one to Lyle, who turns it down.

Ginny's miffed that he pulled out his beer without asking—as he has for years—if she minds. It's no big deal, by now she has shared hundreds of meals with people who drink. And she doesn't challenge him on it, because all afternoon he has seemed in good spirits. He's affable and more relaxed than he has sounded in recent months, and she mentions this. "I didn't want to say it, but on the phone you've seemed a bit low. I worried about depression."

"No, it's not that. I wasn't keeping up with my emotional work. That's what smooths things out for me these days."

"Emotional work?"

"It kind of comes from you, Mamá. Remember how you'd hold a pillow for Miles so he could scream and moan and cough into it? And how he felt better afterward? I was thinking about that and one day tried it for myself. It's something like primal therapy, but not just for childhood trauma. Whatever's eating at me, I scream or cry or contort about it, anything to release the feelings instead of tamping them down."

"It did seem to work with Miles," she says.

"I don't have his troubles, obviously. But there are days when I get sad or nervous and my body goes tight. Nothing loosens me up like this emotional work."

Lyle is intrigued. "How do you start? Do you need some kind of trigger?"

"I think the pillow's my trigger. I just sit down with it."

Lyle stands up and points to the stairs. "May I?"

"Sure. What?"

He runs up the stairs and ten seconds later returns with a pillow, which he hands to Jamie. "Let us be part of it."

Jamie hesitates. He looks at his mother.

"I've been there with Miles," she says. "This can't be any harder."

"It takes a little time. I have to let it build."

He sits quietly, bent forward, the pillow held ready on his lap. His shoulders grow more hunched and he starts to rock faintly, forward and back. Then he breaks. The pillow flies up to his face and he weeps into it, then gives a muffled scream. He gasps for breath, he moans and cries and curls up over his knees. He goes silent for a moment, then starts again, and again. Finally he grows still. When he looks up his face is red, but he's breathing deeply and seems to be at peace.

A few minutes later he explains. "I start with something small, something that isn't going well. But it always comes back to Miles. I know I'm supposed to move on, to live my own life. What the hell, it's been years. But I keep hanging on to him and raging inside about how unfair it is. With this catharsis work I let it out, and at least for a time I feel lighter."

Ginny can see it, how at ease he sits in his chair.

"I loved him," Jamie says. "He gave me everything he could, as long as he lived."

The next day Jamie takes them to visit Frank, the tango dancer who moved back to Altoona to look after his father.

"Five years he hung on," Frank tells them. "But thank you again Ginny, for urging me to go. For suggesting I should do what I couldn't do later. He was a crusty old guy, but slowly he grew calmer. I don't think he knew me at the end, or maybe he forgot that I was gay, or forgot how he felt about that."

"Five years," Ginny says. "I'm moved that you gave him so much. How was life in Altoona?"

"I grew up there, but so long ago I hardly knew anyone. Luckily I met this woman."

"Imagine," Jamie says. "A woman!"

"Trust me, it was nothing sexual, I'm the same gay jay I ever was. But we met over tango, and out on the dance floor we tore it up, or sometimes right there in my father's house. I'd put on Carlos Gardel's *Mi Buenos Aires querido* and we'd dance all over the living room. I don't know, maybe Dad just liked seeing me with a woman, but sometimes tears would come to his eyes. That was a lot of emotion from him, believe me."

"I've always regretted that my sisters and I put our mother in a home," Ginny says. "Though I don't know what else we could have done. I wasn't going to move into her apartment in New York. I doubt if I'd have had the patience for a month."

"That's what I thought at the start. If you'd told me I'd be living with my dad for five years, I think I'd have fled screaming. But we slipped into it gently, a day at a time. And I did come to love him. I was always the weirdo in the family, but nothing's weirder than serious dementia, so it felt like a strange kind of bond."

He stops and looks straight at Jamie. "If I ever start losing it, if I don't know who I am or who you are, just shoot me."

"You're kidding I hope."

"Yes, forget I said that. Of course you can't shoot me. And as long as I spent with my father, it was nothing like losing Miles. You're a prince, Jamie. You and Ginny showed me how to care for someone."

They sit in Frank's living room, another Key West wooden house with no drywall or plaster inside, just dark studs and the backside of the clapboards. Books lie on top of magazines, on top of tables that dot the room. A pair of pants and some shirts hang from the back of chairs. Frank's housekeeping is relaxed.

"And all that time," Ginny says, "you held on to this house."

"Good thing, too. I had to boot the last renters, but I think they understood. Now I'm back, though I don't get out the way I used to. Not like Jamie here, who's so young and supple."

"Frank has some health problems," Jamie says.

"I get tired. I had a case of shingles last month, and that wasn't the worst. I got pneumonia in July and believe me, that's not when you want it. Fever in the middle of summer—*god damn*. I'll have to recuperate some so I can party more."

Jamie gives him a hug. "Whenever you're ready Frank, I'll have some invites. And how about tomorrow, with the Fest?"

"I might make it down to the parade, but I better take a chair. I get tired."

On Saturday afternoon Jamie walks them to Duval. The parade doesn't start until dusk, but the street is already closed to traffic and filled with half-naked people. Ginny is stunned and Lyle delighted. She knows Key West, she's seen how relaxed it can be, but now a couple of thousand people stroll back and forth, the men in Greek robes, loin cloths and animal skins, the women dressed like angels or whores with exposed and painted breasts.

"Nudity isn't allowed on the street," Jamie says, "but if you're painted it's okay."

A guy floats past in a diaphanous cape. A Catholic priest stands in a miniskirt and high heels, with a cross on a chain and a leering laugh, chiding everyone for their sins. A group of black women wear strings of flowers instead of blouses, and a mother and daughter walk naked from the waist up, their breasts painted as erupting volcanoes.

"Okay," Jamie says, "are we ready to join in?" In his small knapsack he has brought a couple of Speedos for him and Lyle, and a skinny pair of panties for Ginny. "We put these on and get painted. Here, over in this store."

The street life is so free, both Lyle and Ginny are ready to join it. Jamie has set things up beforehand with a couple of smiling middle-aged guys who have taken over the store with their paints and brushes, and who go to work on the three of them. They paint Jamie as a zebra, Lyle and Ginny as lion and lioness. The artists are so focused that Ginny never feels embarrassed. She's painted into her beast, with a mouth gaping below her belly. The paint is like a weightless suit of clothing, and when they go back onto the street they're one with the rest of the town. If there's a theme to the party, it's the glory of the human body.

Jamie is more relaxed than he's been since they came. Even more so after he ducks into a bar for a shot of tequila. At the same time he seems quite responsible, carrying their shorts, shirts and wallets in his knapsack. Ginny feels free and Lyle is clearly having fun, alerting her to other minimal and inventive costumes.

"You love this," Ginny says.

"I do! Half the people are at least half naked. And you know me, I like to look. I love how everyone's so relaxed about it."

The street pulses with a growing crowd. "Would you like it if everyone was completely nude?"

He has to think about that one. "Maybe not, with all that dangling. Not so sure about that."

"So you have your limits."

"Come on Ginny, you know I have limits. I keep to them all the time. If something entrancing pulls my eye off too long, just slap me."

"Or I could kiss you."

"Yes, do that." He offers one of his ass cheeks, and she laughs.

Men in drag are all over the street and one of them, a guy in light blue panties and bra, with long hair all his own but no lipstick or makeup, strides up and looks Jamie over in exaggerated approval. "When am I going to get another piece of *that*?" he says.

"When you deserve it."

"I'll turn a new leaf, Jamie. Invite me over to your place sometime."

"No, my house is closed to randy encounters."

"Hey, we're in Key West, loosen up why don't you?"

Jamie gives him an air brush with his fingertips, and the guy moves on. Ginny asks about him.

"That's Valentine, who's on the move every minute. Cruise it and bruise it. I'll stick to better friends."

It's something of an answer to the question she hasn't asked, about his love life. She's still thinking about it when a couple of guys appear with painted faces and chests. They slide their arms around Jamie's shoulders, pinch his nipples and tell him he looks great.

The light is fading and the police have begun to clear the street. The parade starts soon, and Fantasy Fest so far has been as loose and fun as Jamie said it would be. It's almost dark when the horns and sirens start, and the first car creeps into view. It's a black Lincoln Continental, and lying on its hood is a human ornament, a fleshy, completely naked woman painted silver all over, her legs spread wide and a beaming smile on her face. She waves and blows kisses, and the crowd loves it.

A flatbed truck comes next with a steel drum band, three black and three white pannists moving in rhythm. Then a licentious Bugs Bunny float, then one with a dozen young men shaking their half-covered asses. People in the crowd toss bananas at them, along with some streaming rolls of toilet paper. Next comes the mayor on a high-rise pickup, then another band and a collection of drag queens, each vehicle interspersed, down on the pavement, with dancers, jugglers and hula hoopers.

"Nothing matches Key West," Jamie says.

The next day, with everyone recovered, Ginny steps out to buy milk, pancake mix and guavas. She serves breakfast at the table in the back yard, and the three of them call up stories from the night before. But Ginny also has some questions about Frank, who didn't show. The doctor in her is worried. She asks Jamie if he's heard about GRID.

"That's in LA and New York," he says, "not here."

She explains it to Lyle. "Gay-Related Immune Deficiency. They're finding it in gay communities, and the Centers for Disease Control just published a report on it."

Jamie doesn't buy it. "You're not suggesting that Frank has GRID?"

"He's had shingles and pneumonia, which could be an indication. He's had a fever and he gets tired. It's something to think about."

"Do you want to talk to him?"

"No, it's all too early stage. And they aren't really sure about the symptoms. Also, if he has it, it doesn't sound like he's doing much that would spread it around."

"You mean sex."

"Pay attention to it, and if any cases show up here I think Frank should see a doctor."

"I'll talk to him about it, Mamá. But only because of how right you were about Miles and his Lou Gehrig's."

After breakfast they go for a walk, down to Higgs Beach and out to the pier, then along the shore. They've ambled like this since Jamie was two, on Connecticut, Cape Cod and Long Island seashores. Ginny holds hands with Lyle, to include him as she reminisces about her boys rowing their dinghies back and forth in front of the Cantipauk house, about eels in the eel grass, gobby-gunk seaweed fights and walks on the mudflats, a pathless world that appeared and vanished twice a day. There the tide ruled their lives in summer, with fiddler crabs and herons in the marsh, strutting gulls on the cobbled shore and halyards clacking on windy nights. On Cape Cod the fogs were so thick that bodies disappeared only thirty feet away. On Long Island the long blue beach stretched all the way to Montauk. The ocean here evokes the oceans there.

37

The days grow short. The autumn leaves drop and scatter. Ginny works at her clinic, glad to have both job and money. She has a home, a man, a part-time job and four children who love to see her face.

But in December, some hard news. Jamie reports that Frank has died. His body lay in bed undiscovered for two or three days. Another round of pneumonia killed him, the pathologist thinks. Ginny goes back to the Athens Health Department to read again the Centers for Disease Control report from last summer. Frank's bad health still sounds like GRID, and his death as well.

Christmas sweeps her up, and the New Year has passed before she calls Jamie and raises the topic again. He still thinks she's being dramatic. No one in Key West has GRID, he says. It's an East and West Coast problem, a small disaster in a few big cities.

"I'm troubled. Frank wasn't that old, and I don't want you to die."

"I'm perfectly healthy, Mom. I'm not going to die of this whatever-it-is. I run and work out and play volleyball on the beach. I don't drink that much and never touch a cigarette."

"None of that will help if you come down with Kaposi's sarcoma."

"What's that?"

"A cancer found in gay men. They think it's linked to GRID."

"Mom, you're in a panic. Anyway, I don't party like I used to."

"How often?"

"I don't know. Not even once a week."

"And in a month, how many different men?"

"Mamá, you're going to drive me crazy."

"I wish you'd talk to a doctor about it."

"I told you, I don't have a doctor. I haven't been sick in ages."

She can't persuade him of the danger. She lets it ride, but in the months that follow she keeps checking the CDC's Morbidity and Mortality Weekly Report. Homosexuals are dying of this new disease, which is most likely passed via semen. It's an awkward topic for a mother, with the transmission hinging on anal and oral sex. She tries to talk about GRID again on several phone calls, but Jamie won't listen.

In early May an article appears in *The New York Times*: "New Homosexual Disorder Worries Health Officials." The word is out. Many homosexual men are believed to have acquired an immune dysfunction, and to be at risk for both infections and cancers. And the disorder is often deadly. Twenty states and seven countries have reported cases, and many doctors have shown concern. The spread must be stopped, they say.

That's it for Ginny, she must convince her son. The next morning she juggles her schedule, sets up a free week at the clinic, asks Lyle to cover Friday night with the kids and buys a flight to Key West. She doesn't tell Jamie she's coming.

Late in the afternoon, a taxi drops her at his house. He's not there. Off at his studio, she thinks, or at a rendezvous with friends. She tries the door handle and as ever, it opens. For a while she waits on the porch, then goes inside and takes her suitcase up to her old bedroom. She finds some sheets and a pillowcase in the closet where they've always been kept, and makes her bed.

She can't relax. What if he's off with some lover, having unprotected sex? She's brought the article from the *Times* so she can read it to him in person. Doctors and researchers are paying attention, and gays are not. Even so it's delicate, because she doesn't want to make gay men out to be foolish ninnies. Much of the world does that every day.

As the sun sets over palm trees, Jamie rolls up on his bike. He parks and locks it without seeing her, then bounds up onto the porch.

"Mamá!" He takes her in his arms, but his surprise and pleasure don't last. "What are you doing here?"

"I need to talk to you."

"We've *been* talking. You call me all the time."

"But you don't listen. You brush me off like some bug."

"Get over it. You're all heated up about nothing."

She has raised him, she has helped him, she has loved him, but now she wants to bang him on the chest. One minute into her visit and they're facing off like boxers in a ring.

"This disease is real and you could be in danger."

"A shark could eat me in the ocean, but I'm still going to swim."

"Jamie, please, I'm not making this up. The doctors and lab people are trying to look after you."

"They don't know me from Adam."

Someone has stopped on the street, straddling his bike. "Jamie, you okay?"

"Yeah, yeah, it's just my mother."

"Always a treat," the guy says.

Jamie steers her inside. Trying to calm both of them down, he pours them some juice from the fridge. Ginny waves it off, opens her purse and pulls out her clipping from the *Times*. She points to a chair, waits until he sits down and reads him the full article.

GRID, it explains, is an immunity suppressor, and federal health officials worry that tens of thousands of homosexual men may already be compromised and in danger of contracting Kaposi's sarcoma or several deadly infections. Another name for GRID, the article says, is A.I.D., for acquired immunodeficiency disease. Ginny slows down over the key statistics: that male homosexuals are most at risk, that over 300 people have come down with the disease and 136 have died. A New York doctor is quoted. "Gay people whose life style consists of anonymous sexual encounters are going to have to do some serious rethinking."

It's a long and somber article. A plague report, Ginny thinks. "The transmission," she says, is via semen or blood. You're not shooting up with anything, are you?"

"Never. The most I do is smoke a little dope."

"Semen's the danger. Does anyone use condoms? If you don't want to die we've got to talk about these things. You should all be talking."

Jamie stares across the room. "I only hear about it from you."

"That's why I came, to make you listen."

The usual sounds of the town float in from outside, bird calls and random bicycle rings. A family passes by on the sidewalk, the children yelling and laughing. Ginny watches her son. He looks healthy, but thin. She's been watching his body for forty years.

"You get to be older," she says, "and some things don't matter so much. But one thing, always. Your children can't die before you."

"I'm not going to die."

"Of course you are. Just not when I'm alive, please. Can you see how worried I am about this disease?"

Finally he nods. "It does sound a bit sobering."

She wants to take him in her arms. They haven't touched at all, which is unlike them, but she waits. It has to come from him. He's courteous, he warms up some soup and they eat it at the kitchen table. He asks about the twins. They still enchant him, she can see. He asks about Lyle, who's doing fine.

She asks about life without Miles, after all these years.

"He comes to see me sometimes."

"What do you mean?"

"I found a channel who could call him up at will, and now I can kind of do it myself. Don't worry, Mamá, I'm not going wacko. It's just a way of thinking. It's how I keep him close."

He reaches across the table and takes hold of her hand.

.

The next day she visits his studio to see his latest work. There's no sign of any life-inside-a-fruit paintings. Instead, every canvas now features a man, or two. Some are half undressed, a few are laid out either sleeping or dead, she can't tell which. Some are fishing or standing in the surf, or hovering above the street with their sandals not quite touching the ground. A few bear some resemblance to Miles.

"I know it's repetitive," Jamie says, "but men are what I look at. If Miles taught me anything, it's *Paint what you want. What moves you.*"

That night he takes her to a drag show, one of several down on Duval. It's exaggerated and fun, a sexy mockery of the straight world, and there's never a hint that anyone is thinking about some terrible new disease. Has she convinced Jamie of the danger? The two of them walk home in the dark, talking about the characters in the show.

Of course she's not invited, a couple of days later, to his Friday party, the one he goes to almost every week at a different house each time. It's purely for guys in the know and not, god forbid, their mothers. Jamie is apologetic. It's her next-to-last night in town, but he doesn't want to miss out on the party.

"I imagine there's plenty of drinking," she says.

"Sometimes. But don't worry about me, I keep it sane."

She asks him flat out, "Do guys fuck right there?"

He looks away, but she waits for an answer. "Sometimes they do," he admits.

She doesn't ask how careful he's going to be. This late in her visit she doesn't want to be a shrew. Before he takes off she gives him a hug.

Alone in the early night, she heads to the beach. It's where she has always gone. To Compo Beach in Westport, to Nauset Heights on the Cape, to Sagaponack on Long Island. Here she starts at Higgs and walks on to Smathers, where she once made angel wings with Miles. The Southern Cross, as bright as she's ever seen it, hangs above the horizon, and waves lap gently onto the sand. Jamie's never going to leave Key West, she thinks. Why would he? He's surrounded by friends and lives in the house he shared with Miles. But he's too far here from her and Rob. What if he needs help?

The night is warm. The sea is dark and placid. She takes off her sandals and walks barefoot into the water, here where sharks and dolphins swim, here where moon jellyfish often wash up onto the sand, here where she cannot talk to Jamie or try to help him. It's a solitary walk, until she turns and heads back toward the pier and finds that someone is walking toward her. A man, she thinks, and they will pass each other in the dark. But then, the man is Jamie.

"Mamá," he sings out as they draw close.

"What's going on?" she asks.

"I need you to look at something."

"You didn't go to the party?"

"I think maybe I shouldn't."

Already she knows. But she asks, "What's wrong?"

"My chest has been hurting. Would you look at it?"

It's far too dark on the beach. She takes his hand and leads him across the sand to a distant streetlight, and there unbuttons his shirt.

The rash is clear, a bright red streak dotted with bumps that will soon erupt into blisters.

She can't say it. He waits, and finally says it himself. "It's shingles, isn't it."

She still can't speak, but nods. The night is still, the beach empty, the stars invisible. She will walk him home beside the waves.

For my readers:

Dianne Arman
Lady Borton
Sandy Brown
Rebecca Coffey
Lois Gilbert
Paul Kafka-Gibbons
Eddie Lewis
Raul Ramos
Alan Thorndike
Ellen Thorndike
Janir Thorndike

John Thorndike grew up in Westport, Connecticut. His mother was an anesthesiologist, his father an editor and writer, and the house was filled with books. He graduated from Harvard, then took an MA from Columbia. Following two years in the Peace Corps in El Salvador, he married Clarisa Rubio and spent five more years in Latin America, including two in Chile, where they raised chickens and grew potatoes on a backcountry farm.

Separated from his wife and settled with his young son in Athens, Ohio, Thorndike began to write in earnest. He published more than a hundred articles in Horticulture, Country Journal and Fine Homebuilding. His first novel, *Anna Delaney's Child*, about a woman whose son dies in a car crash, was published in 1986. His second, *The Potato Baron*, about a man trying to hold his family together on their farm in northern Maine, appeared three years later. His 1996 memoir, *Another Way Home*, described his wife's descent into schizophrenia and the years he spent raising his son.

In the fall of 2004 Thorndike found that his father's memory was failing and his confusion growing. To keep him out of a nursing home, John left Ohio and moved to Cape Cod, living with his father until the ninety-two-year-old Joe Thorndike died, in John's arms, of congestive heart failure and complications from Alzheimer's. The book that followed, *The Last of His Mind, A Year in The Shadow of Alzheimer's,* is a memoir about the dementia that stripped his father of language, memory and self-awareness, and was a *Washington Post* Best Book of 2009. The novel *A Hundred Fires in Cuba* follows an affair between a young American photographer and one of the heroes of the Cuban Revolution, Camilo Cienfuegos. The World Against Her Skin is a half-fictional evocation of his mother's life, and The Passionate Sister gives her ten invented years.

Author's website: johnthorndike.com

Also by John Thorndike

The World Against her Skin

Winner of the 2023 Eric Hoffer Micro Press Award, and the 2023 Maria Thomas Fiction Award from Peace Corps Worldwide

An "incredibly compelling book" —*The US Review of Books*

"A rousing portrait of a brave, imperfect woman"---*BookLife*

"Masterful...inviting...thought-provoking" —*Midwest Book Review*

A Hundred Fires in Cuba

Kirkus Reviews: Best Indie Fiction of 2018

Eric Hoffer Award, 2019 Winner in Historical Fiction

Independent Publisher Book Awards, 2019 Gold Medal Winner in Historical Fiction

"Thorndike is a talented, experienced writer, and Clare and Camilo especially are fully developed, attractive characters.... A highly recommended rendering of a love affair and mysterious slice of Cuban history." –*Kirkus Reviews* (Starred review)

"The prose is elegantly crafted....A Hundred Fires in Cuba is a sophisticated historical novel that effectively deploys a love triangle to capture the essence of a remarkable figure and the historic period that produced him, laying bare the yearnings of the heart." –*Foreword Reviews*

"With *A Hundred Fires in Cuba*, Thorndike explores his great themes: the mother in extremis, the intrigue of a foreign lover (or two), the beloved child, aging men unmoored, and the complications of passion, passion, passion." –Ted Conover, author of *Rolling Nowhere, Coyotes*, and *Newjack: Guarding Sing Sing*

The Last of His Mind

A Best Book of 2009 —*The Washington Post*

Indie Top 20 —*Publishers Weekly*

2009 GOLD Winner for Autobiography and Memoir —*Foreword Reviews*

"An engrossing memoir...a beautiful book." —*Publishers Weekly (Starred review)*

"A brave, moving story.... Thorndike's prose is serenely beautiful.... An affecting work of emotional honesty and forgiveness." —*Kirkus Reviews*

Another Way Home

"The directness, the honesty, the terrible plain chant of the narrative stunned me." —Doris Grumbach, author of *Fifty Days of Solitude*

"The prose is shapely and elegant, polished to a shine, with never a word out of place or a phrase too many." —*The Chicago Tribune*

"This book sings. It's a burning, beautiful memoir, rich in anecdote and character. And elegantly written. We need to see fathers in this light—tender, caring, committed." —Natalie Goldberg, author of *Writing Down the*

Bones, Wild Mind and *Let The Whole Thundering World Come Home.*

The Potato Baron

Thorndike offers an unabashed good read: exotic travels and love affairs, earthy sex and heart-twisting passages about Austin and Fay's devotion to their gaptoothed son, Blake. Their feelings shift as they are pulled in different directions, revealing Mr. Thorndike's sensitivity to the tortuous process of making and unmaking decisions. The novel unfolds with a finely calculated momentum. The Potato Baron is an intelligent and high-spirited story. In contrast to much of contemporary fiction, it explores characters who have never lost their connection to their work or to each other—and who, when these essential ties are threatened, are willing to fight to get them back." —*The New York Times*

Anna Delaney's Child

"An affecting first novel" written in "lyrically powerful prose." —*The New York Times*

"Ambitious and daring." —*Los Angeles Book Review*

"A novel of grace and style." —*The Columbus Dispatch*

"A terrific novel." —*The Cleveland Plain Dealer*